I0538917

"Quis Separabit"

(Who shall separate us?)
By Ian S Varty
Published by: Ian S Varty

Dedication

In memory of Sergeant David "Bob" Monkhouse, born Carlisle, 1974, Killed in Action (KIA) Nahr-e Saraj, Helmand Province, Afghanistan, 17th July 2010. "Quis Separabit" and "Fare Thee Well".

To all I have served with, who have contributed to my trilogy.

Contents

Acknowledgements

A big thankyou to Jim and Margaret Gardiner for proof reading and editing my three books. Words cannot express how thankful I am for your friendship.

To My family for putting up with my mood swings over the last two years. The early morning and late nights, me tapping away at my keyboard.

To all who have contributed in some way to this trilogy, also a big thank you.

Prologue

It was late 1989. Richard was travelling, once again, to the UK, on yet another course. It wasn't that he wanted additional qualifications under his belt, more that it afforded him a bit of time back in the UK. He had also received a letter from Isaac, who had gone AWOL, while they were in Cyprus. Isaac was on a brief stopover to the UK, before returning to Goa in India, where he was living.

After the course, Richard had planned to visit him, thereby killing two birds with one stone. This course, however, was going to be one with a difference. He would not be learning anything that would benefit him personally, rather taking part in a series of experiments.

The military installation of Porton Down was part of the Government's Defence, Evaluation and Research Agency (DERA), situated slightly northeast of Porton near Salisbury, in Wiltshire, England. To the northwest, lies the airfield of Boscombe Down. The site is believed to be one of the United Kingdom's most sensitive and secretive government facilities for military research, including chemical, biological, radiological and nuclear (CBRN) defence.

'Porton Down originally opened in 1916 as the Royal Engineers Experimental Station, as a site for testing chemical weapons. The laboratory's remit was to conduct research and development regarding chemical weapons agents such as chlorine, mustard gas and phosgene by the British armed forces in the First World War.

By 1918, the original two huts had become a large hutted camp with 50 officers and 1,100 other ranks. Studies in the Great War mainly concerned the dissemination of chlorine and phosgene and, later, mustard gas. By May 1917, the focus for anti-gas defence and respirator development had moved from London to Porton Down.'
(Wikipedia)

Richard had heard all the rumours of the goings-on at the establishment and a great sense of foreboding washed over him, as he drove his car towards the sentry box. The Ministry of Defence policeman checked his ID card and his name against his list. He then directed Richard to the reception area, where he was to book in. Richard thanked him and drove the short distance to the main building. Switching off the engine, he climbed out and took his suitcase from the boot. As he struggled carrying the weight towards the entrance, he asked himself was this going to be worth the free week's leave and the paltry sum he had been offered for his services?

He was one of some 20,000 'volunteers' who had passed through the gates since Porton Down's beginnings in 1916. He had read many articles about the establishment and knew that, in the early days, tests were supposedly carried out to find a cure for the common cold. He recalled one incident, where a young airman, Ronald Maddison, had died, after liquid nerve gas was dripped on his arm by Porton scientists, in an experiment.

Another case was of a young soldier, who had taken part in blister agent testing. He had been dispensed a small drop on the back of his wrist, which had swollen up and measurements taken. That evening, while he was drinking in a local pub, he had brushed against a civilian, the blister had burst and the fluids transferred to the unsuspecting recipient. Later that night, the civilian had developed a blister and the media had a field day with the story. For that reason, Richard had been informed in his joining instructions that no one was allowed to leave camp during their time there.

Richard was booked in by a young lady, in a white lab coat. He was told that he had been assigned to a nuclear testing group. Richard had no idea what this would entail and turned to make his way to the room he had been assigned to. He wandered through the maze of corridors,

5

until he finally found a nameplate with his and another three names on it. Inside the room, one of the bed spaces was occupied and, seeing Richard, the reclining figure climbed off his bed and introduced himself.

'Hi, mate, I'm Ken Stott,' he said, in his strong Geordie accent. It transpired that Ken was another cavalry man, from Richard's local Regiment, the 15th/19th King's Royal Hussars.

On first impression, Richard found him to be an amiable character and they chatted continuously for the next hour or more. Ken was a few years older than Richard. He had a familiarity about him which peaked Richard's interest. Ken explained the reason behind this was that he had served in Cyprus at the same time as Rchard, a few years earlier. One Squadron from the 15th/19th, known as 'G' Squadron, had been attached to bolster the numbers, to provide an infantry size Regiment, to carry out the peace keeping role. Richard then realised where he had seen Ken's face before. The Royal Armoured Corps (RAC) was not a big organisation and peoples' paths often crossed.

Later that evening, their other two roommates turned up. One was from the Parachute Regiment, the other from the Artillery. All four had been selected to take part in the nuclear testing. It was time for the evening meal, so the four set off, to look for the cookhouse. The mess hall was one of the best that Richard had seen. There were white table cloths and it resembled a restaurant, rather than a cookhouse. This was probably down to the place catering for civilian scientists and other support staff who worked there.

Choosing from the various options on the menu, the four soldiers took seats, at a nearby table. The room was only a quarter full; it was Sunday, so Richard supposed there would only be a skeleton staff working. Finishing off their meals, they tidied away and headed back to the room.

The following morning, the 'Guinea Pigs' gathered in the main reception, where they had booked in, the evening before. There were a number of desks arranged throughout the hall, with signs on them. They ranged from Nuclear Testing, Biological Testing to Chemical Testing. The four roommates made their way over to the "Nuclear Testing" desk and their names were ticked off a list. Once everyone had been accounted for, eight in total, they were ushered into a side room. A tall, elderly looking man in a lab coat was waiting for them. He invited them to take a seat and paused, while they settled down.

'Good morning, gents. My name is Dr Steven Gentle and I will be in charge of the experiment we will be undertaking, during your time here.' He paused again, making sure he had their full attention, then continued,

'There has been a nuclear explosion. You have gone to ground, to wait for the effects of the radiation and fallout to cease. What we require of you is quite simple. We want you to count time.'

The soldiers looked at each other in disbelief; realising their confusion, the Doctor went on to explain.

'The time now is 09:00, day 1. We want you to order your meals, according to how your body feels. If you think it is breakfast time you will order breakfast, lunchtime you will order lunch and so on. There is no set length to this experiment but we ask that you try and last as long as you can, so that we can gather some useful data. You can, at any time, ask to be released from the test.'

He then went on to explain the effects of sunlight depravation on the human body. 'One of the effects on the body can be depression, a little like that experienced in winter, known as 'Seasonal Affective Disorder' (SAD). Before we begin, does anyone have any questions?' He ended his briefing, looking about the room at the blank faces. With no questions forthcoming, he asked that they follow him.

They descended a set of stairs, into the bowels of the building, along a long, tiled corridor. On each side of the corridor were metal doors, each with a red light above it. They stopped at each one in turn and one volunteer was invited to enter. The rooms were compact, a little bigger than a cell in a military prison. They were fitted out with a chemical toilet, wash basin and shelves, filled with books. The most noticeable thing was the lack of any windows. The room was lit by a red light and, entering his room, Richard spotted a camera fitted in the far corner, pointing towards the door and bed. He sat on the bed and was shown the intercom he would use to order his meals, or if he had any medical issues or simply wished to end the experiment. As the door slammed shut, Richard felt ominously isolated. He was glad, however, that he wasn't taking part in the chemical trials, this one seemed a piece of piss.

He picked up a book, from the shelf above his bed, settled down and began to read. After what he thought was a couple of hours and feeling his stomach rumbling, he decided to order lunch. Ringing the intercom, he passed on his request. Some twenty minutes later, the hatch, located at the bottom of the door, opened and a tray was passed through. He never saw the face of the person who delivered it but guessed, from the hands, it was a female. He stooped down, picked up the tray as the hands withdrew and the hatch slammed shut. It was obvious there was to be no interaction with the 'lab rats'.

After lunch, Richard hit the buzzer again, to let them know he had finished his meal. Once again, after a short while, the hatch was opened and the tray removed. This continued over what Richard reckoned to be three days. He had read a number of the books provided, the ones that remained held no interest to him. He asked if could be given alternatives, which the unseen voice agreed to. As he read, he was aware of the blinking red light on the camera, in the corner of the room. He wondered if this was for his safety or if they were recording his actions and moods. over his time there.

To alleviate the boredom, Richard took it upon himself to begin an exercise regime. He would spend what he thought was an hour a day, doing sit-ups, crunches and press-ups. The lack of shower facilities meant he had to wash himself at the sink. After so long spent in isolation, sexual urges were rising in him. He finally gave into them and, moving to the corner of the room, under the camera's watchful gaze, he toyed with himself. Images of Birgit flashed through his mind until, at last, he was spent.

Time dragged and become the ritual tedious. Richard could feel himself becoming more and more depressed. He wondered how criminals such as Charles Bronson had managed to cope with such isolation.

On what he calculated to be the seventh day, he pressed the buzzer and informed the staff that he wished to end the test. In no time, the sound of footsteps and the turning of a key in the lock indicated his release. As the door opened, he blinked, his eyes adjusting to the white light in the corridor. He was led away by one of the staff. He was ushered into a room and his health checked over by a medical Doctor. Steven Gentle was also there and asked Richard what day he thought it was. He then asked what time it was. As there were no windows in the room, Richard had no way of telling. He worked out that it was seven days from when he had begun the test, so this must be Sunday. He was amazed to find out he had miscalculated by three days, he had been confined for ten days, not seven. He wondered how many of the group had given in, up to that point. Richard was later to find out, after meeting up with Ken on a training course, that he had lasted two months. What pissed Ken off was that he only got the same pay as the rest of them. Richard looked over his shoulder as he drove out of the establishment, promising himself never to darken its doors again.

The next week was spent at home, with his parents, in the North East of England. It was Christmas time, a time for families, but Birgit was back in Germany. Richard spent the time celebrating Christmas with his family. He had decided to visit Isaac in London on New Year's Day, before returning to Germany. He saw the New Year in and realising it was 02:00, he knew it was time to hit the sack.

At 07:00, his alarm woke him. He rubbed his eyes and swung his legs out of bed. His mother was already up pottering about and he headed into the bathroom, to try and freshen up. The taste of alcohol was stale on his breath and he scrubbed his teeth vigorously, in an attempt to remove it. Placing his shaving foam, razor, toothpaste and brush in his wash bag, he returned to the bedroom and put it in his bag. He had already packed his case and put it in the car the previous night. In the kitchen, his mother poured him a cup of coffee and placed it on the table. The smell of toast browning filled his nostrils but he had no appetite. Knowing that he would be nagged if he didn't eat something, he struggled to eat it when it was offered. They chatted about how things were between him and Birgit. His mother knew only too well the pressure that wives of serving soldiers were under. She, herself, had spent many months, if not years bringing up her children, in the absence of Tommy, her husband. The men were often away for long periods of operational duties and the wives were left to cope. Richard assured her that Birgit and he were fine. She, after all, had her parents only an hour away, if she needed them. Finishing his breakfast, he kissed his mother goodbye and headed out of the door.

It was just getting light as he set off from his home town, leaving behind the familiar smell of the coal fires. He joined the motorway, heading south. After two hours, he was alerted to the fact that there had been an accident on the M1 southbound. The radio announcer advised traffic of diversions. Richard knew the stretch of road well and chose to take an alternative route. Indicating to exit the motorway, he followed the signs for Silverstone and Bicester. This would circumnavigate the M1 and bring him back on, closer to London. Rain started to fall lightly, the temperature now below freezing point.

Suddenly, Richard was startled, he had briefly fallen asleep, probably due to the alcohol intake the previous night. As his eyes opened, he saw what looked like a car bearing down on him. He turned the wheel to the left, to correct his path. The tyres slipped on the icy road and his car careered, to the right. It crossed the other side of the road and hit an embankment, which turned it over onto its side. Richard closed his eyes and braced for the impact. Suddenly, all was silent. The vehicle had come to a halt. Removing his seatbelt, he attempted to get out of the vehicle, which was on its side. As he pushed open the passenger door, he clambered out, only for the door to fall back and knock him inside again. He finally managed to scramble out and, assessing the car, knew he would need recovery. He started to make his way down the road and, at last, reached a garage. He told them the situation and they made a phone call. A recovery truck turned up and took Richard back to the car. Unfortunately, someone who had seen the accident had called the police, who were waiting for him. He was breathalysed and, to his dismay, it turned positive. After being taken to the station, he was given a further two tests, which also proved positive. He was informed that he would need to appear in court, two days later.

The car was a write off and Richard had to make the embarrassing call home to his parents. His father turned up three hours later, to collect him. Tommy was not happy with the situation, and chastised Richard for his stupid actions. Richard appeared in court two days later and was given a fifteen month ban and a £450 fine. This was not to be the end of it, as the police informed his Regiment. On his return, he was given a severe reprimand, lost his commander's pay for the fifteen months and had a block on promotion. This was to prove decisive in the following two years.

Chapter 1 – A New Regiment is Born

Richard, like the rest of the new Regiment, had just returned from a couple of weeks' leave. It was September 1992 and they gathered, for the first time, on the regimental square. There was no band to herald the beginning of this new era, just an eerie silence.

The ramifications of Richard's drink driving incident a couple of years previously had had serious consequences. There were limited commanders' positions available in the sabre squadrons and he had been told that, prior to the amalgamation, he would be returning to HQ Squadron. Richard was to re-join the world of signals and fill one of the positions in the newly formed Command Troop. He had been devastated when he had been given the news but, like all soldiers, knew he would just have to get on with it.

The sound of the RSM bringing the Regiment to attention jolted him from his thoughts. For such a small man, the RSM projected his voice with an awesome force. His name was WO1 Finbar O'Hearn and he hailed from a Roman Catholic area of West Belfast. He had been the RSM of the 5th Royal Inniskilling Dragoon Guards, with whom Richard's Regiment was amalgamating. For continuity purposes, O'Hearn's tenure would only last six months, then he would then hand over to a member of Richard's former Regiment.

As the Regiment stood with the legs locked and hands glued to the seams of their green trousers, they waited for the arrival of the new Commanding Officer. The Regiment's practice of wearing green trousers in various orders of dress (other than combat uniform) was inherited from the 5th Royal Inniskilling Dragoon Guards. Adopted as a former (eighteenth-century) custom of one of its precursors, the 5th (Princess Charlotte of Wales's) Dragoon Guards ('the Green Horse'). It had been a bone of contention among some of the diehards of Richard's Regiment, who saw it as capitulation. Such things were trivial in Richard's mind, he viewed it as just one of many things people did not agree on. The name of the new Regiment had also been a compromise, this had in the past caused animosity from antecedent Regiments.

Prior to the reforms of George III's era, Regiments of the British Army were usually known by the name of their Colonel (e.g. Berkeley's Dragoons, Howard's Regiment of Foot). This resulted in numerous changes in the names of Regiments, creating a great deal of trouble with administering the army - a regiment that had been Jones' Horse one week could become, on occasion, Smith's Horse the next. In an attempt to alleviate the confusion this caused, the Army began to designate its units by numbers, with a word to denote the role of the regiment in question (e.g. 4th Horse, 22nd Foot). The terms "Horse" and "Foot" were employed during this period; it was felt undesirable to use "Cavalry" and "Infantry", since these were of French origin!

In due course, the reforms of 1746 resulted in the reduction of three regiments of Horse to the lower rank of Dragoon Guards as a measure of economy (Dragoon Guards were paid less than Horse). This was then continued in 1788, converting the remaining Horse regiments into Dragoon Guards.

At the end of the First World War, as a further measure of economy, the cavalry were yet further reduced. The 3rd and 6th, and the 4th and 7th Dragoon Guards amalgamated, to form the 3rd/6th and 4th/7th Dragoon Guards, respectively. Meanwhile, one of the three surviving Dragoon regiments - the Inniskillings, (6th Dragoons) was amalgamated with the 5th Dragoon Guards, to form the 5th/6th Dragoons. In each case, two squadrons from the senior regiment would amalgamate with one of the junior (e.g. the 5th/6th Dragoons contained two squadrons from the 5th Dragoon Guards and one from the 6th Dragoons).

The joining of two regiments inevitably produced difficulties for all involved. However, the title "5th/6th Dragoons" caused particular animosity; the former 5th Dragoon Guards resented their loss of seniority (Dragoon Guards being senior to Dragoons), and the Inniskillings, who had carried the city's name proudly since 1751, and maintained a strong connection with Enniskillen, resented the loss of their ancestral association. To make matters worse, the former 5th (Royal Irish) Dragoons had, in fact, been disbanded in 1799, for allegedly refusing to attack Irish rebels during the Irish Rebellion of 1798; the name was thus somewhat disgraced.

Eventually, repeated petitions proved able to sway higher authority, and in 1927 the 5th/6th Dragoons re-titled to become the 5th Inniskilling Dragoon Guards, thereby restoring lost pride on both sides. Furthermore, they went on to receive the "Royal" title in 1935, becoming the 5th Royal Inniskilling Dragoon Guards:

"On the occasion of His Majesty's Birthday and in commemoration of the completion of the twenty-fifth year of his reign, the King has been graciously pleased... to approve that the following regiments shall in future enjoy the distinction "Royal" and shall henceforth be designated:—

5th Royal Inniskilling Dragoon Guards..."

The 4th/7th Dragoon Guards would also receive their much-coveted "Royal" appellation in 1936. (RDG Museum Website)

The tall figure of the Regiment's first Commanding Officer marched briskly on to the parade square. Halting in front of the RSM, salutes were exchanged and the RSM handed the parade over to the CO, after standing everyone at ease. The CO took a deep breath and addressed the assembled troops.

'Good morning, gentlemen. For those of you who don't know me, I am Lieutenant Colonel Dunbar-Smith,' he began; Richard noticed he had a slight speech impediment. The contrasting figures of the tall CO and the much smaller RSM looked almost comical.

For the next ten minutes, the CO went on to explain to the Regiment what he expected of them, over the coming months, during his time as their CO. It would be a busy time of training, vehicle preparation and getting to know one another. In two months' time, they would be leaving for their first exercise in BATUS. 'The "getting to know one another" will be interesting,' thought Richard, to himself. It was to prove more difficult, the higher up the food chain you went.

The CO finished his address and handed back to the RSM, who saluted, smartly, as the CO marched from the parade square. The RSM handed the parade over to the Squadron Leaders, and invited them to carry on. Richard's new Squadron Leader was a Major, called Pat Geraghty, who was from a rough part of Belfast and had come up through the ranks. Richard could tell, from his craggy looks, that he would not like to get on the wrong side of this man. Major Geraghty informed the SSM that he would like to inspect his new Squadron. The SSM ordered the Squadron to move into open order, to facilitate the Squadron Leader's walk between the ranks.

For the next half hour, the OC passed every Squadron member, quickly inspecting them and asking each person a bit about himself. When he came to Richard, he asked his name and what job he had been appointed to. Richard explained that he would be commanding the 'A2 reach echelon command vehicle.' This vehicle was responsible for all logistical support for the Regiment. Its call sign was 42 Delta and it would be located well behind the front lines. Although this was a disappointment for Richard, at least he was still commanding. The OC smiled when he heard Richard's new role, he would be working very closely with this seasoned soldier. Richard had heard stories of his new OC, who had served some time in Aden, now South Yemen. Richard guessed that Geraghty must have served around the same time as his own father. He had also heard that the Ulsterman had a fiery temper to go along with his fearsome looks. The OC welcomed Richard to his new Squadron and said that he looked forward to working with him, in the future.

The inspection over, the OC handed back to the SSM. Calling the Squadron up to attention, he then handed over to the respective Troop Leaders and informed them that they could fall out their Troops. One by one, the Troops were turned to the right, saluted and marched three paces, before breaking off, into individual groups. Richard's new Troop Leader was the Regimental Signals Officer (RSO). He was a tall, lean, fresh-faced, almost arrogant looking individual. Richard would cross swords with this man on more than one occasion and had formed an immediate dislike for him. The Troop Leader then went on to introduce the Regimental Signals Warrant Officer (RSWO) and the Troop Sergeant. The RSWO, Les Gibson, came from the city of Chester. He seemed an amiable type, although there was something about him Richard couldn't put his finger on. The Troop Sergeant, Steve Orchard, appeared to be a happy-go-lucky sort, who hailed from Exeter. His West Country accent seemed alien among the Yorkshire, Irish and Cumbrian accents, which made up almost 95% of the Regiment.

The introductions over, the Troop made their way towards the tank park. It was only a five minute walk. Richard and the rest of the Troop entered the hangar, which housed the vehicles. As in his previous time in Command Troop, he viewed four Sultan Command vehicles, a Spartan, for use as a rebroadcast station, two Challenger tanks and a AFV 432 ambulance. The Troop already knew which vehicles they would be working on and made a bee line towards them. Richard's new crew consisted of John Plumber, Terry O'Neil, Grant Barrow and a tall, gangly guy called Pete Cain. John and Terry were from his former Regiment, whereas Grant and Pete were ex Skins. Richard wondered if each crew had balanced in the same way, as a method of integrating the crews in the new Regiment. There was something familiar about Grant. When he spoke, Richard knew exactly where he had met him before. He had been one of a number of members of the Skins who, along with members of Richard's Regiment, had undergone a local Control Signaller Course, where Richard was one of the instructors.

Their first task over the coming weeks was to fit the vehicles with a new communications system, known as Ptarmigan. At the rear of the hangar, behind each vehicle, was a set of wooden boxes. Inside were all the components, fittings and cables needed to install this new system into the vehicles. Richard could tell from the array of equipment this was not going to be an easy job.

Ptarmigan is a mobile, cryptographic digital and modular battlefield wide area network communications system based on the Plessey System 250 architecture. It was initially designed to meet the needs of the British Army of the Rhine in West Germany and replaced the BRUIN system. The system consists of a network of electronic exchanges known as trunk nodes. These nodes are connected by multichannel UHF and SHF radio relay links that carry voice, data, telegraph and facsimile communications. The Single Channel Radio Access subsystem is effectively a VHF secure mobile telephone system that gives isolated or mobile users an entry point into the PTARMIGAN network. (Wikipedia)

From what Richard had learned about the system while on his Control Signaller course, he likened it to a mobile secure telephone system. He had heard many bad reports of this new system and knew there were reliability issues with it. However, the military had taken it on and Richard and others like him would have to deal with it. For the following weeks, the Troop underwent the task of fitting out the vehicles with the new system.

Everyone, by this time, seemed to gel and working relationships were good from all sides. Richard met a few new characters, one of whom was the brother of the famous Northern Irish footballer, George Best. His name was Ian and he had an uncanny resemblance to the TV presenter Eamonn Holmes. Richard had been told by one of the other former members of the Regiment of the day Ian had joined the Skins. Arriving from an air trooping flight on a Wednesday afternoon, Ian had been met by the football officer, as he had got off the bus. After having welcomed him to the Regiment, he had said what an honour it was for the brother of one of Belfast's most famous sons to be joining them.

'Have you got your kit with you?' the football officer had asked, expectantly.

Looking bemused and not understanding the question, Ian had replied 'What kit?'

Thinking that he was joking the football officer had smiled. 'Your football kit!' the football officer had exclaimed.

'Football kit? I don't even like football!' Ian had said.

'How could this be true?' the football officer had thought, 'the brother of one of Britain's most gifted and talented footballers and he doesn't like football!'

The story had quickly gone round the Regiment and had been met with the same disbelief. However, it was not a joke, Ian hated football. Perhaps it stemmed from the attention his older brother had received while he was growing up. Richard liked the young man, who was very unassuming and didn't in any way use his brother's fame for his own ends.

Another familiar face had followed Richard into the Troop, his old operator from C Squadron, Trev Miller, who had been assigned as an operator on Zero Bravo, the main command vehicle. Richard wondered how long it would be before Trev fucked up, as he had done on numerous occasions in their old Regiment. It would not take long before Richard would find out.

After a number of weeks, Richard noticed that Trev had been missing on a couple of occasions, first thing in the morning. He would appear, out of nowhere, half way through the morning. Richard covered for him with the Troop Sergeant Steve, who had asked where he was. Richard did this out of loyalty to Trev, however his patience was wearing thin. One morning he noticed that Trev was absent, once again. Richard called Dave Elmsall, a young Lance Corporal and commander of the Spartan rebroadcast vehicle, over to him. Whispering in his ear, to ensure the Troop Sergeant didn't notice, he ordered quietly.

'Go to the block and find Trev, will you? If you find the little fucker pissed, lock him up!' he spat the words into Dave's ear.

Dave simply smiled and answered, 'Will do, mate.'

By this time, the whole Troop were well fucked off with Trev getting away with murder but had not said anything, due to Richard's protection of the bloke.

Heading out of the hangar, Dave took one of the others from the Troop with him. They walked briskly, in the direction of the Squadron accommodation block. The pair ascended the stairs and turned left, down the corridor towards Trev's room. Opening the door, the smell of stale urine hit them like a hammer blow. Richard had experienced this on more than one occasion, while they were in the same tank together and Trev had consumed more than his fair share of beer. He was quite prone to emptying his bladder into his sleeping or 'doss' bag. As Dave and his escort entered the room, they scanned the interior. Trev's bed was made up and looked like it hadn't been slept in. Thinking that he had gone into town the previous night and 'copped off' with some German lass, Dave was about to leave. As he turned, he noticed a dark patch on the carpet, behind the sofa, which was in the centre of the room. Moving towards it, he knelt down and felt the dark patch with his fingers. Bringing his fingers to his nose, he almost vomited, when he realised that they were wet with urine. As he was about to stand up, he heard snoring coming from the sofa. Pointing, he indicated to his colleague to help him lift the sofa. As they did so, Trev was revealed, lying in the foetal position, with his jeans soaked in piss. The stench of alcohol and urine was overwhelming.

'Trev, you drunken fucker, get up!' Dave screamed, shaking the pissed up soldier. 'You're in the shit now, mate. Richard said he wants me to lock you up!' he bellowed at the now semi-conscious Trev.

'Where am I? What you fucking on about?' mumbled Trev, as he attempted to get to his feet.

'Richard wants you locking up!' Dave repeated.

Not really knowing what was going on, Trev stared at Dave in disbelief. Dave ordered him to fall in outside. As he descended the stairs, he stumbled and Dave had to grab him, to prevent him falling. The stairs safely negotiated, he stood the hapless Trev to attention, outside the block.

'Right, listen in to my words of command, by the front, quick march!' At a rapid pace, he marched the unfortunate Trev in the direction of the guardroom.

As they passed the tank park, the spectacle drew the attention of those working outside, on vehicles. Richard looked up, as he recognised Dave's voice and his words of command. He shook his head when he saw the dishevelled Trev marking time, as Dave strode behind him. Once he had drawn level with him, he set him off again, at an even faster pace. From where he stood, Richard could see the tell-tale wet patch covering the front of Trev's jeans.

It wasn't the first time Trev had had a 'little accident'. Richard recalled the time when Trev had gone for a night out with some of the Troop to a German disco, in a town about 40 minutes away from their camp. He had been wearing a light coloured pair of Chino trousers that evening. As the night progressed, he had got incredibly drunk. Some of the lads had said that he was just topping up from that afternoon. He had rushed off to the toilet with a worried look on his face. When he had returned, he had acted as though everything was okay. It wasn't until he had taken his place at the bar, that one lad, Ted Hutt, had noticed an appalling smell. One of the Troop had pointed to Trev's chinos, which were now adorned by a dark brown patch around the arse.

'Have you shat yourself, you dirty bastard?' Ted had asked him.

Trev had simply shrugged his shoulders, and ordered another beer. The lad who had been driving that night had refused to take him back. There was no way he was going to let him mess up his seats. The rest of the guys had remonstrated with him, saying that Trev wasn't in a fit state to be left on his own.

This was something that set soldiers aside from their civilian counterparts. No matter how much someone had fucked up, their mates would always be there for them and never leave them behind. So, after much persuasion and having scrounged a plastic carrier bag from one of the barmaids, they had managed to manoeuvre Trev out of the disco and into the car. Having placed the carrier bag on the back seat, they had sat him down on it. They had situated him in the middle of the seat and, as the car set off, the driver, front and rear seat passengers opened their windows. They had driven with their heads out of the windows all the way back to camp, to prevent themselves from spewing from the terrible stench.

Richard's thoughts returned to the present and, as he watched Trev being marched away to jail, he knew he had done the right thing. He had a soft spot for the lad, but enough was enough.

Chapter 2 - Scandal

Almost six months had passed and the Troop had formed a good working relationship. There was no animosity between the members of either of the former Regiments. There was, of course, the obvious mickey taking, from time to time. Richard's colleagues, from his old Regiment, created a nickname for some of the Irish lads. Due to their occasional fiery tempers, they were lovingly known as '1 Amps', which highlighted their explosive natures.

However, word had reached Richard's ears that this harmonious relationship was not the same in the Warrant Officers' and Sergeants' Mess. One of his friends, who worked behind the bar, told him of mass brawls, which had broken out on more than one occasion. This was probably due to the fact that these members of the Regiment had served longer than the lower ranks and had formed a loyalty to their Regiments. That was not the sole reason for disagreements though, all were vying for promotion. Everyone on the tank park was in the same boat, but it did not lead to punch ups, at least not very often.

Trev was asked to accompany the RSWO, Les Gibson, on a trip to Division Headquarters, to change the cryptography devices used in the communication systems. Known as 'Silver Link', this was carried out on a regular basis. The RSWO invited Trev to drive his brand new BMW car. Trev jumped at the chance, as he didn't own a car himself, nor probably ever would, if he continued his drinking habit. On their return, in the afternoon, Trev mentioned that the RSWO had touched his leg, whilst he was driving. Richard brushed the comment off, knowing that Trev could sometimes make something out of nothing.

It wasn't till a week later that Roger Burgess, who had been on his tank in C Squadron, came to Richard with another disturbing story. He mentioned that he had been drinking in the NAAFI bar, the previous evening. The bar was strictly controlled by NAAFI staff, the Regimental Orderly Corporal (ROC) and Regimental Order Sergeant (ROS), who were detailed to see that it shut on time. When it came to the appointed time, the bell was rung and the duty personnel made sure everyone polished off their drinks, then began to shepherd them out of the building. This routine was always accompanied by good natured jeering from the revellers. Richard had performed this duty many times in the past and knew that it could, at times, get a little lively. Roger left the bar and was making his way towards the accommodation, when he bumped into the RSWO, who asked him where he was going. Roger answered that he was off to bed, as the bar had shut.

'I've got some drink in my room, if you fancy it?' he offered.

Never one to turn down free beer, Roger accepted and they took the short walk to the Sergeants' Mess accommodation. Richard had always found it strange that the RSWO was a single man, living in the Mess. This was not unheard of, as some of the SNCOs were married, but unaccompanied, having decided, for one reason or another, to leave their families back in the UK. This was usual for people in their last year of service, so their families had time to settle into civilian life.

Entering his room, Gibson opened the fridge, situated in the corner. It was full of beer and Roger's eyes opened wide at the sight. Taking two beers from the fridge, the RSWO removed the tops and offered one to Roger, who took it, gratefully. Les moved to the expensive hi-fi set up next to the fridge. Placing a CD in the open drawer, he pressed the play button. Not wanting to disturb his neighbours, he turned the volume down to an acceptable level. He stood by the fridge, chatting to Roger, asking him how he had found the transition to the new Regiment. Roger answered truthfully, saying that it hadn't been as bad as he had expected and that the lads were a good bunch. For the next half hour, the pair made small talk and continued to drink. After a while, Les moved from his position by the fridge and sat on the bed, next to Roger.

Richard was told that the RSWO then made a pass at Roger, placing a hand on his shoulder. Richard was shocked at this allegation but, as with the incident featuring Trev the previous week, he had genuine concerns. He demanded of Roger if he had imagined the incident or if he had taken it out of context. Roger was adamant that what he had experienced was not his imagination.

Richard felt sick inside but knew that he needed to act on this information. He walked Roger across the hangar, to their Troop Sergeant Steve. He asked that Roger explain to him what had happened in the RSWO's room. With an embarrassed look and obviously quite distressed, he blurted out the same story he had just conveyed to Richard. Steve's face clouded over with anger, then disgust. Without a word to Richard, he took Roger by the arm and marched him out of the hangar.

Richard stood on his own, wondering why Steve had reacted in such a manner. It was as though the incident was not unexpected. He had noticed, since the Troop had been formed, there had been a certain tension and friction between the RSWO and the Troop Sergeant, but he had dismissed it, without a thought. Maybe there was some underlying reason, something that had happened in the past, prior the amalgamation. Richard returned to his vehicle and crew, keeping to himself what Roger had told him.

The sound of the hangar door banging shut caused Richard to look up from what he was doing. Steve had returned with a rather sheepish Roger. Steve was obviously not in a happy mood; he muttered a few words to Roger, who then made his way back to his own vehicle.

It was not until two or three months later that they were told that the RSWO had been given a posting, in preparation for being promoted. Richard was told later by Steve that when the RSWO had been confronted about the allegation, he had denied it vociferously. As there was no proof that it actually happened, the RSM had to dismiss the matter. It seemed strange that Les had suddenly been given this posting, Richard thought, cynically. He was replaced by a balding bloke from Manchester, called Richard Scalder. He seemed decent and was well respected by the former 'Skins' members of the Troop.

The incident with Roger was dramatic enough but the biggest shocker of all was to come. One of the Troop Corporals, Mark Childcott, was missing for the Troop parade, one morning. When the Troop Sergeant asked if anyone knew where he was, all he saw were shaking heads. Mark was a quiet type, who always seemed to keep himself to himself. He didn't really mix with the other members of the Troop, regardless of which 'side of the fence' they came from. He was a single man, who lived in his own room, in the Squadron accommodation.

Richard had learned, in the time he got to know him, that he was heavily involved in a local children's football team. He supposed this was an outlet from what seemed a very dull life. Mark didn't drink or smoke, just quietly got on with his work. As Steve was trying to ascertain his whereabouts, they were alerted to the sound of someone being marched, at a rapid pace, along the road, past the tank park. Resembling meerkats, the whole Troop, and others on the far side of the park, popped their heads out of the hangars, to see what was going on. The answer to Steve's question was then revealed.

There, was the absent Troop Corporal, missing his beret and belt, marking time, on the road. He was flanked by two burly members of the Regimental Provost Staff. They were hurling abuse at him, telling him to keep his thighs parallel with the pace stick they were holding out, horizontally, in front of him. This was an unusual occurrence, Richard thought to himself. It wasn't every day a Corporal was seen to be treated in such a way. Mark was a fit man but it was obvious from his demeanour that he was finding it difficult to comply with the Provosts' wishes. They had obviously being drilling him for some time, for him to be in this state. Murmurs and whispers passed along the on-looking Troops. The Regimental Police (RPs) ordered him to step off again, only to make him mark time, after five paces. Even at 08:30 in the morning, in the height of summer, the perspiration ran in, down his face. His coveralls were soaked with dark patches around his armpits and down his back. While the remainder of the Troop watched on, Steve made his way over to one of the RPs. Richard couldn't hear what was said at that distance but knew that it wasn't good, as Steve sprinted in the direction of Regimental Headquarters (RHQ).

As the sound of raised voices and boots striking the ground faded away, the Troop returned to the hangar. Little work was done, everyone was speculating about what they thought Mark had done, to receive such a 'beasting.' After twenty minutes, Steve returned and called them all together. What he was to say next would send a shock, not only through the Troop, but also through the Regiment.

'Right guys, before I tell you what I know about Corporal Childcott,' he paused, waiting for them to pay attention. The use of Mark's rank, rather than his name, told Richard what they were about to hear would not good.

'Corporal Childcott has been arrested by the RMP, on allegations of child molestation.'

This drew an almighty gasp from the assembled Troops. Richard's stomach churned and he felt physically sick at the thought. He could tell, from the faces of the Troop, that they were finding it difficult to process the information. Some were visibly angered, clenching their fists by their sides.

'Let's just say that up to this point, it is only an allegation.' That final sentence was uttered with a hint of sarcasm and did not sound convincing. 'If, by any chance, he is released prior to being charged for the offence, I must warn you that no physical violence is to be directed at him.' Again, this came out in the most insincere way possible. Many of the Troop had young kids of the age Childcott had been 'mentoring'. Richard could only imagine the thoughts running through their minds at that particular moment. Steve had finished what he had to say and asked them to go back to work. Richard had yet to be blessed with the birth of a child but he still felt enraged about the whole affair. They knew the news would spread round camp like wildfire and, as they broke to go back to their vehicles, Roger piped up, in his broad Yorkshire accent:

'Bloody hell! We've amalgamated with a bunch of fucking perverts!' That lightened the mood a little. However, some of Childcott's former colleagues failed to see the funny side.

Chapter 3 - Shock to the System

Things settled down after a week or so, although the Troop was still in shock over the news about Mark Childcott. They became the butt of a number of jokes from others Troops in the Squadrons. An imminent vehicle inspection and exercise kept them busy, though. They paraded on the tank park and, after the Troop had been accounted for, the commanders set off, across to the Troop office, to collect the vehicle documents. Richard held back a while before he left, chatting to his crew. When he saw that most of the commanders had returned, he decided to make his own way to the office. Leaving the tank park, he placed his beret on his head and secured his belt around his waist. He always checked that he had all his buttons done up, as he had been hammered previously.

He had passed the RSM early one morning and had greeted him in the prescribed manner.

'Good morning, Sir,' he had acknowledged his superior in a loud, clear voice.

'Good morning to you, Corporal Hunter,' had come the RSM's reply.

They had passed each other by and Richard had continued on. Later that day, he was crossing the drill square, when a voice bellowed out, bouncing off the surrounding buildings.

'You there! Get your top button done up!'

Richard had recognised immediately the voice of the RSM. He had looked around and had seen he was the only one in the direction of where the RSM was looking. He had realised the order had been aimed at him. He had glanced down and had noticed his top button was undone. The RSM had been some 200 metres away, on the other side of the square. Richard had wondered how the fuck he could have seen that from where he stood. Not questioning the hows or whys, he had immediately complied, then had set off, as quickly as he could, to get away from the irate RSM. He had later found out that the RSM had noticed the button earlier, as they had passed, but had decided to keep the fact to himself. These were the kind of tricks that RSM's played, which gave them the illusion of being more than mere mortals.

The Troop offices for HQ Squadron were all in the cellar of the Squadron block. Richard entered from the far end and walked along the red lead painted corridor. He walked into the office, where Steve was at his desk, writing in what Richard assumed was his vehicle maintenance folder. Richard went to the bookcase, which held all the Troops' documents. He checked the registration on the front of the sole remaining folder, to ensure it was indeed for his own vehicle. Happy that it was, he turned to speak to Steve but was interrupted by a loud crack. Steve and Richard looked at each other, wide-eyed.

'What the fuck was that?' Steve exclaimed.

'Sounded like a gunshot to me,' was Richard's retort.

Turning around, Richard popped his head out of the door and looked along the length of the corridor. At the far end, a head appeared out of a doorway. Richard recognised it to be Tony Reagan, one of the commanders from Recce Troop. He must have been working in their stores, at the end of the corridor. There was an eerie silence throughout the passageway. It was so quiet, Richard imagined tumbleweed drifting down it, like a scene from an old cowboy movie. He knew they would have to find out where the sound had originated, so he called out to Tony to start checking the rooms at his end of the corridor. Richard started directly opposite and tried the door of Recce Troop Office. The door was not locked, so he pushed down the handle and walked in. The room was empty, so Richard closed the door and went on to the next room. At the same time, Steve was checking the doors on the left side of the corridor. After a while, all three met back at Command Troops' office.

'It must have come from somewhere,' Richard said, starting to get concerned.

He asked if there were any doors open in the basement. The other two said, apart from the offices and stores they had been using, there were not. Even the armoury, a buzz of activity earlier, was shut and locked up. Richard had seen Recce Troop drawing out their weapons earlier that morning, as they had a day on the ranges planned.

The only other door that had been open was the Recce Troop office, directly opposite theirs. Deciding to take another look, Richard pushed down on the handle once more and went in. As he re-entered, he noticed a pair of combat high boots, protruding from behind the desk on the right of the room. The boots moved. Richard advanced slowly, keeping the desk on his right. As he neared the end of the desk, he peered down.

A man, dressed in NBC kit, his back facing the door lay there. Richard could see what looked like the butt of an SA 80 rifle. There was a dark patch around the top of the body. Richard leaned down, to turn the figure, to ascertain who it was. As he did so, a loud, scrunching noise came from underneath his right boot. Lifting up his boot to examine it, Richard observed a large, white fragment, covered in hair, matted red. His thoughts were confused, trying to figure out what the object was. It wasn't until he looked to his right, at the large whiteboard, showing a list of vehicles, that the penny dropped. The board was covered in a dark red, sticky substance and was dotted with grey matter.

Turning his attention to the figure on the floor, he used his right hand to turn it over. It was then he saw what was left of the head of Recce Troop's TSM, Rob Carney.

Richard's mind went into overdrive, as his finger automatically went to the neck, to feel for a pulse, in the carotid artery. He felt nothing. Why then, had the legs been moving, he thought to himself. Tony Regan, who had been standing in the doorway, had run from the scene, when he had seen the sprawled body. As Richard stood up and turned, Regan re-entered the room. He ran forward to where Richard was standing. He had a first field dressing in his hand and was attempting to apply it to Rob.

'Where do I put it?' he stammered, eventually looking pleadingly at Richard for guidance.

'He hasn't got a pulse, mate,' Richard offered and, with that, rushed out of the room, asking Steve to secure the area, to prevent anyone entering.

Rushing up the stairs to the ground floor, he slammed through the double swing doors at the top. Sprinting the short distance to the Squadron office area, he burst into the SSM's office, who looked up, at this unannounced intrusion.

'You after me?' the SSM, Ian Humphries, asked, annoyed at this very rude intrusion into his domain.

Catching his breath and gathering his thoughts, Richard blurted out, 'It's Rob Carney, he's shot himself!'

The look on the SSM's face went from one of annoyance to one of surprise. Looking down at his desk, he paused for a moment, before looking up at Richard.

'Right, okay, make sure you secure the area. I will get on to the Medical Centre and contact the Regimental Medical Officer (RMO). You are to make sure no one goes in or out. Do you understand, Corporal Hunter?'

Richard nodded, turned about and sped back out of the office and returned to the scene. Steve had already closed the doors that led out the side of the building and was guarding the door to Recce Troop Office. Tony Regan was wandering around aimlessly, like a zombie, the first aid field dressing still clutched in his hand. He had been

33

close to Rob and the shock of seeing his body had obviously hit hard. Richard made straight for him and placed his hands on his shoulders, to try and calm him down. He explained that the SSM had been informed and the RMO would be arriving shortly. Tony stared blankly at him.

They were interrupted by the sound of footsteps on the stairs, from above. The doors flew open and the Squadron Leader, along with the SSM and the RMO, strode towards Steve. A brief conversation ensued, then all three entered the room. Steve beckoned Richard and Tony over and told them they needed to wait in Command Troop office with him. As they walked back into the office, Richard invited Tony, still in shock, to sit down. When Tony was settled, Richard's legs gave way and he slumped against a wall, on his haunches. The adrenalin of the last ten minutes left him and his legs had turned to jelly. The smell of blood and brains clung to his nostrils. He felt like being sick but nothing would come up.

After what seemed an eternity, they were joined by the Squadron Leader, SSM and RMO. The RMO asked if everyone was all right; noticing that Tony obviously wasn't, he asked him to accompany him upstairs. The Squadron Leader and SSM thanked Richard and Steve on their professionalism and, with that, left the room. Steve and Richard stared at each other, in an awkward silence, until Richard decided to break the mood.

'Well, that's something I didn't expect to see today when I arrived for work,' he said, in an attempt to ease of the situation.

Steve nodded in agreement. He had served with Rob for many years, prior to the amalgamation. He sat down at his desk, quietly contemplating, when they were disturbed by two men, assigned by the SSM to guard Rob's body, until the ambulance arrived to take him away. They said the Padre was upstairs and was available for a chat, if they wished. Steve told Richard to go up and see him, he needed a moment alone. Richard agreed and left him to his thoughts.

Arriving back upstairs, Richard was greeted by a sympathetic smile from the Padre. He motioned, with a jerk of his head, to an open door, to his right. Richard followed him and the Padre closed the door behind them. The Padre motioned Richard to a chair in the corner, then asked if he wanted a brew. Richard nodded his assent. He disappeared out of the door and returned a short while later, carrying two cups of steaming, hot tea. He offered Richard one and sat down in the chair opposite him. The tea tasted sweet, as it trickled down Richard's throat.

'You feeling any better?' the Padre asked.

'A little,' Richard answered, looking down at the floor.

'I know what you have experienced in the last hour was not pleasant, something like that never is,' the Padre offered, in a gentle tone.

'Why did he do it?' Richard enquired of the man of the cloth.

'No one, not even God, can answer that one, I'm afraid. Things must have been desperate for him to have taken this path. All you need to know is that there was no way you could have prevented it,' the Padre explained.

It was then Richard realised he had begun to blame himself for what had happened and harboured feelings of animosity toward Rob, for putting him in this position. The Padre seemed to pick up on his thoughts. Looking him straight in the eye, out of the blue, he asked,

'Do you want to go home? I think it may be a good idea, as something of this magnitude can have an effect on a person's feelings. I would suggest you get a few stiff whiskies down your neck and try to have a good night's sleep.'

Pausing a moment, Richard looked up from the floor before answering, 'I think you may be right, Padre. I don't think my mind will be on the job this morning.'

'You've made the right decision. Try to rest. It might be an idea to pop in and see the RMO tomorrow morning, for a chat. You know my door is always open, Richard. Feel free to visit anytime, if there is anything you want to talk about. I'll go and see the SSM and explain what's happening.' With that, the Padre stood up and left the room.

Richard waited a minute, before draining the remaining tea in his cup. He exited the room and went across the hall, to the Squadron Clerk's office and asked if he could use his phone, to call home. Knowing what had happened earlier, the Clerk said, 'Of course'.

Richard thanked him, picked up the receiver and dialled his home number. Birgit was pregnant with their first child and was due to give birth in two months' time. The phone rang three times before being picked up. As soon as Richard explained what had happened, she said she would set off, to pick him up. At that time, they were still living in their old married quarters. Since the amalgamation, not everyone had moved, due to the lack of housing in their new station.

It would take her around 45 minutes to make the journey, so Richard said he would meet her outside the block. As he left the Clerk's office, to go back to the Troop Office, he was met by the SSM, who told him the RSM wanted to speak to him. Richard thought that he probably wanted to sympathise with him, but this could not be further from the truth.

Standing to attention in the doorway of the RSM's office, he announced his rank and name. The RSM looked up from the paperwork on his desk.

'Corporal Hunter, come in and close the door,' he said, in his deep Yorkshire accent.

WO1 RSM Andrew Halifax had been in Richard's Regiment but had been away on posting at the time of the amalgamation. He had taken over from the old RSM, after a few months and had been there now for about four weeks. Richard remained standing to attention, as he was not offered the seat he was expecting. The RSM eyed him closely, before asking a question, which shocked Richard.

'The Padre informs me you want to go home. Is that right, Corporal Hunter?'

Not expecting this, Richard's mind was racing, which delayed him answering the question. Surely this wasn't a trick question, he thought to himself, before answering.

'Yes, Sir!'

'Don't be such a pussy. You're a soldier, lad, and this is your job. Now fuck off out of my office and get back to the tank park!' He spat the words out, without a hint of compassion.

Coming to attention again, by smartly banging his right foot into the left, Richard did a full 180 degree turn and marched out of the office. He descended the stairs, still in shock at the callous attitude of the RSM. He went into the Troop Office, where Steve was still at the desk. Richard quickly explained what had happened with the Padre and what the RSM had said. Steve gave a wry smile and shook his head, in disbelief.

'You get yourself home, Richard. Take the Padre's advice. I have few things to tie up here and I think I may be doing the same. If you don't feel up to it tomorrow, let us know.' Steve said, thoughtfully.

Richard thanked him and turned to leave, to head back upstairs and await the arrival of Birgit. He didn't have long to wait, before she pulled up, got out the vehicle and threw her arms around his neck, in an attempt to console him. He didn't have the words to say how he was feeling and simply opened the door and got into the passenger seat. The journey back to their quarters was taken in silence.

Chapter 4 - The First Gulf War

Richard sipped on his third whiskey, since getting home. He could feel the warmth of the smooth Irish glide down his throat and across his chest. It had been nearly two years since he had witnessed death so close up. He drained the glass and leaned forward to refill it from the bottle, on the coffee table. As he lifted it to his lips, his mind drifted back to early 1991 and the First Gulf War.

It was the second week in February and Richard, along with others from his Regiment, stepped off the aircraft, at the Dhahran airbase in Saudi Arabia. They had left Germany in almost freezing temperatures but, as they stepped off the plane, the heat hit them like a sledgehammer. They struggled under the weight of their Bergens and webbing, every pace drawing more sweat from their bodies. They were there as Battlefield Casualty Replacements (BCRs). With Richard, was Dusty, his fair skinned, ginger haired mate from his time in Cyprus. Both were joining the Royal Scots Dragoon Guards (RSDGs). Richard was taking command of a tank, whose own Commander had been sent back to the UK, following the death of his father. Dusty was to join the same Troop as a driver, replacing an unfortunate who had fallen from the turret, while putting up a cam net. It wouldn't be long before Dusty had his own little accident.

They were met by the SQMS of A Squadron, the RSDGs, who was waiting, by a Land Rover. As they approached, he spotted their cap badges and walked forward, to introduce himself.

'I'm SQMS Tom Howard,' he said, extending his hand.

'Richard Hunter and this is Dusty Miller,' Richard replied, taking his hand.

'Good to meet you boys, throw your kit in the back and we'll be off'.'

Doing as they were asked, the pair heaved their heavy Bergens over the tailgate of the Land Rover and climbed in. They were sweating profusely by this point. It hadn't gone unnoticed by the SQMS. He handed them each a bottle of water and advised them to get it down them. It would take a week or more to acclimatise. They knew they needed to consume anything up to ten litres of water a day in these temperatures. They drained the first bottle and were handed them another. The drive to the Squadron's location took them around three hours. The dust from the arid desert was filling the back of the Land Rover. Richard took a Shemagh from his Bergen. The large, square cloth, usually worn as a scarf or head covering to protect from the elements, is a traditional Arab dress but is worn by soldiers of all nations, to protect them from harsh weather. He quickly wound it around his neck and, within moments, had covered his face and mouth from the invasive sand. Dusty hadn't had the foresight to being one with him, so had to cover his mouth with his beret.

By the time they pulled into the Squadron's location, they were covered in dust and looked as though they had been in the desert for weeks. Their once shiny boots were now the colour of the ground they now stood on. Taking their Bergens from the back of the vehicle, they followed the SQMS to a Troop of tanks, set up in all round defence. The sound of aircraft screeching overhead caused them to duck down. The SQMS didn't flinch.

The air war had begun on the 17th of January. The following day, Iraq had launched a SCUD attack on Israel, heightening tensions in the region. The US had deployed Patriot missiles to both Israel and Saudi Arabia, as a defence against these attacks. The biggest fear the Coalition Forces had was of chemical attack. The Troops had been given a cocktail of different drugs, as a counter-measure to such attacks. As they crossed the ground nearing the tanks, a voice called out from Richard's right.

'What the fuck you doing here, you English bawbag?' in a dialect and voice which Richard recognized from way back.

Turning to look for the source, Richard smiled, as he saw the rugged figure of Steve Angus, striding toward him, a massive grin on his face. Their paths hadn't crossed since they had passed off the square, at Bovington, some eleven years earlier.

'Fucking hell! I wasn't expecting to see your ugly mug!' Richard replied, as the two embraced.

'Likewise, buddy, how's things with you?' the burly Glaswegian asked.

'They're good, mate. We're here to join 1st Troop,' Richard said, pointing to Dusty.

'Yeah, I know. I saw your name on the BCR list and knew it could only be you. I'm 3rd Troop, we're a couple of hundred metres to your left,' he pointed across the desert, to where three tanks were situated.

'You'd better report in, to your Troop Leader. We should get a chance to catch up later. The word is that it won't be long before we start to advance north.' He patted Richard on the back and made off, in the direction of his Troop.

Richard and Dusty continued to follow the SQMS, who led them to one of the tanks. Lifting up the cam net, he invited them to join him. Richard saw two men engaged in conversation. One of them wore three chevrons on a slide on the front of his desert smock and the other, two pips. These were clearly the Troop Leader and Troop Sergeant. Looking up at the newcomers, the Troop Sergeant smiled, seeing the SQMS. A few words were exchanged and they turned round, to greet the new arrivals.

'I'm Chic Brompton. This is Lieutenant Carrgrove,' the Troop Sergeant introduced himself and the Troop Leader. 'Good to have you with us. I will take you to your vehicles and introduce you to your crews.' He beckoned them to follow him. Although the Troop Leader hadn't said a word, Richard's first impressions were that he seemed a decent type. In reality, the Troop Sergeant was the one in charge of the Troop.

Chic firstly took Dusty to meet his new commander and crew, while Richard waited, on the other side of the cam net. He returned shortly and took Richard to meet his own crew. As they crawled under the cam net, two figures, sipping mugs of tea, turned round. One was stooping, as his head almost touched the cam net above him. He must be almost six and a half feet, Richard thought to himself.

'This is Neil Gardiner, your operator,' Chic motioned towards the big man, 'and this is Hamish Warren, your driver.'

Richard's new crew members eyed him curiously, obviously making an assessment of him. It wasn't going to be easy to get a rapport going with his new crew. Richard knew how closely a tank crew bonded and it would be difficult to fit into their commander's shoes.

The introductions over, the Troop Sergeant left them, returning to his own vehicle. For the next half hour, the three chatted about how things had been, since they had deployed. His two new crewman said that it had been monotonous, since their arrival. They had spent the first couple of weeks making their new home as comfortable as possible. They had either stolen from or exchanged equipment with a nearby American unit who, as always, were better equipped than their British counterparts. This was a constant source of irritation to Richard; the British Government seemed to neglect its Troops.

The Squadron was now well into an established 'hide routine'. The Commanders and operators rotated the radio watch, while the gunners and drivers provided the ground sentries, which was where Dougie, his gunner, was, Hamish explained. Richard asked where the trench was and Hamish informed him it was about 100 metres away, just forward of their position. He picked up his webbing and weapon and told Richard to follow him. Lifting up the cam net, they made their way forward, to the position.

Arriving, Richard was impressed at the way the trench had been dug and fortified with sandbags, providing some form of protection from small arms and artillery fire. Entering the trench from behind, the young man occupying the position turned round. He smiled, as he recognised Hamish.

'You're not on stag, yet,' he remarked.

'No, pal. I've brought our new commander to meet you,' he said, motioning toward Richard, who shook the gunner's hand.

Richard passed the next couple of minutes making small talk with him. Dougie seemed very laid back, but professional at the same time. All in all, Richard was happy with his first impressions of his new crew. Patting Dougie on the back, he said he would see him later, when he finished his stag.

For the next week, Richard slowly acclimatised, the boredom only relieved by the constant Nuclear, Biological and Chemical (NBC) drills, carried out on a regular basis. The Iraqis were known to have used chemical weapons in an earlier conflict with Iran. When the lads had been back in camp, NBC had always been treated as a bit of a joke. It was no joke now, everyone carried out their drills earnestly, as if their lives depended on them.

As the week progressed, their daily briefing from the OC became more serious, with the likelihood of an advance drawing ever closer. Their notice to move times (NTM), had been reduced to 30 minutes. From experience, they knew that something was about to happen. The previous day, Dusty had been on sentry duty in the Troop trench. After a short while, a shot had been heard and the Squadron stood to. It came to light later that it had originated from 1st Troop trench. When Chic, the Troop

Sergeant, had gone to investigate, he found Dusty, rolling about the floor of the trench, in agony.

It transpired that Dusty had placed his loaded submachine gun (SMG) onto of a box of ammunition for the general purpose machine gun (GPMG). He had turned around, in the trench, and his webbing had caught the weapon and dislodged it, from the box. As it hit the ground, it released a round, which entered Dusty's leg, just below the knee. He had to be extracted from the area and back to the UK. For him, the war was over and he would never live the incident down.

That evening, they were given a brief by the OC and a set of orders, which included a move north, in the early hours of the following morning. They were to advance with the Staffords as their infantry, toward an Easting, known simply as '73'. The area they would be advancing across was a flat, trackless desert, giving limited protection. Providing reconnaissance would be elements of the American 2nd Armoured Cavalry Regiment. They would be advancing against the Iraqi Republican Guard. Going through the plan in detail, the OC made sure everyone was happy with the tasks they had been given. After answering a series of questions, he advised them to try and get their heads down, if they could.

The Commanders dispersed, to go back and brief their troops. On the short walk back, Richard's pulse began to rise. It was the ultimate aim of every soldier to test himself in battle, however, trepidation welled up inside him.

The news imparted to his crew was met with a mixture of bravado and nervousness. Richard tried to put any fears they had to rest, saying that everything would be fine. The Coalition air power had subdued the Iraqi Air Force and taken out a lot of their strategic assets. This wasn't to say it would be a stroll in the park.

The crew settled down, on the back decks of the tank, after pulling down their cam net, under the cover of darkness. They tried to catch a few hours' sleep, before the battle ahead. Richard sat in his Commander's seat, his headsets on, listening in for any change to the battle plan. He dozed looking at the markings on his map. Coming awake, he checked his watch and decided it was time to wake the crew. It was an hour before 'H Hour' and the crew were stirring, putting away their sleeping bags. They clambered into their crew positions and waited for the order to start their engines. The American reconnaissance screen had already crossed the start line and reports were beginning to be sent back.

At first light and ten minutes before they were due to advance, the order came for them to start their engines. The sound of the generating engines and gun kits being switched on echoed across the desert. Richard settled into his seat and once again looked at his map. As the sound of the gun kit came on line, he checked his sight, ensuring the gunner had started up the thermal imaging system. He scanned the area in front and several heat signatures could be seen, in the distance. Satisfied that all was in order, he asked Neil if he had all his stowage and, in return, received a big grin and a thumbs up.

'Hello, Charlie Charlie, this is Zero Alpha, move now!' The sound of the Squadron Leader's voice in Richard's headset confirmed the Squadron's order to move off.

'Right, Hamish, let's go,' he said, into his microphone and the Challenger leapt forward.

The wind had picked up and they were steering into a full blown sandstorm. They would be relying on their thermal imaging sights to aid them identifying the enemy and with navigation. The whole Squadron were moving in line abreast, making best speed, under the conditions. As they trundled northwards, they were being continually updated on the American reconnaissance movement, ahead.

By midafternoon, the reconnaissance units came into contact with elements of the IRG. Deviating from their orders, they began to engage the enemy. They had been engaged a complex of buildings, which they had destroyed with direct fire from their main armaments and TOW Missiles, from the Bradley APCs. There was a line of Iraqi tanks dug in, all facing south. The recce screen held their attention, while they waited for the rest of the armour and infantry to join them.

A set of quick attack orders was sent over the air by the OC. The Squadron halted, to give themselves time to decode them. Richard was busy, scribbling down the orders and waited for Neil to give him the decoded version. Once this had been done, he found their Troop was to provide fire support, as two other Troops rolled through the objective, with the infantry of the Staffords. The Troop took up a position and identified a line of roughly 30 tanks facing them. Richard laid Dougie on to one of the tanks, which appeared as a huge heat signature, in the centre of his sight. Dougie confirmed he had seen it and went through his drills. The gun drove up, with an ellipse, around the target. Hearing the clang of the breech closing and the sound of loading from Neil, he pressed the firing mechanism.

'Firing now!' he shouted, excitedly.

The sound of the gun spitting flame and the ensuing pressure wave were but a background noise and feeling, so concentrated was Richard on the target to his front. In a flash, the impact of the round slamming into the tank whited out his sight, for a split second. All he could see was intense heat, emanating from the bulk of the destroyed Iraqi tank.

'Target, next target right, go on!' he shouted into his microphone.

This was repeated by Dougie and for the next twenty minutes, they laid down fire on the dug-in Iraqi forces. Five minutes before the infantry and close support tanks were due to advance and take the position, the artillery unleashed a bombardment unlike anything Richard had witnessed. How the hell could anyone survive that, he thought to himself. As the shelling ceased, the infantry in their warrior APCs and two Troops of tanks rolled toward the position. There was little if no resistance from the opposing forces. 200 metres minus of the objective, the infantry dismounted and began to fight through the Iraqi line of defence. The tanks followed them up, laying down suppressive fire on what was left of the armour and dug-in infantry. The landscape was a sea of smoke and burning vehicles.

Once the position had been taken, the remainder of the Squadron was given the order to move through the defences and carry on their advance north. As Richard's vehicle lurched forward, the adrenalin coursing through his body gradually subsided. He had given no thought to the men on the receiving end of the onslaught, such was the nature of being a tank soldier. Unlike the infantry, engagements were normally at a distance and no one saw the face of his enemy. Now, as they rolled through the position, he witnessed the carnage they had wrought. Vehicles were burning, charred remains of bodies were strewn all around. The stench drifted across the desert.

This had been his first experience of war as it really was, not as played out on some video game. As Richard drained his glass of whiskey, he realised why the suicide that day had hit him so hard. The smell of the blood and body matter had been reignited in his brain. Trying to put it to the back of his mind, he refilled his glass and closed his eyes.

Flashbacks to the horror of war have to be endured by soldiers, throughout their lives.

Chapter 5 - Troop Tests & NBC

Two weeks had passed since Rob Carney had taken his life. Richard had managed to put it to the back of his mind. The following week, the Regiment would be going on exercise and the Sabre Squadrons would be entering an annual competition known as 'Troop Tests'. It involved numerous military tests, from vehicle recognition, NBC, first aid, night navigation, hide drills to advance to contact. Random others would be thrown in. It would not involve Command Troop, although Richard had been selected, with a couple of others, to run the NBC stand, in recognition of the qualification he had gained, having spent a couple of weeks at the Defence CBRN Centre at Winterbourne Gunner.

As Richard had driven into the sleepy Wiltshire town of Winterbourne Gunner, he had smiled to himself, recollecting the time he had spent years earlier, at Porton Down, to the north. At that time, he had been taking part in Chemical and Nuclear trials.

On this occasion, he would be learning how to teach the very serious subject of Nuclear, Biological and Chemical Warfare. It was a Sunday evening and, as he approached the gates to the establishment, a Ministry of Defence Policeman left the cubicle he occupied. He motioned for Richard to wind down his window and asked him what he was looking for. Richard explained that he was on a course, starting the following day. Checking Richard's ID card, the MOD policeman directed him to his accommodation. Richard thanked him, engaged first gear and headed off, in the direction given.

The living accommodation was a set of wooden huts and were basic, to say the least. The course was for Senior Non Commissioned Officers (SNCO). Richard had been pushed up to local Sergeant, to enable him attend the course. He had expected to be living in the Warrant

Officers' and Sergeants' Mess, but this was obviously not the case. As he searched for his room, in the hut he had been directed to, he was pleasantly surprised to find that he had his own room. As he unpacked his suitcase and placed his clothing in his locker, he was interrupted by a voice:

'What about ye?' Richard recognized the familiar Belfast brogue.

Turning, he saw a well-built man, who appeared to be in his mid-twenties. Walking towards him Richard introduced himself and the stranger reciprocated. His name was John, a Sergeant in the Royal Irish Rangers. That unit had been stationed in a town not far from Richard's, prior to amalgamation. Richard and others from his Regiment had served with them in Northern Ireland, when they had asked for volunteers. He had had a great tour with them and still kept in touch with some. He threw some names at John, who knew most of them. They hit it off straight away and agreed that, as soon as they were unpacked, they would go for a drink in the Mess.

The Sergeants' Mess was small, but very comfortable, with sofas and soft chairs arranged around the room. John and Richard stood at the bar, waitng for the barman to finish serving. Once finished with his customer, he turned to the pair, asking what they would like. Richard opted for a pint of Guinness, so John ordered up. They chatted for a couple of hours, then were joined by others, starting the course, the following day. Introductions were madeand the small group passed the time drinking, until the bar shut, promptly, at 11pm.

The course assembled in the main lecture theatre, with around twenty students in attendance. They were given an introduction to the course and an overview by the camp commandant, an RAF Wing Commander, the equivalent of a Lt. Colonel in the Army. Richard wondered what the officer had done, to deserve being posted to this shithole. The course members came from all three services, but were predominately Army personnel. The course overview and content covered, the students were asked to follow a Warrant Officer, who would be their instructor for the rest of the day.

The Instructor, WO2 Williams, was from the Royal Regiment of Wales. He led the students from the lecture hall to a Portacabin, set up as a classroom. Asking them to take a seat, he busied himself with some paperwork on his desk. Richard sat next to John and glanced around the class. There was an array of different uniforms on show, Army, Navy and RAF. Williams asked them to write their names on the white piece of folded card, placed on their desks.

'Do you have a pen, Sir?' came a loud voice, from the back of the room.

There was a deathly silence, until Williams answered, 'Have I got a fucking pen? What fucking jelly head turns up on a course without a pen?' Then, seeing the parachute wings on the red beret on the desk, he nodded. 'A fucking Para, I might have known!' he bellowed, throwing a pen from his desk, in the direction of the class retard.

This caused the class to erupt into fits of laughter, at the expense of the Para, who simply smiled back at the instructor and thanked him. The lad's name was Mick and, although he wasn't the sharpest tool in the box, seemed to be a good laugh. Richard didn't know it, but they would be in the same group, for the final test exercise.

The instructor then asked each of them, in turn, to stand up and give a five minute talk, about themselves. Richard had become used to this, it was known as an ice breaker. Some people were better at it than others and it didn't prove a problem for Richard, who was already an instructor in two other disciplines. When it came to Mick the Para's turn, it became evident that he was a thick as he had seemed earlier. The men having spoken, the instructor began the lesson, by going through chemical safety rules.

'If you experience a bombardment of any kind; sight hostile or low flying aircraft; see suspicious mist, smoke, droplets or splashes; smell anything unusual; notice symptoms in yourself or others, such as dimness of vision, irritation of the eyes, running nose, sudden headaches, increased salivation or tightness in the chest; or, if you hear an alarm, you are to carry out the immediate action drill (IA):' he paused, looking about the room. 'You will stop breathing, close your eyes, turn your back to the wind, lean forward and remove your helmet and hood. Put on your respirator, blow out hard and shout Gas! Gas! Gas!'

Williams demonstrated the actions as he voiced them. 'You would then decontaminate your hands and put on your gloves; check the adjustment of all your clothing; finally, check your detector paper, for any signs of liquid.' he finished the short demonstration.

Asking if there were any questions, he then instructed the class to get into their full 'Individual Protective Equipment' (IPE), which consisted of a set of trousers with braces crossed over the chest and tied in a bow, a jacket, with an attached hood with a drawstring, a set of black over boots and two pairs of gloves, an inner cotton pair and a rubber outer pair. Once everyone had changed, he drilled them, for the next hour, on the immediate action drill. After numerous run-throughs, he asked the class to retake their seats. Then, he called Richard to the front of the class and, once in place, Williams started to bang two mess tins together. This was one form of alarm that could be given and Richard reacted immediately, going through the IA drill, in sequence. Once finished, he faced the instructor.

'Did anyone see anything wrong with the drill that Sergeant Hunter just carried out?' he asked the class. A few people put their hands up, pointing out minor things he had missed. Richard knew that he had not done it all perfectly but, for a first effort, it wasn't bad.

'That was a good drill, Sergeant Hunter, you can sit back down.'

Richard loosened the drawstring of his hood, took off his respirator and sat back down, next to John.

For the rest of the morning, they went through the full decontamination drill. It was summer and it was hot and sticky wearing the full IPE equipment, but they would get used to it, by the end of the course. At midday, they broke for lunch. Dropping the books they had been given that morning off, they made their way to the Mess.

As they walked through the doors, everyone put their berets on the hooks provided. Richard had noticed one of the class who was very quiet and would never wear his beret, sauntering around, as if he didn't have a care in the world. If Richard had behaved like this in his own camp, he knew he would be up in front of the RSM. They grabbed something to eat from the hot-plate and sat down, together. The conversation immediately turned to the course. Some of the RAF lads were whining already. They had been ordered to attend and were not there by choice. Richard smirked to himself, he had volunteered for this and many other courses, purely to get back to the UK, for a few weeks on the piss. It also would stand him in good stead for assessment to pass annual tests. Known as 'Army Training Directives' (ATD), there was a number that had to be passed each year.

Lunch over, the afternoon was spent going through how to fit a respirator correctly. Once they had mastered this, they went through the rules of respirator maintenance. Then, they were told when they were needed to change their canisters.

The final part of the afternoon was spent going through alarms and the different signs used, to denote Nuclear, Biological and Chemical attacks. By the end of the day, Richard's head was reeling, with all the information which had been forced in. They were tested every morning, to ensure they had retained the previous day's lessons. Richard had a decent memory and would only spend half an hour, after the evening meal, revising that day's coursework.

After this, he and John hurried to the Mess and spent the rest of the evening, getting pissed. An hour before closing time, the quiet guy who didn't like wearing his beret came into the bar and ordered a pint. They had established he was known as Taff, because he was from south Wales. He hadn't been in class for the ice breaker session, so they knew little about him. He mostly kept himself to himself, although one of the Welsh Guards seemed to know him and engaged him in deep conversation. At exactly 11pm, the shutters came down on the bar and the students wandered off, to bed.

The rest of the week was spent going through the symptoms and treatment of NBC casualties. It was very in-depth and unlike normal first aid lessons. It was something new to Richard and kept his mind busy. He had to study harder at night, to make sure he passed the morning tests.

They were also shown the various pieces of equipment which could be used for detecting and monitoring different agents. One of these was the Chemical Agent Monitor (CAM), a portable, hand-held device capable of detecting blister or nerve agent contamination on persons, equipment and elements of the surrounding environment. Another was the Nerve Agent Immobilised Enzyme Alarm and Detector (NAIAD), which emitted an audible alarm, allowing personnel to take the necessary protective measures, including the donning of individual protection equipment, before they being exposed to a potentially hazardous dose of chemical warfare agent.

During one lesson, just before lunchtime, a figure entered the classroom, and whispered to the instructor, who nodded and looked towards the back of the class.

'Sergeant Price, the Commandant wants to see you in his office,' he barked, looking directly at Taff.

'For fuck sake!' Taff grumbled, as he got up from his seat and, with his hands in his pockets, ambled out the room.

'I hope it's not bad news,' Richard thought to himself and, turned his attention back to the lesson which was about to come to a close, for the morning. After the instructor had finished his last lesson, he dismissed them for lunch.

They rushed out the classroom, thankful for the fresh air. It was a boiling hot day and the classroom was stifling. As they began to eat their lunch, they were joined by Taff. He put down his plate and, without speaking, began to eat. Not knowing what had happened between Taff and the Commandant, Richard thought it best not to open his mouth. If Taff wanted to say anything, he would. The meal over, some retired to the comfortable sofas and chairs, to watch the news or read the newspapers. It wasn't long before the lunch hour was over and they needed to be back in the classroom. As they left the lounge, to exit the building, they retrieved their berets, from the coat hooks, by the door.

'Well, I'd better put this on,' Taff said, picking up a sand coloured beret, from one of the hooks. It wasn't until he turned round, that Richard saw the winged dagger of the Special Air Service. It came to light that this had been the reason the Commandant called for him, and had ordered him to wear headdress, when walking about camp. This rigidity was alien to members of 'The Regiment', who had a much more laid-back approach to military dress.

Richard had suspected there was something different about him. He knew that every evening, Taff came into the Mess at 10pm and had learned he had been out on a two hour run. Taff drank no more than two pints and would disappear, to bed. The SAS were a different breed, highly motivated and not many passed their rigorous selection process. Even after passing selection, they kept their standard of fitness at the highest level. Taff was a classic example, unlike the rest of students on this course, who had not seen the gym nor a pair of trainers, since they had started.

The end of the first week was to culminate in what was known as a 'degradation' exercise. The course had been told to assemble in the lecture theatre, wearing three layers of clothing and their IPE, carrying their respirators. It was just after lunch and the temperature was higher than it had been, since their arrival. They took their seats in the lecture room and one of the staff closed the black curtains, to block out the sun. As the Chief Instructor began to speak, the sound of metal on metal rang out across the room. Instinctively, everyone tore open their respirator haversacks and, holding their breath, donned their respirators. Pulling up the hoods and securing the drawstring, they sat up and faced front. The Chief Instructor went on to explain the symptoms and causes of wearing full IPE, for an extended period. As he went through symptoms such as alienation, the feeling of confinement and tunnel vision, Richard began to sweat. He had taken part in an NBC exercise and trial previously, so hadn't thought this would bother him. After twenty minutes, he wanted to tear the mask from his face. Calming himself and steadying his breathing, the panic began to subside. He continued to sweat, due to the heat in the room and his three layers of clothing.

As the lecture drew to an end, everyone was inspected, to make sure they were wearing three layers and their full IPE. They were then separated into four teams of five and led outside.

Crossing the road, they stepped onto a playing field, where different obstacles and games were set up. Richard's group's first task was to be tethered together by one leg, one man in front of the other. They were to carry an ammunition box up and down a series of bunkers. When they reached the end, they had to navigate all the way back to the start. It was a comedy of errors, as the team tried to keep in step, while climbing up and down the bunker banks. By the time they were finished, they were soaked in sweat and were then moved on to the next exercise or game.

They were to dribble a rugby ball around a slalom course, then kick the oval ball into a football goal. It was hilarious to watch, but wasn't fun to take part in. The exercises went on for around two and a half hours. They were encouraged to drink, frequently, during them. However, they had to carry out the correct drills shown during the week. They were not allowed to remove their respirators, so had to drink using the straw built into their respirators.

After the staff had decided that the exercise had run its course, they asked one candidate to carry out a residual vapour test, using the equipment supplied. They were relieved to hear that everything came back clear, even though they hadn't expected anything else. Surely they would not release an agent in an open area, so close to a civilian, built up, area? The instructors gave the all-clear, everyone pulled back their hoods and removed their respirators. The warm breeze on Richard's face felt heavenly, as he wiped away the sweat from his eyes. The Chief Instructor went on to tell them there was no need to repeat this exercise back in their own Units, this was just to let them experience what it would be like to wear the equipment for long periods. With that, he wished them a good weekend.

The rest of the course flew by and, before long, they were beginning the final test exercise. This would last 36 hours and be a mixture of Nuclear, Biological and Chemical test scenarios. The teams of five had been issued with various items of monitoring and protective equipment.

The list included one NIAID per team, which weighed the same as a small Shetland pony. Richard's group included Mick, the Para, who, on seeing the NIAID, piped up.

'I'll carry that,' he said, a wide grin lighting up his face.

'You're welcome to it,' Richard said. The rest of the team breathed a sigh of relief. They reckoned this went to prove that Paras were good for something.

The first stand that Richard's group went through was a nuclear one. They were housed in a bunker and briefed that there had been a nuclear explosion. They were to take cover, to wait for the fallout to subside. For the following couple of hours, they would go around the surrounding areas, taking readings. On their return, one person, the designated team leader was to check their personal dosimeters, a wrist device which monitored exposure levels to radiation. All these figures were plotted on a chart, to enable the team leader to work out how much each individual had been exposed to. Although fictitious, this was a good training exercise.

For the rest of the day, they rotated through the various stands, marking areas of chemical and biological contaminations and going through the various decontamination drills. The final stand was a seven mile hike, carrying all their equipment, which culminated at the top of a hill. Mick the Para was in his element, loving carrying the NIAID on his back, tabbing his way up the hill. Reaching their destination, they dug in, to simulate an infantry section setting up a defensive position. Once they were settled in, the instructors threw a thunderflash into their midst, to simulate a bombardment. They quickly donned their respirators, carrying out their IA drills. Having done this, the team leader ordered a couple of the team to start monitoring for chemical agents. After two hours, the directing staff told the team there was no sign of any liquid. The team leader instructed one man to carry out a 'residual vapour test', which came back clear. He then removed his mask and the rest watched to see if he contracted any symptoms. To their delight the all clear was given and the remainder unmasked. The exercise and the course was over and Richard was thankful. It had been a hard couple of weeks, but it meant that he would never have to undergo another NBC test in his career.

With these thoughts, Richard sat on the edge of a wood on Soltau training area. He was waiting for the rest of the Troops to come through his NBC stand, during their Troop tests. The first ones who had passed through looked tired and a little pissed off. They had spent the previous night on a night navigation test, which included going through a replen and finishing with hide drills. They had had minimum sleep and were a little tetchy, to say the least.

The unmistakeable sound of the Challenger engines could be heard in the distance. Growing ever louder, two tanks came over the crest, 500 metres ahead. He thought to himself that one of the tanks must have broken down. It wasn't until they drew closer, that Richard recognised the crew of the first vehicle. It was the CO's tank, along with the Regimental Second-in-Commands. As they pulled up in front of him, the crews dismounted and made their way over, to where he was standing. The two crews smiled as they saw Richard, obviously thinking they were going to have an easy time, being part of Command Troop. No sooner had they settled than Richard banged two mess tins together. The grins left their faces, as they grasped for their respirators. They were already wearing their NBC suits, in accordance with the current threat level. Richard observed their drills critically, making sure that everything was in order and being carried out in a timely fashion.

'Right, guys, a good start, an excellent IA drill!' he beamed, having inspected everyone's dress. 'What I want now is for you to do a full personal decontamination.'

The Troops nodded their understanding and began to go into their drills. Firstly, decontaminating their gloves and any area they were going to touch. They were working well. As they removed their helmets and placed them between their legs, Richard wandered around them, trying to find any mistakes he could mark them down for. This was proving difficult, until one idiot removed his respirator to decontaminate his face. Stupidly, he had left the respirator face up; if there had been any falling liquid, it would have fallen inside. Richard took a decontamination puffer bottle, filled with fuller's earth, from his pocket. As the offender began to decontaminate his face, Richard emptied half the contents of the bottle into his upturned respirator. He stood back and waited until the unfortunate, Aidan Manx, replaced his respirator. As he did so and blew out, he ingested a lungful of fuller's earth. He was coughing and spluttering and the others turned round, to see what the problem was. When they saw the eyepieces of his respirator covered in the powder, they burst out laughing.

'Right, you lot, this is not a laughing matter,' Richard spoke, trying to be restore order. 'If this had been for real and it had been a liquid agent, Aidan would have been incapacitated.'

He continued by listing symptoms which Aidan was now showing.

The rest of the crews recognised at once the symptoms and what had to be done. One, Tony Hart, took out a combi pen from Aiden's respirator haversack and simulated putting it into his thigh. Combi pens contained an antidote against nerve agents and the Troops carried three each. Three was the maximum which could be administered or the casualty could contract atropine poisoning, which was just as lethal.

Happy that they had carried out the drills correctly, Richard moved on to the next task, a chemical recce. He gave them an area and some monitoring equipment and signs. For the next twenty minutes, they surveyed and marked the given area. Richard followed them every step of the way, marking on the clip board he carried. The last task he gave them was to fully decontaminate their vehicles, using some buckets and a stirrup pump. This equipment was carried by all the vehicles, except the plastic buckets which Richard supplied, to make things a little easier. The crews mounted their vehicles and prepared the equipment. Starting from the top of the turrets, they worked their way down. It took a lot longer than Richard had given them to complete the task. Once he was satisfied, he called an end to the exercise.

'Right, you can unmask and pack away your kit. That was a good effort, you have been the best, so far,' he congratulated them.

He didn't know it, but they would go on to win the Troop tests. However, they had a few more stands to go. One of these was provided by the Officers' Mess staff. They would have to knock off the top of a champagne bottle with a cavalry sabre, drink the contents and bob for apples. It may not have been a military task, but it was a light-hearted end to the exercise. As Command Troop were not part of a Sabre Squadron, the title of winners of the Troop tests was given to a Troop from A Squadron, much to the disgust of the CO's and 2ic's crews.

Chapter 6 - Fatherhood

Richard returned from exercise and arrived back at his flat, to be greeted by a heavily pregnant Birgit. As usual, he was made to stand outside the door of the flat and remove his clothing, until he was down to his boxer shorts. He was then allowed to enter and was led to the bathroom, where his wife had run him a bath, filled with sweet scented bubbles. While he climbed in and washed away the dirt and grime of the past two weeks, Birgit busied herself, putting his dirty clothes straight into the washing machine. She had commented once that they were so filthy they probably could march there on their own.

As soon as she had started the washing machine, Birgit returned to the bathroom, armed with a glass of sext, complete with a floating mat. This had become a bit of a treat after exercise and Richard lay there, sipping the sparkling wine. Birgit left him to it and went back to the door, to retrieve the rest of his clothes, from his rucksack. As she bent down, she knew something was amiss. A dark patch had appeared on her jeans and she quickly realised her waters had broken. Calling out to Richard to come quickly, she leaned against the wall, panting as she had been taught. The contractions seemed to come every minute or so. Richard's head appeared out of the bathroom.

'What's wrong?' he asked, grumpily, having been disturbed from his relaxing soak.

'I think I'm going into labour!' Birgit said, panting between the words.

Not knowing what to do or say, Richard exclaimed 'Fucking hell, you could have picked a better time!' which drew a look that could have slain a dragon. 'Okay, okay, I'll get dressed,' he said, not wanting to make the situation worse than it already was. Throwing on a pair of jeans and a t-shirt, Richard grabbed the bag Birgit had packed in anticipation of this day.

Being German, she was always very efficient and always planned ahead. They spent their Friday evenings planning a shopping list for what they would eat, the following week. They went shopping for only those items on the list. Richard always managed to sneak a few little treats into the shopping trolley, which always drew a look of disapproval from Birgit, as that deviated from her plans. Richard, secretly, did enjoy the structured way of life, it reflected his military lifestyle. "A place for everything and everything in its place", was a motto he lived by. The pair were a good match and their marriage was a strong one. Like all married couples, they did have their arguments and the first year had been a struggle. The spouses and families of soldiers were often a forgotten part of the military. They were an essential part of army life. If a soldier's family was not happy, this often spilled over into his work life. Richard didn't know it then, but this facet of military life would become a big part of his own career, as his time with the army drew to a close.

Richard threw the bag over his shoulder and helped Birgit down the stairs. He placed the bag on the rear seat, opening the passenger door for gasping Birgit. She struggled to put the seatbelt on, so Richard did it for her. Jumping into the driver's seat, he engaged the gears and drove out of the estate. It was less than a twenty minute drive to the local German hospital in heavy traffic, so at this time of day it should only take half that. They were quite fortunate with Birgit being a German citizen, as the nearest military hospital was almost an hour away.

As they pulled up in the car park, Richard leapt out and assisted Birgit, from the car. They made their way, slowly, toward the hospital entrance and followed the signs for maternity. The staff on the maternity ward were very calm when the couple arrived at reception. There was an exchange in German between Birgit and the female on the desk. Although Richard could speak German, the medical terms they were using were unknown to him. After Birgit's details had been noted, they were taken to a room by one of the midwives. She gave Birgit a gown and asked her to undress. She complied and eased herself onto the bed.

Feeling like a spare part, Richard said he was going for a cigarette. He leaned over and kissed Birgit, saying he wouldn't be long, then turned and left the room. He had felt helpless and was thankful to be out of the room.

Finding an area where he was allowed to smoke outside the hospital, he withdrew a cigarette from its packet and lit it, his hands shaking. Inhaling a deep lungful of nicotine, he slowly began to calm down. He wasn't a heavy smoker, but suspected that, over the course of the next few hours, he might be making a few trips outside. Stubbing out what was left of the cigarette in a nearby ashtray, he made his way back inside. It took him a while to get his bearings and find his way back to the maternity suite. Locating the room, he quietly knocked on the door, opened it and put his head round, to make sure he had indeed found the right one. Birgit seemed a little calmer now and was alone. She was still breathing a little heavily but did not seem to be in as much pain.

'They said that I have gone into labour, but it might be a while, before the baby comes,' she smiled, as he approached the bed.

'It'll be over soon enough,' Richard replied, trying to reassure her. It was only then he realised he had not informed camp that he probably wouldn't be in for the next couple of days. There was time enough for that, he thought. Taking Birgit's hand in his, he sat on a small chair, next to the bed. As he did so, Birgit had another contraction and squeezed his hand tightly, causing him to wince, in pain. He wondered if this was Birgit getting revenge on her man, to reflect the pain of childbirth.

For the next couple of hours, he stayed by Brigit's bedside, stroking her forehead and holding her hand. Every now and then, a midwife came in and examined her. They re-assured her of the progress of her labour, offering pain relief, if required. Birgit consistently replied that she didn't want any and the midwife left the room. She asked Richard to get something for her, out of the bag they had brought. As he fumbled about, looking, he couldn't find the item anywhere. It wasn't like her to forget something, he thought to himself.

Having heard the latest conversation with the midwife, he knew the baby's arrival was not imminent, so decided to nip home and gather a few more things for Brigit's stay. He told his wife he wouldn't be long and left the building, letting reception know where he was going. The receptionist glared at him, incredulous that he was leaving his wife on her own.

It took Richard over twenty minutes to get home, as the traffic had got busier. It was well past lunchtime and he realised that he hadn't eaten since he had returned from exercises. He quickly made himself a bacon sandwich, which he devoured. Gathering together a few more things for Birgit, he stuffed them into a bag and locked the door to the flat. It had been eight hours since they had left, that morning, for the hospital.

Back at the hospital, he entered the room to find Birgit, a picture of serenity. She smiled as he sat down next to her, taking his hand in hers. The calmness was down to Birgit having sucked on gas and air, just before Richard arrived. She informed him that there had been no change with her labour and it that it could be a few hours yet. Richard nodded. He just wanted it to be over with, as he was sure his wife did.

It was another eight hours before Brigit's contractions were close enough for her to be taken into a birthing room. Walking into the room, Richard looked around, wide-eyed, at the apparatus and equipment. There were tools laid out in sterile, silver trays. It was more like a medieval torture chamber than a delivery room, he contemplated. Birgit was now in severe pain and the nurses suggested an epidural. She hadn't wanted any pain relief prior to this, apart from gas and air. The pain was now so bad that she would take anything. It had been sixteen hours since her first contractions and she was now feeling the effects.

An anaesthetist prepared a needle, in readiness for administering the pain relief. As soon as the injection had been inserted and the blessed relief delivered, Birgit felt much better. The relative tranquility was short lived, as her contractions increased. She squeezed Richard's hand so hard, he thought she would draw blood with her fingernails. Perspiration ran down her forehead. Richard wiped it away with an antiseptic wipe. Conversation between the midwives and Birgit was getting more and more animated, as she was getting very close to delivering.

Richard looked at the clock on the wall and hoped that Birgit could hold on, just a little longer. It was April 20th, a date that had always stuck in Richard's mind. From his beloved history lessons at school and his fascination with the Second World War, he knew April 20th, 1889 had been the date of Hitler's birth. Richard simply did not want his first child to be born on the same day. It looked as though he wouldn't have a choice, as Birgit gave one more, desperate push.

A midwife reached across, to her right and picked up what looked like a pair of kitchen scissors. The snipping sound reverberated around the room. Richard closed his eyes, the grip of Brigit's hand on his intensified. The midwife uttered a few more encouraging words. Brigit's head lolled to one side, a picture of relief. The midwife was busy cutting the umbilical cord and stood back, holding the form of a new-born baby. The sound of Richard's daughter's cries overwhelmed him joy. He had never thought that he would feel like this. He stared open-mouthed, as the midwife beckoned him over.

She handed the tiny bundle into Richard's outstretched arms. He peered into his daughter's eyes, the colour of coal. As he held her, a stream of black liquid coated the white gown he was wearing. His daughter had emptied her bowels, all over him. He fought back the need to retch, at the same time finding the situation amusing.

He passed the baby to the midwife, who cleaned her up once more and presented her to Birgit. Gazing at his wife cuddling their child and the new-born's perfectly formed features, Richard could see immense pride and love, the bond between a mother and baby. He disrobed and cleaned himself, then joined them both at the bedside. He leaned forward and gave his wife and baby a kiss on their foreheads.

They were left alone for a moment, until the nurses came back and took away their daughter, so she could be properly checked over.

Leaving the staff to tidy his wife, Richard rushed from the room, letting her know he would not be long away. It had been seventeen hours since they had arrived at the hospital and, outside, Richard drew heavily on the cigarette, between his lips. The last hour had whizzed past but would be one he would remember all his life. He would remind his daughter, in the years to come, how she had shat on him, on their first meeting. After a second cigarette, he returned to the ward, in time to see Birgit being wheeled back into her room. He joined her at the bedside and their new-born daughter, Sonia, was brought in and given over to Birgit. They both stared lovingly at her; it had been almost three years since they had started to try for a baby and the day was finally here.

On the drive home, Richard put on the car audio and placed a CD into it. The sound of *Informer*, by the Canadian reggae musician Snow, blasted out. He had no idea why he picked that particular CD but he played the song, over and over again. In years to come, when he thought back to that day, that song would always enter his head.

Placing the key in the door of their flat, Richard turned it and entered. It seemed strangely quiet, as he padded down the hallway. Crossing the living room, he opened the drinks cabinet. Taking out a glass, he poured out a generous measure of whiskey.

Birgit hadn't manged to hold on until after midnight but Richard didn't care, he had his first child.

Making himself comfortable on the sofa, he lifted the glass to his lips. Before sipping the amber liquid, he raised the glass in a toast and, in a quiet voice murmured,

'Happy birthday, Adolf.'

Chapter 7 - Canada Once More

Sonia was three weeks old. As Richard packed his bags, once again, for a trip to Canada, it hit him he would experience, first-hand, one of the downsides of being in the military. Many personnel missed seeing their children grow up, which was one of the reasons many left the services prematurely. Having being brought up in a military environment, Richard had seen this himself.

He had his own child now and the cycle was repeating itself. He took a photograph of his wife and daughter from an album, in the living room. He slid it into his top pocket and made sure the button was securely fastened.

He had already selected a number of albums to take with him, top of the pile was his beloved *Informer*, which he packed, with a portable CD player, in the small bag he would take on the plane. His preparations complete, he returned to the living room to say his farewells.

Birgit was on the sofa, nursing Sonia. She had been no trouble since her birth, being put to bed around 7pm, and waking, once a night, to be fed feed. As Birgit was breastfeeding, she let Richard sleep on.

As he leaned over to kiss them both, he noticed tears in Birgit's eyes.

'What's wrong?' he asked, concerned.

There was a pregnant pause before Birgit replied. 'I'm not sure, you going away has never bothered me up till now,' she whispered, careful not to disturb her sleeping infant.

'It'll be okay. I'll be back before you know it,' Richard tried to reassure her, 'your family are just up the road, if you need anything.'

The sound of a car horn outside the flat heralded the arrival of one of Richard's neighbours. He had arranged a lift into camp because Birgit needed their car and he didn't want to drag her and the baby into camp. He descended the stairs and climbed into the waiting car. As they drove away, he looked up at the windows of the flat, to see Birgit waving him goodbye. For the first time in his life, he didn't want to go away. Of course, that was not an option.

The plane touched down at the familiar Calgary Airport. It was mid-June and the weather was a blistering 32 degrees Celsius. This was in stark contrast to a few years earlier, when Richard had contracted frostbite. He glanced down at his left boot, as they disembarked the aircraft. His foot still reminded him of that time, when the temperature dropped below freezing point.

This exercise would be the exact opposite. They would have to contend with searing hot conditions, on the open expanses of the prairie. It was the time of the Calgary Stampede. The Airport was busy, with incoming tourists.

The Calgary Stampede is an annual festival held every July. The ten-day event, which bills itself as "The Greatest Outdoor Show on Earth" attracts over one million visitors per year, and features one of the world's largest rodeos, parades, stage shows, concerts, agricultural competitions, chuck-wagon racing and exhibitions. Richard had managed to go once before and found it to be an amazing experience. He wasn't sure when he would get his R&R this year, so was unsure if he would manage again.

The journey to Suffield and Crowfoot Camp was an uncomfortable one. The coach, which normally had air conditioning, was playing up. By the time they arrived, Richard was dripping with sweat. Collecting their luggage from the baggage truck, the men found their rooms. Richard had lost count of how many times he had entered these huts, over the past eleven years. Nothing ever changed and, after throwing their kits on the beds, the new arrivals walked to their RMP briefing.

The ice cold water cascaded down Richard's body, as he leaned against the tiled wall, in the shower room. His body was telling him to go to sleep. From past experience he knew if he went to bed now, he would wake up in the early hours. He grabbed his towel from the hook, put on his flip flops and returned to the room. As in the bus, the air-conditioning wasn't working, so he began to sweat again.

'How long before you're ready, Besty?' he called out to Ian Best.

'Two minutes!' came the reply, in Ian's thick, Belfast accent.

They finished getting changed and walked to the guard room, where the Provost staff manned the desk. Richard asked if they would call a taxi. As he waited, he looked around the room, bringing back memories of the time when he had spent a few days in one of the cells. His thoughts were disturbed by the Provost Corporal.

'It'll be ten minutes, at the front gate,' he informed them, returning to his newspaper. He seemed annoyed that he had been interrupted from his "busy" work schedule.

Richard and Ian sarcastically thanked him for all his help. Why were members of the Provost such a bunch of dicks, thought Richard. As they approached the exit from camp, the taxi was already there. Richard jumped in the front, saying that Ian could pay on the way back. This agreed, he told the driver the destination. The two friends chatted throughout the familiar journey. As the taxi pulled up outside the Gaslamp pub, Richard drew a twenty dollar bill, from his jeans' pocket and handed it over, to the driver.

'It's 25 dollars, bud,' came the voice from the cab.

'Feckin' hell, it was only eighteen dollars last year!' Richard replied, digging into his pocket again, to retrieve another note. He handed it over, begrudgingly, and the two went inside the pub.

It was just around 11:00am and there were only a couple of locals in, at this early hour. Richard, politely, nodded his head, in acknowledgement. The response was an inaudible mumble, which didn't sound too friendly. The locals didn't like squaddies but put up with them, for the sake of the town's economy. If it weren't for the Battlegroups which passed through every year, the town might probably cease to exist.

Both ordered a pitcher of beer and sat down at a table, in the corner. Richard began to feel tired, after the first couple of glasses.

'Fancy a walk over to the Captain's Cabin?' he asked Ian, in an attempt to try to stir himself.

'Aye, why not? It's dead in here,' Ian answered, polishing off the last of his beer.

The two picked up their empty pitchers and glasses and returned them to the bar. Thanking the barman, an ex-squaddie, who had settled in the town, when he left the forces, they made for the door. The glare of the summer sun blinded Richard, emerging from the dark, dingy bar-room.

A short walk across the rail-tracks found them outside the Captain's Cabin. Usually a quiet bar, Richard had often used it, when he wanted to get away from the testosterone fuelled pubs teeming with soldiers. Unlike a lot of the bars in town, it was friendly, as well. As they walked in, the girl behind the bar looked up. Recognising Richard, she smiled.

'Hello there, stranger,' she greeted him, 'whiskey, is it?' impressively remembering what Richard normally drank in the bar.

'Good to see you, Kirsty. Didn't think you would still be working here,' he replied. 'I think we'll just have a couple of beers to start off with. Don't want to kick the arse out of it on our first day,' he laughed.

'You take a seat and I'll bring it over,' Kirsty indicated a table.

The Cabin had a few more customers in, talking local politics, the weather and other usual subjects debated in drinking establishments. Having spent many happy hours listening to locals in bars; and engaging himself in their debates in the past, Richard reckoned no nationality was as opinionated as the Canadians. The discussions had, at times, got a little heated, normally after he had consumed his body weight in alcohol. Having integrated himself when he was last here, he had built up a friendship with some of the regulars and he raised his hand in recognition, as two of them entered the bar.

Ian and Richard passed the next half hour recounting stories of visits gone by. It wasn't long before they were rolling about, laughing at some of the scrapes they had been in or witnessed. The pitcher was almost empty and Richard ordered another, before grabbing something to eat. As he stood at the bar, waiting for Kirsty to finish serving another customer, a wicked thought entered his mind. Ian never liked anyone knowing about his famous sibling. Football was a big thing with Canadians, and they kept an eye on results in the English and Scottish leagues. Richard leaned over to his right, where two drinkers were deep in conversation.

'I don't want to butt in,' he whispered, surreptitiously, 'but do you know who that lad is I'm sitting with?'

They shrugged their shoulders, saying they had no idea.

'That's the brother of George Best, who used to play for Manchester United,' Richard triumphed.

'Get the fuck out of here!' one of them yelled, at the top of his voice, causing everyone in the bar to look round, at a puzzled Ian.

Ian stared over in Richard's direction, not knowing why everyone in the bar was gaping at him. Richard stood grinning and it didn't take long, for the penny to drop.

'You bastard!' he shouted, knowing the cat was out of the bag.

For the next 30 minutes, he had to field questions about his early life and growing up with such a talented, famous sibling. Ian was a quiet person and, unlike his brother, didn't like to be in the limelight.

After a while, the two made their excuses and prepared to leave. Just before they did, Paul Hunt and Phil Taylor, from the Regiment, entered the bar. They propped themselves up at the counter and began a furtive conversation with Kirsty. Richard noticed that she was agitated and there followed raised voices. Abruptly, the two exited. Richard made his way over to Kirsty, to find out what had just occurred.

'Is there a problem?'

'Not anymore, there isn't,' she said, smiling. 'Those two jokers only wanted to provide security for the place, while the Battlegroup is in town,' she laughed.

Richard knew that the pair, had run the doors, on a couple of nightclubs, back in Germany. They were obviously chancing their arm, to make a bit of cash, before the Regiment deployed on to the prairie. Kirsty and Richard laughed at the proposal, till Ian joined them and they left, in search in food.

The next week was spent, as usual, preparing vehicles, for the exercise. Everything had gone well on the handover takeover of equipment and vehicles. Preparing command vehicles was a lot easier than preparing the main battle tanks.

It took more time because of the equipment required to set up and run a Battlegroup complex. They needed to check the generating units they carried were all in working order; and the penthouses, attached to the back of the vehicles, were serviceable. All radio equipment was tested, to ensure effective communications. It would be rather embarrassing if the CO tried to contact one of his commanders and, due to poor preparation, he was unable to do so. That would not be viewed in a favourable light. The rebuke would be passed down the chain of command, as the saying goes, "shit always rolls downhill!"

The Battlegroup gathered on the 'dustbowl' at the top of camp, ready to move out, at their allotted times. The heat had risen and it was now in the high 30s C. A warm wind, known as a Chinook, swirled around the dustbowl, blinding the troops. Richard pulled down his goggles from the top of his helmet. He wrapped his Shemagh around his face, preventing the dust from getting into his mouth and nose. Now protected against the elements, Richard awaited the order to move out. He called down inside the vehicle, to make sure everyone was ready for the move. Terry, John and Grant gave him the thumbs up. Pete Cain, their driver, gave a burst of revs on the accelerator, confirming he, too, was ready.

'Hello, Charlie Charlie One, this is Zero Alpha, move now, out!' the CO gave the order for them to head off on to the area. He had chosen to take his Land Rover, rather than travel on his tank. The Regimental Second in Command, had decided to command his tank, for the move, as his Land Rover was in the workshop having repairs done.

With a belch of black smoke and a cloud of dust, one by one. the Sultan command vehicles entered the area. They took the Rattlesnake Road, past the Exercise Command Centre at Brutus, to Wells Junction, which would be their home, for the first few days of the exercise.

As soon as they arrived, the RSWO arranged the command vehicles in a 'cruciform' arrangement, so that the penthouses could be pulled out and joined together. This provided an area inside, where tables could be laid out, allowing the CO to give his briefing to his Squadron and Company commanders and support arms. It was also an area used for planning and a board, with a map of the area, was set up, for the CO and Operations Officer's use. This left the command vehicles free for their operators and

Watchkeeper, usually a senior NCO or Officer. The operators provided the role of 'scribes' and logged any messages that came into Battlegroup command. They would rotate, with two operators and a Watchkeeper on at any one time, reduced to one operator and a Watchkeeper, in silent hours.

Every evening, each Squadron, Company and support arm were required to send their vehicle locations back to Battlegroup. Each vehicle had a unique 'Zap Number', which was painted on its side. These numbers were even issued down to trailers, in order that all vehicles could be accounted for, at the end of a day's firing. Live firing areas could not be opened or go to 'green', until all vehicles were accounted for. This process often went on for hours; safety was taken very seriously by the BATUS training staff. There had been occasions when vehicles had been reported as accounted for, only for firing to be halted, as vehicles, either lost or broken down, were found in a live firing template.

It took a couple of hours for the complex to be set up, with the generators running, to charge and run radios and vehicle batteries. The Troop looked to put up their 'bivvies', four man canvas tents, normally secured to trees. However, on the prairie, there was hardly a tree to be found, and were so scarce, they were marked on maps. Enterprising crews attached their tents to the sides of their vehicles, while others began to get a meal going. When they were in locations like this, all the crews cooked communally, sharing rations, as well as cooking and washing up duty. They were to be together for the first three days, then the Echelons would remain, while the main command vehicles would follow the exercise, from two to five kilometers behind the rearmost troops.

Richard had eaten his evening meal and was washing it down, with a welcome mug of coffee. As he drained the last drops from the mug, he felt his stomach start to gurgle. He couldn't believe it, they had been on the area less than a day and he needed a crap! Reaching the front of his vehicle, he opened the long bin, bolted on the front. He extracted a shovel and roll of soft toilet paper, a luxury every crew carried, as the toilet paper in the ration packs, was like tracing paper.

Locking the bin back up again, Richard turned into the dark wilderness. Going on a 'shovel recce' was all a part of life on exercise and was an event which had resulted in many humorous episodes. Experienced men would walk a short distance downwind and simply dig a hole. Some made use of oil containers, fashioned into portable toilets, hung off the gun crutch, at the rear of the vehicles. When the nature took its course, they would simply use these improvised devices.

Richard chuckled to himself as he walked, recalling the time when one young officer, on his first exercise, had wandered off, to relieve himself. Particularly shy, he had walked almost a kilometer from where the vehicles had leaguered up, for the night. His crew, knowing where he was going, had taken great delight in starting up the vehicles' GUE and starting the gun kit. They waited until they knew he would be in position to do his business. Then, flicking a switch, they opened the armoured door to the searchlight, located on the side of the vehicle. The searchlight was a powerful beast and moved in relation to where the gun barrel was pointing. Much to the young Subaltern's embarrassment, his ablutions were on show to the whole Squadron, as the searchlight bathed him and the surrounding area in spotlight.

Richard stopped, around 30 metres from the vehicles. He took the shovel and began to dig in the hard, arid ground, dry as a bone, from the last few months of constant sunshine. Satisfied it was deep enough, Richard began to undo his coveralls. Pulling them down, he took hold of the arms, placing them in front of him. Once, in the early days, he had made the mistake of not doing this and had shat all over the sleeves. As he began to force the waste from his body, he was disturbed by a high pitched sound. He felt a stinging on his exposed backside, whirled round to find that he had chosen to take a dump, right in the middle of a swarm of mosquitoes! At that time of year they were a plague all over the training area. He quickly tried to finish the shit, while being bitten what felt like a thousand times. Hastily cleaning himself with the toilet paper, he pulled up his coveralls, filled in the hole and sprinted back, in the direction of the Troop.

When he arrived, he replaced the shovel and paper in their bin. He headed inside the complex, where there were enough lights, to see what damage had been inflicted. Dropping his coveralls, he bared his arse. The sight was met by a cry of derision by a Regimental Signals Officer, acting as Watchkeeper.

'For fuck's sake, Corporal Hunter, do you have to?' he asked, shaking his head, in disgust.

'I've just been bitten to fuck by a load of mozzies! How bad does it look?' he proffered his rear end to the operators, in the back of the Sultan.

'Fucking hell! It looks like the surface of the moon! Put some cream on it, before it gets infected,' one of the operators suggested, laughing.

Pulling up his coveralls, Richard rushed to see the medic, parked with his AFV 432 ambulance, to the side of the complex. Examining Richard's predicament, the medic handed him antiseptic cream, insisting that he wasn't going to apply it himself. Richard thanked him for his concern and left with the tube in hand, to find a quiet spot to apply the treatment. 'What a start to the exercise,' he thought to himself, as the soothing cream took effect.

For the next couple of days, while the tanks completed their 'Confirmation of Accuracy by Firing' (CABF), Command Troop practised 'stepping up', a procedure where one vehicle, usually Zero Charlie, detached itself from the complex and moved forward, to simulate following up, behind the Battlegroup. Once in position, it reported back to the main command complex, who then moved, to join it.

This meant they always maintained control of the Battlegroup, while the other vehicles were moving. At times, it was necessary, due to the distance between command Troop and the main forces, to deploy a Rebroadcast (Rebro) vehicle, a Spartan light tracked vehicle, also of the CVRT class.

On this occasion, it was commanded by Dave Elmsall and driven by Joe Gordon, whose job it was to situate themselves in a suitable position, to enable them to pass through or rebroadcast all communications, thereby extending the normal working range of the Clansman radios. It was a job to be envied, because the men were mostly left to their own devices.

Dave, who liked a drink or two, took great advantage of this and had, in the past, been reprimanded for being 'worse for wear' on exercise.

One day, their vehicle caught fire. Richard knew that had happened to his father's tank and how serious the repercussions could be.

Although the vehicle was not carrying live ammunition, its petrol engine meant there was a real danger of an explosion, if it were not brought under control. Dave was astonished to see Joe shoot out of his driver's cab and set off, across the prairie. He should have pulled the fixed fire extinguisher, which would have flooded the engine compartment. Dave, despite having consumed a number of beers that morning, quickly sobered up. He jumped down from the vehicle and pulled the handle of the extinguisher. After a few moments, he lifted the engine decks and threw in a couple of portable extinguishers. Quickly, the blaze was put out and Dave called across to Joe, who trudged back to the vehicle, with a sheepish look on his face. He was greeted by the mother of all bollockings from Dave, for dereliction of his duties.

This done, the pair laughed, in relief, about their lucky escape. Dave got on the radio and called the REME to come and inspect the vehicle. It transpired that the engine was so severely damaged, a new one was required, which put them out of the exercise, for a couple of days. This new was met by delight from Dave, who cracked open another beer.

The Operations Officer, Captain Schneider, had, for the last week, been complaining about the amount of people who had been crapping close to the command complex. The Troop leader of Recce Troop had picked up on this remark, when he attended a CO's briefing, the previous evening. On his way to Battlegroup HQ the following day, he passed one of the infantry soldiers, taking a dump. He approached him and asked him, when he was done, if he could have the turd. The infantry soldier looked bemused, but agreed to his request. As the Troop leader scooped the dark lump into a bag with a shovel, he giggled to himself. As he returned to his vehicle, he heard the perplexed soldier mutter something along the lines of, 'fucking gay cavalry officers'.

Reaching Battlegroup HQ, the Troop leader made his way to the side of the canvas complex. He placed the turd on a shovel and slipped it under the tent, to a spot beneath the desk, where the Ops Officer was sitting. Giving the shovel back to his driver, who was crying with laughter by this point, he nonchalantly walked into the complex, as if butter wouldn't melt in his mouth.

A few minutes passed and the CO was reaching the middle of his briefing. The rest of the commanders, by this time alerted to what had happened, were watching the Ops Officer. His nose twitched, he began to sniff the air, complaining about the troop's poor personal hygiene. As the smell got stronger, he was heard to utter, 'Its definitely getting worse, it's almost as though someone has laid one inside the tent!' At which point, he looked down, to see the steaming turd adorning his freshly polished cavalry boots.

'Oh, for fuck sake!' he exclaimed. The whole briefing group, including the CO, erupted into raucous laughter.

Incidents like this was what Richard loved about serving. He lived and worked with people who could make any situation funny, including the officer class. The story quickly spread throughout command Troop and the Recce Troop leader attracted great kudos, for having pulled off the joke.

The exercise now began to grow in intensity and neared its final week. The heat was unbearable, with no trees to give shade. It had been a week since the last shower run, the fetid smell from the unwashed men was almost tangible.

The main Battlegroup command complex were now following behind the lead Squadrons and Companies. Richard and his crew had pulled back to the rear echelon location, some fifteen kilometres behind the main forces. Although they were some way behind the Battlegroup, they still had to maintain tactical awareness. All the echelon vehicles had their camouflage nets erected and sentries posted. Those not on stag slept, during the day. The echelons' main tasks of refuelling and resupplying food and ammunition were carried out in the hours of darkness. It was a job that few appreciated. They were lovingly known as REMFs, an acronym for Rear Echelon Mother Fuckers, a title they did not deserve, or like, in the slightest.

Richard and his crew were part of this organisation, so were tarred with the same brush. This rankled Richard slightly and he longed to be back on tanks. Little did he know, but a twist in fate would see him remaining where he was, for a while longer. For the next week, they carried out their task of keeping lines of communication open with the forward elements of the Battlegroup. All requests for replenishments were passed back from command Troop, via the various Squadrons, Companies and support arms. These were then passed on to HQ Squadron Leader, who commanded the echelon.

Richard and his crew rotated the duties of listening out, on the radios. Two people would man the net, while the other two slept. Working in command Troop had given Richard a better overall picture of the makeup and tactics of an armoured unit. This would stand him in good stead in years to come.

The boredom was broken up by little things the Troops found amusing. One was trying to capture gophers or prairie dogs, which inhabited most of the training area. Richard wondered why these creatures continued to inhabit and build homes in such a dangerous pace for them. With the heavy armour rumbling overhead and artillery fire raining down on their underground burrows, it was a wonder they survived, in such numbers.

It was midday on the penultimate day and Richard sat in the command vehicle, with the back doors open, trying to ventilate the enclosed space. He watched, inquisitively, as two members of Motor Transport Troop crawled forward, on their stomachs. One had a shovel in his hand, while the other held something bright yellow. As they neared one of the many burrows in the ground, the soldier with the small yellow disc began to break it up. Richard recognised it as processed cheese or 'cheese possessed', as it was popularly known. The soldier laid a couple of bits outside the entrance to one of the holes. An age passed, as the two soldiers waited patiently, lying in the burning sun. Richard lost interest and returned to the book he was reading. He would look up every now and again, to see if there had been any change in the situation. Once, a small head appeared out of the hole, sniffing the air. The soldiers had ensured that they were downwind of the burrow. Satisfied it was safe to emerge, the gopher left the burrow and began devouring the cheese that had been left there. One of the soldiers leapt to his feet and, in one swift movement, swung the shovel, in the direction of the gopher. Richard winced, as it connected full force with the rodent, sending it flying through the air. It landed about 10 metres away, twitched a couple of times and lay still. This provided great amusement to the pair of assassins, whose laughter could be heard across the echelon position. Although the sight of the creature flying through the air was comical; and the creatures were seen as vermin, the act itself did not sit well with Richard. The feeling lasted around a minute before he put it out of his mind and returned to his reading.

At the end of the exercise, Richard bumped into one of his friends, who was, at the time, serving as one of the safety staff. He told Richard of an incident which had happened during the exercise. One of the safety staff on a 'Warrior' Armoured Personnel Carrier had hit a bump. The driver's hatch springs had failed. The driver had his hands out of the cab at the time. The hatch slammed into them, resulting in him having all his fingers, less a thumb and a little finger, crushed. He joked that it looked something like a Cornish pasty. By the time Richard's friend arrived, the driver had received an ampulet of morphine. Despite the wounds, he was more concerned about being placed into the helicopter and returned to the UK.

The driver lost three fingers in the incident and was worried about being kicked out of the Army. Laughingly, his visitors reminded him that he would be ideal for the stores, as his hand was now the perfect tool for counting out the prescribed blankets. Soldiers were famed for making light of bad situations and Richard pissed himself, when he heard the story.

Chapter 8 - Calgary Stampede

It had been a week since they had left the prairie. The Troop had worked tirelessly, getting the vehicles ready to hand over. That had all gone smoothly and the men were now getting ready to go on R&R.

Richard had arranged to go to the Calgary Stampede, with his old gunner Roger and Glen Campbell, an operator on the Intelligence Officer's vehicle. Glen was from Leeds and, like most soldiers, enjoyed a good drink. Richard had matured a little, having reached the dizzy heights of Corporal. He knew that he would have to try to reign in Glen, to prevent him from dropping them all in the shit. He chuckled to himself when he thought of the numerous times he had gone on R&R and others had been looking out for him.

They had arranged a taxi to meet them, at the main gate, in half an hour. Richard had packed a few things in a rucksack the previous evening. Most of the blokes travelled light, choosing to buy clothes while they were away, as mementoes of their visits. Richard had numerous pairs of jeans and fake Lacoste t-shirts, bought while serving with the UN in Cyprus. He pulled a pair of jeans out of his locker and slipped on a bright pink Lacoste t-shirt.

'You're not fuckin' wearing that, ya bender!' Glen ridiculed him.

'Why not? I'm in touch with my feminine side,' Richard laughed.

'What chance have me and Roger got to tap off, with you dressed like someone out of Wham?' Glen shouted across the room, drawing howls of laughter from the rest of the Troop.

'Just get yourself ready,' Richard answered, 'our taxi is due in 25 minutes.'

The three mates picked up their bags and made their way to the front gate. The taxi was already there, to take them the two miles down the road to a road-stop café, on the edge of the trans-Canada highway. From there, they would take a Greyhound bus to the bright lights of Calgary.

They only had a short wait at the pickup point and climbed aboard the bus, within twenty minutes of having left camp. The bus was almost full, so the three friends had to sit apart. Richard wasn't bothered, he nodded to the person sharing the seat with him, then pulled out his Sony Walkman. Despite the sound of Bon Jovi ringing in his ears, he closed his eyes and drifted off to sleep. He was rudely wakened by Roger, shaking his shoulder:

'Richard, we're here! Time to get off!' he shouted in his ear, removing the earphones from his head.

Quickly packing away his music into the bag he had placed beneath his feet, Richard and his pals got off the bus.

In March 1912, Guy Weadick arrived in Calgary to pitch a 6-day spectacle titled the "Frontier Day Celebration and Championship." Weadick, a successful vaudeville performer who had travelled throughout North America and Europe as a trick roper, envisioned a world-class rodeo competition that would celebrate the romance and culture of the "disappearing" Old West. He received support for the event he called the "Stampede" from four prosperous southern Alberta ranchers: A.E. Cross, George Lane, Pat Burns and A.J. McLean, collectively known as the Big Four. First held in September of 1912, the Stampede featured roping and bronc events with competitors from throughout the North American West. Women participated in the saddlebronc and trick riding competitions. Members of the Treaty 7 Nations participated in the events as well. The title of world champion bareback bronc rider went to Tom Three Persons of the Kainai (Blood) Nation who was the first person to stay on Cyclone, the famous horse unbeaten by 129 other riders before Three Persons rode him to a standstill. Despite the rainy

weather, the first Stampede drew large crowds and was a
success.

Due to the onset of an economic depression
followed by the outbreak of the First World War, Weadick's
hopes of making the Stampede an annual event were
dashed. But in 1919, the Big Four and Ernie L.
Richard'son, the Secretary of the Calgary Exhibition,
called him back to the city to hold a Victory Stampede that
would celebrate peace and the end of the First World War.
Once again, the Stampede was a successful rodeo
competition and western event.

In 1923, the Stampede joined with the Exhibition
holding one event – the Calgary Exhibition and Stampede –
in July. This was also the first year of the pancake
breakfast, started by Jack Morton offering breakfast to
visitors and locals alike from the back of his chuckwagon
parked downtown. Within a few years, attendance broke
200,000 and the spectacle continued to grow into the
Stampede we enjoy today. It remains a celebration of the
Old West out of which Calgary grew and showcases the
modern, multicultural and cosmopolitan city it has become.
Like the Stampede, Calgary's past and present are firmly
rooted in the traditions of western heritage and values.
(Calgarystampede.com)

It was a short taxi drive, from the bus depot to the
Elbow River Creek Hotel, their accommodation for the
next four days. The hotel was set in a picturesque location,
on the banks of the Elbow River. The establishment was
nothing much to write home about but had been
recommended by a friend, Keith, from B Squadron. He had
met a French-Canadian girl called Monique, who had been
working there on his first visit, the previous year.

They had spent four days having wild sex and he
had planned to see her again. On his return from the prairie,
the hopeful lover decided to give her a call. Monique
answered and he was horrified to recognise a familiar

voice, in the background. When he asked her who it was, she told him it was a friend of his from the Regiment, who had spent the night drinking, in her apartment, with her and her friend. He demanded to speak to his so-called friend, who proceeded to protest his innocence, insisting nothing had happened. The poor sod was distraught and called mate all the names under the sun. However, a week later, true love resumed and the incident didn't stop Keith going to stay with her on his next R&R.

As the friends entered the hotel foyer, they made for reception and booked in. After receiving their keys, they decided to have a quick beer, before getting showered and taking in the sights. It was early afternoon and the bar was already half full. Waiting for the girl serving to ask for their order, Richard spotted the name tag, on her uniform. Listening intently to her conversing with a customer confirmed that it was the same Monique the B Squadron lad had told them about. After she finished serving her previous customer, she turned to them, smiling the smile all good bar staff show, in any bar in the world.

'Can I take your order, please, sir'? she asked, in her distinctive accent.

'Can we have three Budweisers?' Richard asked, politely. 'By the way, I think you know a friend of ours, Keith, a British Soldier?'

'My God, yeah, of course I do! Did he give you my name?' she enquired, timidly.

'Well, he recommended the Hotel but, yes, he did mention that the two of you had met, last year.'

Monique blushed, visibly and smiled. She turned and opened the coolers, situated at the rear of the bar. Taking the tops off three Buds, she handed the bottles to the friends, who stood, grinning at her. Richard suspected she must be wondering what on earth had Keith told them.

Within minutes, they had polished off their drinks, bade farewell to Monique and made their way to their rooms. Glen and Roger were sharing, while Richard had decided to take one by himself. He thought this best, as he had a tendency to snore loudly, when drunk. They arranged to meet back downstairs, in an hour.

Opening the door to his room, Richard was pleasantly surprised at its size. For the bargain price of 25 dollars, you got a lot of room for your buck, he thought. Similar to America, everything here was of ample proportions, from meals, drinks to, at times, very large women. He threw himself on the bed and lay staring at the ceiling, relaxing for a moment. He had spent some time in Canada over the past twelve years and this was one of the better hotels he had frequented.

He thought back to a time he had been in Edmonton, a few hours north of Calgary. He and a friend had stayed in a motel called Cecil's. It had cost them five dollars each, for the night. The ambience and decor reflected the price and after one night there, they had decided to move out.

Here was somewhat different. He was looking forward to the next three days. Rising from the bed, he unpacked his clutch bag. He placed the clothes in the wardrobe and, taking his towel and wash kit, made his way to the bathroom.

After showering, Richard turned on the TV and flicked through the channels. This was the first time he had stayed in a room on his own, so he made the most of it. The lads often shared rooms, to keep the price down, to allow more money for beer and entertainment.

He cast his mind back to the last time they had stayed in Calgary, when there had been four in one room. They had turned on the radio for some background music. They had listened to a local station, where the presenter had been hosting a 'call-in' about chat-up lines. The roommates had been taking it in turns, to use the shower. One of them, Jim, nick-named Bucky, had said he was just popping downstairs and, with a cheeky grin on his face, had departed.

The others had rotated use of the bathroom, until they were all ready. It was only then, they had noticed Jim was still absent.

''Where's Bucky?' one had asked.

'He said he was just popping downstairs but didn't say what for,' Richard had replied.

Just as he had said this, their attention had been drawn to the DJ, on the radio.

'Our next caller is Jim, all the way from England. Hi there, Jim, how are you doing?'

'I'm great, mate,' came the dulcet Yorkshire accent.

'Well, Jim, as you know, we are talking about chat-up lines. Do you have a favourite you use?'

It went quiet for a moment, before Jim answered:

'Aye, I have one that normally works for me.'

Again, he had paused for effect:

'I normally walk up to a lass, look her straight in the eye, then ask "All reet love, do you fancy going halves on a bastard?" '

The DJ hadn't been expecting anything like this and, as the show was live, he was late cutting Jim off. There was an awkward silence, until he regained his composure. 'Well, that was Jim, all the way from England. Now for a little music.'

The friends had looked at each other, not believing what they had just heard. Then, as they had realised it had really happened, the room erupted with laughter, only disturbed by the sound of the door opening and Jim standing there, proud as punch.

The memory caused Richard to chuckle, as he pulled on his jeans and a bright green Ben Sherman shirt. Lacing up his shoes, he checked he had his wallet and room keys. Closing the door behind him and making sure it was secure, he knocked on the door adjacent to his. It was opened by Glen, who, even this early, had a glassy look about the eyes. He invited Richard in and one glance at the half demolished mini bar in the room, explained Glen's state.

'For fuck sake, Glen! Am I going to be babysitting you for the rest of the night?' Richard asked, jokingly.

'That would be a first. We will probably end up carrying you back!' Glen replied, grinning from ear to ear.

Once Roger was ready, they took the lift down to reception. It was early evening and the friends were feeling a bit peckish. They decided to find a bar or restaurant, where they could line their stomachs, for the night ahead.

At Reception, they were given a name of a restaurant, on the main strip. It was within walking distance, so they thought they would stretch their legs and get a bit of exercise. The sun was still blazing against the backdrop of the city's high-rise buildings. The streets were full of people, either returning from work or, like them, tourists in town for the Stampede. After a fifteen minute walk they arrived at the Embarcadero, situated just off Macleod Trail, on 17 Avenue South East.

The area was one of the main tourist spots and was a hive of activity. It was a quaint looking building from the outside, surrounded by a light blue, wrought iron fence. Some of the clientele were sitting outside, making the most of the summer weather. They spotted a spare table and Glen made a bee line for it.

'Don't you think we should wait to be seated?' Richard said, in the tone of a school teacher reprimanding a young pupil.

'Fuck that, I'm starving!' was the answer.

Shrugging his shoulders, Richard pulled out a chair and sat down. Within moments, a pretty girl appeared at their table and asked if they would like to see the drinks menu.

'Can we just have three pitchers of beer and three glasses?' Roger said.

'Sure, no problem. I will be right back with the menus,' the girl, a little surprised at the order, scurried off inside.

Richard looked around at the rest of the diners, who were either chatting or getting stuck into their food. It hit him that around three quarters of them were dressed in Country and Western dress. All around was a sea of checked shirts, Stetson hats and cowboy boots. Some of the women were downright gorgeous, a refreshing change from Medicine Hat.

He began to think of Birgit, back home with their almost three months old baby. This was the first time in his career that he wanted to get back, as quickly as possible. He was interrupted from his thoughts, as the waitress placed down the three pitchers of beer. She handed them each a menu and asked them to let her know when they were ready to order. They thanked her, poured a glass each from one of the pitchers and began to browse the menus.

Richard was not a big fan of pasta but adored seafood, so he skipped the first couple of pages and went directly to the fish dishes. It took them only a few moments to make their choices and Glen caught the attention of the young girl. Glen and Roger were adventurous and ordered buffalo wing starters, followed by burger and fries. Richard chose oysters to start and a seafood linguine as his main course. This drew a hail of abuse from the other two, who accused him of being a snob.

By the time the starters arrived, two of the three pitchers were empty and they decided to order another. Glen was getting louder, although they had only been out for an hour. They began to tuck into their starters and Richard quickly realised why the receptionist had recommended the place. It had a great reputation for seafood and it didn't disappoint. The three made short work of their starters, leaving only the bones of the Buffalo wings and the oyster shells on their plates. These were hastily retrieved and taken away by the server, who asked if they had enjoyed their starters.

When the main courses arrived, there was a gasp from Richard, when he saw the size of the burgers. When the plates were placed down, the burgers stood around six inches, or more, in height. To hold their contents, and to prevent them toppling over, skewers had been placed through the centres. Roger and Glen cackled like maniacs, rubbing their hands together, in anticipation.

Although Richard had debated whether or not to have pasta, his seafood linguine was one of the best meals he had ever eaten. As he mopped up the remaining juices from his bowl, with the freshly baked Italian bread, he licked his lips.

Looking across at the other two, he noticed they were struggling with their huge meals. Conversation had died between them, as they attempted to finish their food. Being Yorkshiremen, they were loath to leave anything and, with the aid of a couple more glasses of beer, they managed to clear their plates.

When the bill arrived the friends split it three ways. The wonderful meal had only cost around 30 dollars, including the beer. It was a great start to the evening. They tipped the waitress and said their goodbyes. Standing at the edge of the road, they waited for a passing taxi. Spotting one, Richard raised his hand, to draw the driver's attention. The taxi driver acknowledged he had seen them and pulled over. The friends jumped in and made themselves comfortable; Richard, acting the responsible adult, took the passenger seat.

'Cowboys Nightclub, please,' he told the driver.

'Sure, no problem,' the driver answered and, placing the car in drive, pulled away, into the traffic.

It was a short journey up Macleod Trail and on to 12 Avenue SE. Arriving outside the club, Richard paid the driver and gave him a tip. This tipping lark was alien to Brits but they knew it was part of the culture in this part of the world.

The front of the building was like an old Greek or Jewish temple, with its triangular topped porch-like entrance, a pillar on either side. The remainder of the frontage of the club was completely covered in glass panels. The sun was dipping below the horizon, by this point, although it was still early. On either side of the entranceway, stood two giants, dressed in western outfits. Their Stetson hats would have looked ridiculous on anyone of a diminutive stature, however suited them. As the three friends approached, one, obviously a doorman-come-bouncer, stepped forward, preventing them from proceeding. He eyed them up and down, examining their attire.

'It's five dollars entrance, guys. You pay at reception, just inside,' he advised them, satisfied that they weren't too drunk and were respectable enough.

They nodded in acknowledgement and made their way inside. The young man behind the glass fronted cubicle smiled, as they stood in front of him and asked for three tickets. He punched the cash register, then stamped each of their hands, to show they had paid. He then asked how many drinks tickets they wanted. The three looked at each other, never having experienced this before.

'How many do you think we need?' Glen asked, cheekily.

'Depends what kind of time you want. The average guy will normally spend around 50 dollars. So do you want 50 dollars' worth each?' he enquired, looking at them, in turn.

'Aye, why not? We can always buy more when we need them!" Roger replied, raising his voice, to make himself heard above the sound of the music, reverberating from inside.

The young guy handed over a series of tickets to each of them and they stepped inside. Although it was early, the place was already three quarters full. The first thing that hit them was the amount of good looking girls there. The ratio of female to male must have been about three to one. They strolled briskly and with purpose, towards the nearest bar, one of many dotted around the main dance floor. There were three stunning looking girls working behind the bar. Richard thought he had walked into a model shoot, as they were all scantily clothed with denim shorts and half cropped tops. All were wearing cowboy hats and boots.

Attracting the attention of one of the girls, Glen barged the other two lads out of the way. Glen was getting more and more boisterous, Richard thought. The sight of half-naked women would only fuel the flames. Glen ordered three pitchers of beer and three shots of tequila. Hearing their accents, the barmaid became intrigued:

'Where are you guys from?' she asked.

'The UK,' he responded and, seeing the confused look on her face, qualified the statement with 'Yorkshire, in the North of England.' This seemed to make more sense to her and she beamed from ear to ear.

'That's awesome. Great to have you in our city, I am sure you will have a super time,' she replied.

'I'm sure we will, if all the girls look like you!' Roger countered, in a seductive voice, which earned a giggle from the waitress.

Taking the lemon wedges and salt the waitress had placed on the bar, the guys licked the back of their hands. Tipping a pinch of salt on the wet area, they licked the salt off, threw back the shot of tequila, then placed the lemon in their mouths. This reminded Richard of the time in Cyprus when he had consumed 24 of these in an afternoon. He hoped tonight's session would not led to the same hangover the next day.

The first round of drinks lasted only twenty minutes and Richard took his turn at the bar. On his return, armed with another couple of jugs of beer and a round of tequilas, he noticed that Glen was missing.

'Where's he gone?' he asked Roger, who was scanning the room at the female talent surrounding them.

'He's over there, talking to that lass!' he shouted in Richard's ear, above the music.

Just as Richard looked in the direction Roger had pointing, Glen walked across, arm in arm with what could only be described as a 'buxom cowgirl'. She was sporting a wide brimmed Stetson, tight fitting t-shirt, jeans and cowboy boots. She was of ample proportions, her face was pretty, with an olive tinge. She was wearing a push-up bra, her cleavage looked like it was about to spill over.

'Guys, can I introduce Jenny?' Glen said,

Roger stepped forward to shake her hand but was surprised when she leaned forward and, rubbing her chest against him, planted a kiss directly on his cheek. He turned crimson as, although he was quite outspoken, he was very shy when it came to women. Richard gave her a peck on the cheek and said it was good to meet her. Jenny motioned towards another girl, at the bar. She held up five fingers, indicating that she should get drinks in for them all. The other girl, obviously her friend, joined them, carrying a tray of shots. Her name was Sally and she was similarly attired as Jenny. This was not surprising, as most of the girls in the club were in Western dress. Handing the drinks out, one by one, Jenny raised her glass in a toast.

'Bottoms up!' she yelled, and they all clinked their glasses together and downed them in one.

'I hope hers is, later,' Glen grinned at Richard.

The five went toe to toe for the next hour, each buying a round of shots. The room was now full of revellers and the Stampede spirit had kicked in.

Country and Western music was blaring and the dancers were on the floor, taking part in a massive line dance. With a mischievous look on his face, Glen downed the drink he had in his hand and shot off, in the direction of the dance floor. Taking up a position in the middle of the dancers, he began to squat on his haunches and, with a flick of his right and left heels, proceeded to repeat the movement. This caused those around him to stop and stare, wondering what the hell this crazy bastard was up to.

Richard saw one of the male dancers walk over to Glen and shout in his ear. Glen stopped immediately, rose from the squatting position and shouted something back. The face of the big, burly cowboy changed visibly. He shook his head and stormed off. Richard wondered what had just occurred but knew it was not good. Glen returned to them and Richard enquired what had been said.

'He asked me what I was doing,' Glen responded. 'I don't think he was too happy when I said I was shit kicking,' he finished off the explanation.

Richard cringed at this revelation and immediately scanned the room, for the giant cowboy. It wasn't long before he spotted him, on the corner of the dance floor, in the company of another three, each the size of a heavyweight boxer. They were pointing at Glen. Richard knew what would happen next and braced himself. Letting Roger and Glen know that things were going to kick off, he told them to follow him. After having participated in many bar fights in the past, either with locals or other Units, Richard knew their best tactic was to take a position from which they could stand their ground.

The three walked towards the bar and ordered drinks, then turned, to face the dance floor. From here, they knew that no one could get behind them.

Four massive shapes were walking, from the dance floor, in the direction of the bar. One, towering at over six and a half feet; and dressed in a lumberjack shirt, dungarees and sporting an almighty beard, had a look of thunder written across his face. The only thing he lacked was an axe, Richard thought. Reaching the bar, they stopped and directed their attention to Glen.

'Can I help you, mate?' Richard asked, trying to acting as peacekeeper.

The lumberjack didn't even look at Richard, staring directly into the eyes of Glen, who stood there, smirking. The stupid grin on his face wasn't courage or bravado, it betrayed the fact that he was steaming drunk.

'This little guy thinks he's a comedian!' the menacing colossus screamed, covering Glen's face in spit.

'He's just had a few drinks too many. Can we get you guys a beer, if we've upset you?' Richard asked, still trying to calm the situation down.

The giant turned to face Richard, glaring in anger and snorting like a bull.

'I might have guessed, fucking English fucking....!'

Before he could finish, Roger booted him in the stones and, with a sickening look on his face, he sank to his knees.

There was no turning back now, Richard knew. He threw a left hook at the jaw of the guy nearest him. To his amazement, he didn't go down, but his head flew to the left. Glen aimed a kick directly at the lumberjack already on his knees, ensuring he wouldn't get up. Then, jumping over his body aimed a blow at a third opponent.

The fracas caught the attention of some of the other drinks and, suddenly, the place was a mass brawl. The two girls that had been with them had long since fled for cover.

Glasses were flying, tables and chairs thrown and punches and kicks aimed. The three Brits fought their way through the crowd and almost managed to make it to the exit, where they were met by two bouncers, who threw them out, unceremoniously.

Standing outside, the friends checked themselves over for any damage and, suddenly burst into fits of laughter. They looked back inside, through the glass windows, at the melee they had started.

'That was some start to our break, you fuckwit!' Richard aimed the admonishment directly at Glen, who smiled a drunken smile and shrugged.

It was late. The friends decided they would get a taxi back to the hotel, for a nightcap. Across the road from the club was an Asian, leaning on a rickshaw, a bizarre sight in the middle of a Canadian city. Confirming he was free, the three squeezed into the small compartment with Richard and Glen seated, Roger lying across their laps. As their driver pulled them along the street, Roger was shouted 'Mush! Mush!'

It took around 40 minutes to get back to the Elbow River Creek Hotel. The journey cost them an exorbitant 50 dollars and they wished they had called a regular cab.

Entering the hotel Richard stated that he was going to bed, as the other two went into the bar.

Richard woke early the next morning. He stretched and yawned and, as he did so, felt an ache over one eye. It was then he remembered the altercation in the Cowboy Nightclub, the evening before. He chuckled to himself, wondering if he and his mates would ever learn?

Grabbing a quick shower, then dressing, he went to wake the other two. They would, no doubt, still be fast asleep, as he didn't expected the drinking to have finished, after a quick nightcap. They had planned to go for a pancake breakfast, one of the many events hosted at the stampede. He left his room and knocked on Glen's and Roger's door. Hearing nothing, he knocked again, louder.

'It's open!' came Glen's voice. Richard opened the door and went in.

Noticing Roger was not in bed, he wished Glen good morning. He was answered by a grumble and the motion of covers being pulled back over Glen's head. Telling him to get up, Richard threw back the quilt, to be greeted with the sight of Glen's naked arse.

'Get a shower and get some clothes on!' he shouted, taking great delight in his buddy's obvious discomfort.

'I see Roger is up and at em!' he announced.

Glen, confused, looked across at Roger's freshly made bed. 'I didn't hear him get up. I left him in the bar, talking to that Monique, about two o'clock,' he replied.

'Well, if he has tapped off with her, he knows where we are going. He can bloody well meet us there,' Richard said curtly, unimpressed.

Glen struggled out of bed and quickly showered, while Richard turned on the TV and watched the local news. Nearly all the items were about the Stampede, the major local hot topic. When Glen had showered and dressed, they left, locking the room and headed for the lift.

As they neared it, they heard a muffled voice, calling for help. The pair exchanged glances, both recognising it. They looked around, trying to ascertain where it was coming from. They opened a door to the stairwell, thinking maybe Roger had fallen down the stairs, in a drunken stupor. Finding it empty, they returned to the area near the lift.

'It's coming from somewhere near here,' Glen said, becoming concerned. The cry for help was heard again, this time louder than before.

'It's coming from in here,' Richard said, pointing at a round door on the wall, opposite the lift. It was the door to the laundry chute, which the maids used, to throw dirty

linen in. The chute went all the way down to the basement, where the laundry was collected, to be taken away.
Opening the door cautiously, Richard peered down inside. In the gloom, he could just make out the pale face of Roger, staring up, with pleading eyes.

'Help us out, mate, I'm stuck,' he implored. Richard, relieved, could do nothing to contain his amusement. He turned to Glen, who also staring down into the opening.

While Glen held his legs, Richard was lowered into the chute. He held out his arms, in order that Roger could grab them and, with Glen's help, they managed to haul their mate up and out, into the corridor.

As he lay panting for breath, Richard asked what had happened. Roger confirmed what the other two thought. He had been returning to his room when he spotted the laundry chute door. In his pissed state, he had thought it would be a great idea to take a slide down it.

Due to his size, he had got stuck, in the position where they had found him. He had been there about six hours. Glen and Richard thought this was one of the funniest things they had seen in a long time and took the piss out of Roger constantly, for the rest of the day.

After lining their stomachs on a mountain of pancakes, the three friends attended the Stampede parade. This was held on the first Friday of the event and was the official opening, with local politicians, dignitaries and various hangers-on who come out of the woodwork on these sorts of occasions.

For the next three days, they visited all the attractions; rodeo, bull riding, barrel racing, steer wrestling, tie down roping, saddle bronc and bareback riding. They also toured an authentically built Indian village, which had been erected from the 'Five Nations', who were represented in that area of Canada, one of the most popular attractions of the Stampede.

Richard was looking for a gift to take back to his newly born daughter. He came across a dress, made from original buffalo hide but when he saw the price and checked his finances, he realised he couldn't afford it. Instead, he purchased a pair of tiny moccasins, made from the same material.

The three days passed in a blur but were an enjoyable experience which would live with them for the rest of their lives – particularly the sight of one of their number stuck in a laundry chute!

Chapter 9 - Rugby Injury

No sooner had the Regiment returned from Canada, than they were off, again, on exercise on Soltau.

As the father of a new born baby, Richard was beginning to get more and more disillusioned with military life. A high percentage of people who left the military, gave parenthood as the reason for doing so.

Once again, Richard kissed his wife and child goodbye and set off, for another week away, to be followed by an indoor exercise, at the Brigade Battlegroup Trainer (BBGT), located at a camp, twenty minutes away, in Sennelager.

Before they had deployed to Canada, Richard had put his name forward for voluntary redundancy. The British Army of the Rhine (BAOR) had been drawing down its forces, in line with the perceived lessened threat from the Warsaw Pact. This had been the final phase of the draw-down and many people had seen it as an opportune time to leave and begin a new career, in civilian life.

When Squadron Leader Pat Geraghty had heard that Richard had applied, he had sent a message, saying he wished to have a chat. Richard hadn't known why he had been summoned and had been a little apprehensive. Pat was a fiery character, at times unpredictable. However, the two had struck up a good working relationship, over the first few months after amalgamation. What you saw was what you got with the OC and Richard respected him, greatly.

As he had marched smartly into the OC's office, he had halted, a pace before his desk. As Richard had thrown up a salute in the prescribed manner, the OC had looked up, from his paperwork.

'Stand at ease, Corporal Hunter,' he had said, smiling. Richard had relaxed slightly. 'The reason I have asked to see you is your application for redundancy. Before this can be submitted to the CO, I need to sign it. You may or may not know that you are top of my list to be promoted to Sergeant, on the next promotions board. You have obviously thought hard about this before coming to a decision, do you mind telling me your reasons?'

Richard had gone on to explain the reasons for his wish to leave and the OC had nodded as he listened. 'Well, if I can't persuade you to retract it, then all I can do is sign it. You will be sad loss to the Squadron,' he had said and, picking up his pen, he had applied his signature to the document. He had then informed Richard that he was free to fall out. Richard had thanked him, had saluted and had left the room.

Although that had occurred almost two months previously, the CO wouldn't be making his decision until after the BBGT exercise. 'This could be my last exercise,' Richard thought to himself, as he guided the Sultan command vehicle across the familiar landscape of the Luneburger Heide. He had spent so many happy, and some not so happy, times on this desolate place. The rhythmic movement of the vehicle rising and falling and the sound of the engine caused him to smile. It had been a long time since his first trip over the very same ground and the evenings spent keeping a lookout for the infamous 'drop bears'. He had played the same joke countless times himself on new, unsuspecting, young soldiers.

The rest of the A2 Echelon had remained in Rheinsehlen Camp but the Regimental Signals Officer had decided that Richard's vehicle would deploy on to the area. He was just being bloody minded, as there was no reason for them to do so. Richard thought the reason behind it was that they had a history of not seeing eye to eye.

On an earlier exercise, Richard's vehicle had been operating on its own, away from the main Command Troop HQ. Richard had thought it a good idea for the crew to have an impromptu party. After having consumed a large amount of alcohol, he had decided to call up the RSO and give him a piece of his mind. His crew had tried to talk him out of it but he ignored their advice. Dialling the number for the main command vehicle on the secure Ptarmigan telephone system, he had asked the operator if he could speak to the RSO. After a few moments, the RSO's voice had asked Richard what it was he wanted. For the next five minutes, Richard had ranted at the RSO, saying what an arrogant, autocratic, cockwomble he was and that he was not interested in the careers of the soldiers under his command.

With every word of abuse that had crossed Richard's lips, his crew had cringed, trying to get the telephone handset from his grip. It was too late by that point and the damage had been done. On their return to camp, Richard had been invited to an interview 'without coffee' with the RSO. He had been given the biggest dressing down of his life and had been told, in no uncertain terms, that his career would not advance. Richard had not been bothered, as he had planned to leave anyway.

The exercise flew, they returned and were on the last day of the BBGT indoor exercise in Sennelager. The big topic of conversation was the following day. The CO would be informing those who had applied for redundancy whether or not they had been successful. For Richard, the next twelve hours dragged by. He was glad when they were boarding the coaches, for the short trip back to their camp in Paderborn.

As he lined up outside the CO's office, the atmosphere was very solemn. One by one, they were called in by the RSM. Finally, Richard's name was called and he marched smartly into the office. Halting a couple of paces in front of the desk, he was told to stand at ease, by the RSM.

'Corporal Hunter, I have considered your application for phase 3 redundancy. I believe that you have a promising career in front of you, therefore I am declining your application,' he said, allowing a moment, for the news to sink in.

Richard hadn't been expecting this, especially after his run-in with the RSO. He had secretly hoped that the incident might have helped his application, but it wasn't to be. He thanked the CO for his confidence in him, saluted and marched out of the room. He was bitterly disappointed, especially when he found out that a number of people had been given redundancy, who had not even applied.

The following week, Richard was preparing for the inter-Squadron rugby tournament, one of the many sporting competitions held every year. They were always fiercely contested matches and Richard was looking forward to it. It was a distraction that helped to take his mind off the news received a week before and an outlet to vent some of the aggression he was feeling, at that point.

In the first match, HQ Squadron were drawn against A Squadron, who also made up around 50% of the Regimental team. HQ had a number of players who also played at Regimental level, so the contest would be a hard fought one.

The first half flew by, the teams very evenly matched. A Squadron were one try ahead, just before half time but HQ had been awarded a scrum right on the opposition's 22 metre line. As the scrum half placed the ball into the scrum, Richard readied himself. He was playing at standoff and would be the first to receive the ball, assuming they won the scrum. The HQ Squadron hooker heeled the ball back, to his second row. The number eight, at the rear of the scrum, was a gigantic bloke called Angus. He was the Light Aid Detachment Commander, known as the EME and, who played regularly for the Royal Electrical and Mechanical Engineers Corps team. He had also represented the Army on a few occasions. He guided the pack forward, keeping the ball between his legs, as they crept ever closer towards A Squadron's try line.

Around ten metres out, he picked up the ball and peeled away from the scrum. Making a gain of another couple of metres, he passed the ball out to the scrum half who, in turn, expertly passed it on to Richard. Seeing the opposition's defence was thinly stretched, Richard decided to make a break, for the line. As his opposite number closed in toward him, he turned to pass the ball to his right.

Just as the ball left his hands, he was taken off his feet, as the A Squadron standoff landed, with the full force of his weight, on top of Richard. He felt a sharp pain in his back, as he fell awkwardly and the air was expelled from his lungs. He didn't hear the sound of the cheers, as his team crossed the try line. The whistle sounded for the end of the first half and Richard gingerly made his way to the side line, for the half time team talk and refreshments.

By the start of the second half, Richard knew that something was not quite right. Every time his foot hit the floor, he felt a jarring pain in his back. It wasn't long before he put up his hand, to indicate to the team manager that he had a problem. He was immediately replaced and advised to go and get himself checked out at the Medical Centre.

On arriving at the Med Centre, he was assessed by one of the Regimental medics, who came to the conclusion that Richard had probably torn a muscle. He was prescribed some Brufen tablets, for the inflammation and pain, the army's answer to almost 90% of all injuries. Richard collected his medication and returned to the rugby field, in order to see the end of the match. The score was still the same and, as the whistle sounded, HQ Squadron won by that single try. Although they would go on to win the tournament, Richard played no further part. He didn't know it then but that was be the last game he would ever play, due to his injury.

Two weeks later, Richard's injury had still not healed and he paraded at the gym, for the six monthly basic fitness test (BFT), which took the form of a three mile run.

The first mile and a half was run as a squad, in as near to fifteen minutes as possible. Then, they turned around and ran another mile and half, in their best time. Richard's age group were expected to complete in ten and a half minutes.

He knew after the first mile that something was wrong and, halfway through the second mile and a half, he dropped out, as he was in so much pain. As he had failed the test, he was given a week to recover, then had to re-take it. Again, he was unable to complete the run, due to the pain. He was ordered to the Medical Centre, to ascertain his fitness to attend remedial PT. This time, he was seen by the Regimental Medical Officer (RMO), who confirmed that it was probably just a muscle strain and passed him fit to attend the remedial lessons.

Richard's confidence was further dented by his transfer to the Technical Stores Department, as he was not fit enough, at that time, to remain on tracked vehicles. It was a great blow to his ever-faltering career. Things seemed to be going from bad to worse.

Chapter 10 - Quartermaster Technical Department

For the next three weeks, Richard spent his time at Deepcut Barracks, on the 'All Arms Storeman' Class One course. It was a desolate and dull camp, full of Echelon Mother Fuckers. This wasn't something he had envisaged doing, when he first joined up, eleven years ago but, true to character, he threw himself into the course. He learned everything: ammunition, Miscellaneous Stores Account, Equipment Table; how to issue and receipt stores. Basically, the job entailed passing bits of paper from one tray to another. Remarkably, he found that he had a natural talent for it, which was just as well, as he would be in that job for the next two years, until he could get fit enough to return to armoured vehicles.

Successfully completing the course, Richard was returned to Germany, to join his new Troop. It was headed up by Finbar O'Hearn, their first RSM after amalgamation, who had been promoted to Captain and was now the Technical Quartermaster. He had a small team, run by a WO2, Paul Hunt. Richard met the rest of the Troop, on first parade, on his first day.

Their Troop was singled out for inspection, by the OC, Pat Geraghty. As they were told to stand fast, they waited for him, to begin the inspection. Richard was next to a Trooper he had known before the amalgamation. His name was called Walter Damon but was known, for some unknown reason, as 'Mandy'. Richard had heard stories about Mandy converting to Islam, just after amalgamation. The Squadron Leader, having served in Aden in the 1960s was quite conversant in Arabic. As he stood in front of Trooper Damon, he greeted him in Arabic.

'As-salāmu ʿalaykum, Trooper Damon.' In Arabic this means "Peace be upon you," a standard salutation among Muslims, routinely used whenever and wherever they gather. The words were met by a deafening silence. The OC's face reddened as he repeated the greeting, again receiving a blank stare from the attention-seeking Trooper. The typical response to the greeting, "Waʿalaykumu s-salām" ("and upon you, Peace") was not forthcoming.

'Sergeant Major, lock up this piece of shit, will you?' he turned to the SSM, who smiled and, with glee, told the hapless Trooper to remove his belt and beret. In rapid time, he marched him, in the direction of the guardroom.

The OC laughed out loud, as he stood in front of Richard, welcoming him back, from his course. He went on to explain that the RSO had removed his name from the promotion list for Sergeant, after the incident on exercise. Richard suspected that this might have happened and, with his current injury, knew it may be some time before he would be promoted.

The parade and inspection over, the Troops were fallen out and returned to their respective places of work, with the exception of Trooper Damon, who was, at that point, being 'beasted' around camp, by members of the Provost staff.

When Richard entered his new office, he was introduced to his workmates. Two he was going to be working closely with were ex-Skins. The first was a full Corporal, like Richard, called John Cash, an apt name, as he had a habit of putting most of his wages in the first gambling machine he could find. The other was a Lance Corporal, Billy McQueen, who originally came from the staunchly Protestant area of the Shankhill Road, in Belfast. Billy had become infamous throughout the Regiment, after having put an orange sash over the then RSM, now their boss. As Captain O'Hearn hailed from the Catholic area of the Falls Road, there was always friendly banter about the sectarian divide. The prank had been carried out on St. Patrick's Day, when the Corporals' Mess had been invited into the Warrant Officers' and Sergeants' Mess. The then

RSM had taken it all in good spirits, much to the surprise of his Mess members.

Shortly after Richard had made the acquaintance of his new workmates, they were joined by Trooper Damon, sweating like a pig, who received no sympathy from anyone in the Troop. Damon was well known for seeking the limelight. Converting to Islam was just another case in point. Strangely, Richard would meet him many years later, and the transformation in the man would have Richard lost for words.

For the next few months, Richard got to grips with how the Troop worked. They were preparing for an upcoming tour of Northern Ireland, once more. Richard was disappointed he would not be patrolling the streets of Belfast, where they were to be stationed.

The Regiment began their training for the deployment and, while they carried out their patrolling and search skills, the echelon Troops, who were to support them, started their own training.

This was something new to Richard, as one of the main tasks for the echelon would be supplying the Troops with equipment. This meant travelling round the various camps, collecting and delivering stores. To aid them, they were schooled in the use of covert cars, vans and trucks. Most of their time would be spent in civilian clothing, to try to blend in with the local population.

The day before their first lesson, Richard recalled an incident from 1988, which had involved the killing of two Royal Signals Corporals, travelling in civilian clothing, in a covert car.

The killings had taken place against a backdrop of violence at high-profile Irish Republican funerals. Heavy security presence was criticised as instigating unrest, leading authorities to adopt a "hands off" policy, with respect to policing IRA funerals.

The killings took place against a backdrop of violence at high-profile Irish republican funerals. A heavy security presence was criticized as instigating unrest, leading authorities to adopt a "hands off" policy with respect to policing IRA funerals. On 6 March 1988, three unarmed IRA members preparing for a bomb attack on the band of the Royal Anglian Regiment were killed by members of the Special Air Service (SAS) in Gibraltar during Operation Flavius. Their unpoliced funerals in Belfast's Milltown Cemetery on 16 March were attacked by Ulster Defence Association (UDA) member Michael Stone with pistols and hand grenades, in what became known as the Milltown Cemetery attack. Three people were killed and more than 60 wounded, one of the dead being IRA member Caoimhín Mac Brádaigh (Kevin Brady). Mac Brádaigh's funeral, just three days after Stone's attack, took place amid an extremely fearful and tense atmosphere, those attending being in trepidation of another loyalist attack. The attendance at the funeral included large numbers of IRA members who acted as stewards.

The two Royal Signals Corporals (Howes and Wood), were driving a silver Volkswagen Passat in civilian clothing. It is thought that they drove into the funeral procession by accident, as it made its way along the Andersontown Road toward Mill Hill Cemetery. As they entered the funeral procession they realised their mistake and tried to turn off down a side road. Unfortunately the road was blocked and they reversed at high speed to extricate themselves. Their path was blocked by a black taxi, and the procession believed they were under attack from Loyalist paramilitaries. As the crowd surged toward them, they began to smash the windows, and attempt to drag the soldiers from the vehicle. Corporal Wood drew his pistol and fired a shot in the air. The crowd momentarily dispersed, but quickly regrouped and both he and Corporal Howes were pulled from the vehicle, disarmed and beaten.

They were then taken to the grounds of the nearby Casement Park where they were subjected to further beatings, stripped to their socks and underpants, and searched. Here, the IRA took control of the situation. The corporals were mistakenly identified as members of the SAS - the British Special Forces unit that had killed three IRA members in Gibraltar two weeks earlier. The corporals were subjected to further beatings, before being thrown over a wall and driven in a black taxi to waste ground less than 200 metres away. Once there, the two men were killed by members of the IRA. Corporal Derek Wood was shot six times and stabbed four times in the back of the neck. Corporal David Howes was shot five times. (Wikipedia)

It was with these memories in the back of his mind that Richard attended his first training period, in 'covert car drills'. Their instructor, 'Taff', had, for many years, served as an operator in 14 Intelligence Company, known simply as 'The Det'. He had a wealth of experience, which he was eager to impart to his new students. Richard and the rest of the guys were dressed in jeans, t-shirts and bomber jackets, enabling them to conceal weapons. Over the course of the day, they were taught advanced driving skills: sustained high speed driving, using a vehicle as a weapon, controlled crashes, skid recovery and anti-ambush skills. Taff gave them different scenarios, from an explosion to the vehicle, to an ambush by armed terrorists. They rotated, in groups of four, one driving, one in the front passenger seat and two in the back. As an 'ambush' was initiated, they had to make the decision either to fight through it or attempt to drive away, following the guidelines Taff had given them. The skills to be learned over the next few weeks could mean life and death, 'over the water'. They gave the lessons their full attention and, by the end of training, they were all proficient in each drills.

The training over, the Troops bade farewell to their families, once more. Although Birgit was accustomed to this by now, parting was never easy. It would be six more months until Richard saw his daughter again; he had witnessed her first steps but knew he would miss out on other milestones. Because this part of military life was difficult for those who had young families, wives bonded closely and often spent time in each others' houses. It was a friendship that matched, perhaps even surpassed, that of their husbands. They leaned on each other for support in those lonely times, when the men were away. Although Birgit didn't know it yet, she would feel the loss of those friends more than Richard would miss his mates, once he had finished his time.

The Hercules transport plane touched down at Aldergrove Airport, to the north of Belfast. The Troops boarded the trucks which would take them to where they would be billeted or housed, for the coming months. Most of the Regiment would be working out of Girdwood Park, bordering the Roman Catholic area of Ardoyne and the Protestant Shankhill Road. The Technical and Main Quartermasters' departments were stationed in a naval base, known as Moscow Camp, on the edge of Belfast Lough, on the airport road, which ran alongside the City Airport. To the north-east was Palace and Kinnegar Barracks, in the Hollywood area of the city. As they turned off the main western by-pass, on to the airport road, Richard could see the massive cranes, owned by Harland and Wolff, builders of the ill-fated Titanic. The camp was set by the side of the water, small and, from all appearances, very basic. As the Troops disembarked the trucks, they were deafened by the sound of an aircraft landing.

'I see this is going to be a quiet six months, then!' Richard had to shout across to John Cash, to make himself heard.

'I think you could be right,' John replied, laughing.

The Quartermaster, Tommy Steadman, was waiting to greet them. He was Belfast born and bred and also from the Shankhill, like Billy McQueen. He indicated that they should follow him and he took them to a green, one storey, prefabricated building.

'This is your accommodation, your names are on the doors. Get yourselves settled in, the evening meal will be in two hours' time. The cookhouse is that building, there,' he pointed across the road.

There were sixteen staying in the Naval Camp. Some were members of Motors Transport Troop, the rest Quartermaster and Technical Quartermaster staff. The Senior NCOs, from Sergeant upwards, had their own rooms, while the rest shared, two to a room.

Richard had been paired with John Cash. They found their room and began to unpack their gear. The rooms were comfortable enough, with a locker each and a TV. By the time they had everything squared away, it was time for the evening meal. Taking their knives, forks, spoons and mugs, they made their way to the cookhouse building.

Richard was surprised how light and homely the place was. As they neared the hotplate, some Navy personnel eyed them, cautiously. The three Armed Services, didn't always see eye to eye but knew they were going to have to live together, so it was better if they got along. John and Richard selected from the hotplate and, as they were about to take a seat, noticed that cutlery and cups were provided. This wasn't normal practice in an Army cookhouse, as cutlery would quickly be depleted, squaddies nicking them, to use on exercise.

The food smelled absolutely gorgeous and Richard couldn't wait, to tuck in. He decided to break the ice and sit at a table, beside a couple of the matelots. As they sat down, Richard and John introduced themselves. The sailors, over the next ten minutes, got chatting and gave them a brief run-down of the camp and its facilities. As Richard listened, he shovelled food into his mouth, not believing how good it tasted.

'Why the fuck is your food so good here?' he asked the sailors, inquisitively, drawing a confused look.

'This is normal, mate, We say the reason is that if you're a chef on a ship and fuck it up, there's nowhere to hide!' Richard liked that but formed the opinion that the Navy must have a different budget to the Army.

After the evening meal, Richard took a stroll around the camp, to familiarise himself with its layout. Following this, the newcomers attended a briefing by the Quartermaster on how things ran. It was reasonably laid back and those who weren't detailed either collecting or delivering stores were free to their own devices. This would take some getting used to, mused Richard, who had been used to patrolling streets or surrounding countryside, for hours on end. The briefing over, he decided to have an early night and hit the sack.

The next morning, Richard reported to the office with John, to check out the duty sheet for the week. As he scanned the page on the board for his name, he observed that his first job of the day was to take a 10 tonne trolley jack down to the main force, in Girdwood Barracks. Collecting the jack from the small detachment of mechanics, Richard and John loaded it onto the back of a civilian removal truck, with a rolling blind door, at the back.

'Should we get some straps to secure it?' John asked.

Richard thought for a moment, before answering, 'I don't think so, it's not Soltau training area we're going over, just main roads, through the city.'

On the Ops office wall was a map detailing the city, highlighting the sectarian areas. Known as tribal maps, some areas were marked in red, indicating 'no go' or 'out of bounds'. The maps were continually updated, from daily intelligence reports. They discussed the quickest and safest route to take. Coming to a decision they both agreed on, they sent the route over the air. This was received by the Regimental Intelligence cell, stationed in Girdwood Barracks. After a minute or so, they received an answer:

'Tango 42 Alpha, your route is clear.'

Richard acknowledged receipt, then the pair made their way, to the loading bay. Personnel travelling in unmarked vehicles were armed, usually with Browning 9mm pistols. The two checked each other, as they loaded their weapons. Richard was wearing a shoulder holster, as he was wearing a jacket. He ensured the safety catch was applied and placed his weapon in the holster. Climbing aboard the vehicle, Richard, as commander on this occasion, took the passenger seat. John started the engine and quickly checked that all the lights were working. Satisfied the vehicle was fit for the road, they drove off out of the camp gates.

Leaving the harbour area, they joined the A2, heading west, towards the city. Richard constantly checked the mirrors, to ensure no suspicious vehicles were tailing them. As they continued on to the western by-pass, the traffic was starting to build up. The road ahead climbed gradually and John manoeuvred the vehicle, into the slow lane. As he did so, an almighty crash could be heard from the rear. Richard looked at John, wide-eyed, thinking that perhaps they had been hit by an IED or RPG attack. He told John to accelerate out the area, which he did, without hesitation.

Once clear of the bridge that crossed the river Lagan, Richard asked John to pull over, in order to assess any damage. Cars passed them, beeping their horns, drivers gesticulating at the rear of the vehicle. Richard jumped from the passenger door and rushed to the rear of the truck. His heart sank when he saw the concertina blinds had been ripped open, on one side. He knew this had been no terrorist attack but an error of judgement, on his part. Looking inside the vehicle, his fears were confirmed. It was empty. Their cargo had rolled back, during their ascent of the hill and had crashed through the flimsy rear door. Trying to retrieve the situation, John suggested they get to the next roundabout, urgently, and do a U-turn, to try and find the missing trolley jack. Richard nodded his agreement.

It took them a full ten minutes to retrace their way through rush hour traffic. They scanned for any sign of the bright yellow jack. To their disappointment and disbelief, it was nowhere to be seen. Being commander of the vehicle, Richard knew the blame was going to land firmly on his shoulders. Biting his lip, he directed John to make another U-turn and head back along their original route, to Girdwood Barracks.

On arrival, the pair ran straight to the Ops room. It was essential to report the loss of the jack, as quickly as possible. Although they hadn't been able to find it, the last thing Richard wanted was for the IRA to discover and booby trap it.

After he had reported the incident to the duty Watchkeeper, a message was sent over the Belfast net, informing people to keep an eye out for the missing trolley jack. For the next half hour, the two had to deal with the inevitable abuse and piss-taking from everyone, as the story spread.

Richard was not looking forward to the return trip to Moscow Camp, to explain his actions to the QMT.

Chapter 11 - "There will never be peace here"

It was four weeks since the incident with the trolley jack. As Richard had expected, he thought been given a severe roasting by Finbar O'Hearn, the QMT. He had learnt from the experience, something not all soldiers chose to do.

The days were dragging, the routine was monotonous and repetitive. Richard cursed his rugby injury and wondered how long it would be until he was back to full fitness and in a sabre Squadron. When he had any down time, he spent it in the small gym, set up on the camp. He often got up early, met one of the blokes from MT and put in a quick hour in the gym, before breakfast. Although running was still painful, he could manage weights and cycling. The MT lad was John Prestwick, a very likeable Mancunian with a dry sense of humour. He, like Richard, had boxed, prior to joining the army and the two would often spar, in the makeshift gym. John had prepared a programme of training for Richard and he stuck to it rigorously, when time allowed.

The only other source of entertainment on camp was the NAAFI bar, which had gambling machines, pool, darts and the usual pastimes. Although there was a 'two can rule' while on duty, on down time a blind eye was turned, as long as they didn't kick the arse out of it. John Cash could always be found in the vicinity of the fruit machines. Richard had watched him, over the period they had been there and was convinced that he had a gambling addiction. He had been paid that particular morning and had given half of his money to members of the Troop, Richard included, for debts accrued since the previous pay day. What he had left was now being fed into the slot machine.

'Don't forget to hold your plums!' someone shouted out, from the other end of the bar. Richard cackled like a witch, finding the jibe highly amusing. It was a saying which stuck throughout the tour and it followed John throughout the rest of his career.

Living in close proximity to others or sharing a room for extended periods often led to disagreements. The Quartermasters' department were quite lucky in this respect, as they were billeted two to a room, a different kettle of fish from those in Girdwood Barracks. Most of the Troops lived in what was known as the 'Sub', a hardened shelter with no windows, designed to protect them against mortar attacks. It was very cramped, even a little claustrophobic and private arguments often spilled into hostility. Once the air was cleared, the protagonists made up and things would return to normal.

The relationship between John and Richard became strained, at times, normally coming to a head when Richard was on time off, having had more than the two cans permitted. He had become friendly with a number of members of the RUC, who visited the QM, from time to time. They were old school friends of the QM and they would often reminisce, over times gone by.

Richard witnessed something being passed over by the RUC guys. He said nothing but waited until they were about to leave. Plucking up courage, he approached one and asked if the bottle he had spotted was potcheen. The policeman eyed him suspiciously at first, then his face broke into a broad grin.

'It was indeed, son,' he answered, in a deep Belfast brogue, 'would you like me to drop you off a bottle next time I'm here?'

Richard paused for a moment, wondering if it was a trick question, as he knew the spirit was illegal. Coming to the decision that the RUC man wouldn't have spoken if the offer wasn't genuine, he accepted, 'If you don't mind,' he said, apprehensively.

'No problem, my man. I'll drop it off this time next week,' and with that, he strode towards the unmarked car and his colleague, who was waiting with the engine running.

As good as his word, the policeman dropped off a bottle for Richard each week, from that point on. The supply became John's worst nightmare, Richard was obnoxious when he had too much drink in him.

The first time Richard sampled the fiery brew, he called to mind its origin.

Poitín (Irish pronunciation :), anglicized as potcheen or poteen, is a traditional Irish distilled beverage (40%–90% ABV). Poitín was traditionally distilled in a small pot still and the term is a diminutive of the Irish word pota, meaning "pot". The Irish word for a hangover is póit. In accordance to the Irish Poitín technical file it can only be made from cereals, grain, whey, sugar beet, molasses and potatoes.

Poitín was generally produced in remote rural areas, away from the interference of the law. A wash was created and fermented before the distillation began. Stills were often set up on land boundaries so the issue of ownership could be disputed. Prior to the introduction of bottled gas, the fire to heat the wash was provided by turf. Smoke was a giveaway for the police, so windy, broken weather was chosen to disperse the smoke. The still was heated and attended to for several days to allow the runs to go through.

The old style of Poitín distilling was from a malted barley base for the mash, the same as Single Malt Whiskey or Pure Pot Still Whiskey distilled in Ireland. The word Poitín stems from the Irish Gaelic word "pota" for pot, this refers to the small copper pot still used by Poitín distillers.

In more recent times, some distillers deviated from using malted barley as a base of the mash bill due to the cost and availability instead switching to using treacle, corn and potatoes. It is believed this switch led the deteriorating quality and character of Poitín in the late 20th century.

The quality of Poitín was highly variable, depending on the skill of the distiller and the quality of his equipment. Reputations were built on the quality of the distiller's Poitín, and many families became known for their distilling expertise, where a bad batch could put a distiller out of business overnight. It has been claimed that the drink can cause blindness, but this is possibly due to adulteration rather than lack of quality. (Wikipedia)

As Richard sipped on the clear liquid, he watched TV. John was reading a book but would look up, from time to time, to see how his roommate's mood changed. Richard had gained a reputation, throughout the Regiment, of having a "twin brother", only ever appeared when alcohol was involved.

As he drank more of the potent brew, he felt his body relax. After a few more glasses, his vision began to blur and it wasn't long before his mind started to wander. He thought back to when he commanded a tank and cursed his injury. As the drink took a firmer grip, he felt the anger rising inside. He mumbled to himself, causing John to look up from his book. John knew Richard's twin would be making an appearance. He put down his book and prepared to rise from his bed. Retrieving the trainers from under his bed, he quickly laced them up, taking care not to make eye contact with Richard.

'Where the fuck are you going?' Richard exclaimed, bursting for an argument.

Glancing up from the floor, a worried look on his face, John timidly replied, 'Thought I would pop into the NAAFI for a pint, do you fancy one?' hoping his offer would be rejected.

'Nah, I've got this to keep me company,' Richard smiled back, 'Don't you go spending all your money on those bandits again. I'll see you later,' the parting comment sent a shiver through John's body. He hoped Richard would be fast asleep by the time he returned and left the room.

John returned after last orders, to find Richard fast asleep, the empty bottle discarded, on the floor.

Two days later, Richard was tasked, with Billy McQueen, to deliver batteries for radio equipment to Girdwood Barracks. As usual, they met in the small Ops room, where they studied the map and intelligence report. Both agreed on a route and Richard picked up the handset, giving the intended itinerary to Girdwood Ops room. Once they had been given clearance, the two made for the loading bay. It was a warm summer's day and Richard was wearing jeans and a shirt, which wasn't tucked into his jeans but hung loosely, to conceal the pistol, in the waistband of his jeans. After loading their weapons, Richard ensured that the Browning was secure and hidden from view.

A week ago, they had been collecting someone from one of the Belfast train stations. They had parked directly opposite the entrance and waited. 30 minutes after the expected arrival time, their passenger had still not emerged. Richard had made the decision to go into the station to check if there were any delays. Asking his driver to keep the engine running, he had opened the door and, checking the traffic, had sprinted across the road. As he had entered the station, he had noticed that his presence had drawn attention of commuters. For the life of him, he could not understand why they were giving him such funny looks. After learning, at the ticket office, that the train was running late but would arrive in five minutes and thanking the rather helpful young lady, he had turned to return to the car. As he had approached it, he could see that the driver, John Prestwick, was a little agitated. He was gesturing for Richard to hurry up and get in. As he had opened the door and had taken his seat, he had turned and had asked.

'What's wrong with you?'

'Your weapon's showing, for fuck sake!' John exclaimed, panic in his voice.

Richard hadn't known but, as he had exited the car, his shirt had ridden up, revealing the butt of the pistol in his jeans. This had explained why people in the station had staring at him. Feeling embarrassed and exposed, he had nervously looked at his watch. As he did so, their passenger had emerged, from the station. John had pressed the horn, to attract his attention and he had crossed the road to the car.

'Drive!' Richard had shouted. John had slung the car in gear and had raced away, from the scene. They never mentioned the incident but the car they had been using could have become compromised, had they been spotted by a member of or sympathiser of the local IRA.

'How many fuck ups can I make during this tour?' Richard had thought to himself.

The memory was fresh in his mind, as the car they were driving left the west link and entered the city centre. While they always varied their route, there was only one way into Girdwood, so, on this trip, they took a slight detour. Normally, the most direct route would be to go down the Crumlin Road, but Richard had decided to take the Shankill, then turn right, along Agnes Street, which would take them directly on to Cliftonpark Avenue and Girdwood Barracks.

As they turned right on to the Shankill Road, they were greeted by a cacophony of sound and the sight of brightly coloured uniforms. Richard realised straight away that it was a Loyalist march. The sound of the flutes and drums reverberated between the houses and shops running the length of the Shankill. They both realised quickly that their route was blocked, so sat nervously, waiting for an opportunity to drive on. As this was a Protestant area, the situation was not as bad as they been on the Falls Road.

Glancing across at Billy, Richard noticed that the sweat was running down his brow. He was looking very nervous, so Richard tried to calm him down.

'It's okay, mate, we'll get through shortly, once the parade has moved on.'

'Anyone could recognise me!' Billy shouted and made a grab for his pistol, attempting to cock it.

Richard leaned over, grabbing the weapon, to prevent Billy completing the action. 'Put that fucker away, you retard and calm down,'

Billy did as he was told, but remained very nervous, glancing left and right, at the crowds who lined the streets. He pulled down the baseball cap he was wearing, to partially conceal his face. They sat patiently, waiting for the bands to move off and allow them access to turn right on to Agnes Street. The road was too narrow for them to do a U-turn and, as this would only have drawn more attention to them, they sat it out. Fifteen minutes later, they were screaming down Cliftonpark Avenue and screeched to a halt, in the car park of Girdwood Barracks.

The two headed straight to the Ops room, where Richard demanded to speak to the person who had given their route the all clear. The man who had been on duty was from the Intelligence cell and, when he realised his mistake, apologised profusely. This did not placate Richard, who tore him a new arsehole.

The tour was nearing its end and Richard was thankful. The mundane tasks and lack of excitement had frustrated him. One of the main incidents the Regiment had been involved in was a full scale riot in the Ardoyne. Richard hadn't been involved but had spent the time in the Ops room in Moscow Camp, listening to the events unfolding, on the radio. The Regiment had sustained a number of injuries during the riot but, thankfully, no fatalities. It had lasted almost 24 hours and the Troops were on their chin straps by the end of it. It only made Richard want to get back to being fully fit again, so that he would not miss out on any more of these type of operations.

With a week to go, before their return to Germany, Billy asked if Richard fancied Sunday dinner at his parents' house, that weekend. Richard thought this was a grand idea, it had been about two months since his last R&R. Billy said that he would have to clear it through the QM, Tommy Steadman. He went off to get permission and returned shortly, with the approval. They were given the Saturday afternoon off, as well, and were to return to camp, no later than 22:00 on the Sunday. Richard had a word with John Prestwick and asked him if he could drop them off, just outside the harbour, on the Sydenham Road. From there, they would be picked up by Billy's father, at an appointed time.

On the Saturday, they dressed in scruffy, civilian clothing, to blend in with the local populace. Drawing their weapons from the armoury, they met John, at the guardroom. From there, it was only a five minute drive to the main road, where he dropped them off. Richard asked Billy to make sure his weapon was concealed and then checked Billy. Richard didn't want a repeat of the train station incident. After the pick-up time came and went, Richard got a little apprehensive. It was a long walk back to camp, if Billy's dad didn't show. They didn't have any way of communicating with him, nor were there any telephone boxes in the vicinity.

'Here he is!' Billy cried out, pointing to a red Ford Escort, indicating for it to pull over.

Opening the doors to the car, Billy took the passenger seat, while Richard jumped in the back.

'What about ye?' Billy's father greeted them. Billy replied that he was grand and introduced Richard.

Billy's dad, a likeable character, was called Joe. The three chatted, as he steered the car along the Newtonards Road, passed the Knock Golf Club, towards

124

their destination, Newtonards. Billy's family lived on a Protestant, Loyalist estate in the town. Many had moved from the Shankhill, many years before. Parking outside the picket fence which surrounded the front garden, the three entered the dwelling. It was nothing special, much like many council houses in the UK.

'Do you want to put your guns in the safe?' Joe asked them, nonchalantly.

Richard thought it strange that Joe had known they were armed and had asked the question in such a casual way.

Unloading their weapons in the back garden, they returned to the house and placed the guns and magazines in the safe. Joe locked it, turned to them and asked if they wanted a beer.

For the next couple of hours they chewed the fat about the troubles in the Province. Joe was happier when he learned that Richard came from a Protestant family. The conversation turned to the political situation in Northern Ireland. There was a deep rooted suspicion on both sides of the sectarian divide, neither side trusting the other. Richard quickly understood the deep hatred that ran between the Protestants, who wished to remain loyal to the Crown and the Catholics, who wanted a united Ireland. As the beer flowed, Joe produced a bottle of Bushmills whiskey. The debate became more and more heated. Richard knew that Billy was a staunch Loyalist, but had never seen him so animated as now.

By early evening, they had almost demolished the 24 pack of beer and the bottle of 'Bush'. Unanimously, they decided to walk to the local off licence, to replenish supplies. Storm clouds were brewing, as they left the house, which gave their surroundings a sombre, sinister atmosphere. Strolling through the streets, they turned left, on to waste ground, which Billy indicated was a shortcut to the off licence. Richard's attention was drawn to two teenage lads, one of whom, bizarrely, was carrying a car door in his hands. When Richard overheard part of their conversation, he could not believe his ears.

'Right, you're the Fenian and I'm the Prod,' the taller, older looking of the two said, passing the car door to his pal, who accepted it, reluctantly; the taller lad walked back ten paces. He knelt down and picked up a couple of stones, laid in a pile at his feet. With all his strength, he pulled back his arm and directed the first missile at the younger youth. It struck the car door with a resounding bang. Another stone quickly followed, until the pile was gone and the small teenager was crying out for him to stop.

'Enough! Enough! You're the Fenian and I'm the Prod now!' he screamed and his friend grudgingly swapped places with him.

As this was going on, Billy and his father had been busily chatting away. It wasn't until Richard piped up, that they stopped their conversation:

'There will never be peace in this country as long as that goes on!' he exclaimed, staring at them. He would take their answer to his grave.

'While what goes on?' the father and son answered in unison, matter-of-factly. This episode with the youths re-enforced to Richard the hatred which existed, from an early age and which was nurtured until adulthood.

The following morning, Richard was wakened in bed by Billy's mum, who brought him a cup of tea. He had a mouth like Ghandi's flip flop. They hadn't finished drinking until around three in the morning. He thanked Billy's mum for the brew and she left him to bring himself round. After draining the contents of the cup, Richard toddled off, to the bathroom, where he quickly showered and shaved. Taking out a new pair of boxers, shorts and a shirt from his bag, he descended the stairs. Billy was already up, with his dad, reading a newspaper. They wished him a good morning and asked how he had slept.

'Like a log.'

'I'm not surprised, the state of ye last night!' Joe chuckled.

Richard felt his cheeks flush and knew he was blushing. He just hoped that he hadn't said anything to upset anyone. The incident with the two teenagers was still fresh in his mind, the later events somewhat blurred. The smell of bacon wafting from the kitchen caught Richard's attention. He wasn't a man for a big breakfast but the smell was making him salivate. In a mere few minutes, the three men were called through by his mother, who had laid out the plates on the dining room table. She had prepared a full 'Ulster Fry', with all the trimmings. Richard got stuck in to the two fried eggs, lightly browned potato, soda bread, pork sausages, crispy bacon, black and white pudding and juicy, red tomato. He mopped up every bit of juice with the soda bread. He thanked Mrs McQueen for her excellent culinary skills and was told he was very welcome.

After a leisurely walk and a few pints in the local pub, Billy, Joe and Richard returned to the family home. Once again, a meal awaited them and they piled in. For Richard, the rest of the day was spent snoozing, on the sofa.

The time finally came for them to return to camp. They withdrew their weapons from the safe, loaded up and climbed into the car. The journey back was completed almost in silence. Billy knew it could be some time before he had the chance to come across the water, to see his parents again. They were dropped off outside the camp gates and, showing their IDs to the sentry, were allowed to enter. This rounded off the tour, soon they were flying back to their camp in Germany.

Chapter 12 - Warminster & Rehabilitation

Two months had passed since his return from Northern Ireland. Birgit surprised Richard, with the news that she was pregnant with their second child. Conception had obviously taken place when Richard had been on R&R from Ireland. In the forces, a baby boom often occurred in the months after a Regiment was deployed overseas. A lot of the families' children were born very close together. Their child was due in six months and, as the Regiment was preparing to leave their current posting and move back to the UK, things promised to be hectic.

Most of the Regiment was be stationed in Tidworth, one of the major garrisons in the UK. Richard knew it well, as he had lived there when his father served and the Regiment had been posted there in the mid-1970s.

This was Richard's first posting to the UK and the first time that Birgit would live in England. He was still part of the Quartermaster Technical department and had been chosen to support the Demonstration Squadron, who were stationed in Warminster. The process of moving was all part of army life and one that Richard had known all his days. Several weeks prior to leaving, they were issued with flat-pack, wooden boxes, known as 'MFO' (Military Forces Overseas) boxes. In typical military fashion, they were allocated just enough screws to assemble the boxes. If anyone managed to damage any while putting the boxes together, he was screwed. Where Richard worked, these sort of items were readily available. He had acquired a couple of extra boxes and had built them. They lay ready in his cellar. Over the following weeks, he and Birgit packed up their possessions one by one. Moving was a real pain in the arse, but one he was well used to. Families were given money for the inconvenience, to sweeten the move. The contracts for conveyance of furniture and boxes were given to a number of removal companies, one of whom,

Pickfords, arrived early one morning, to collect the family's belongings.

The removal men performed were like a well-oiled machine. The three men, armed with bubble wrap, tape and packing paper, descended on the flat. Birgit and Richard stood back and let them get on with it, supplying them with brew ups, on a regular basis. The crew made short work of loading up the furniture and boxes and were away by lunchtime.

For the rest of the day, Birgit and Richard spent their time cleaning what had been their home, ready for the handover, in two days' time. As they had no bed to sleep in, the army paid for them to stay in a hotel, for two nights. For the next two days, they returned to the empty flat and spent from morning to late evening scrubbing, painting and polishing everything in sight. They knew the standard required for the handover and didn't want to incur any penalties for not being ready to 'march out'.

The estate warden, responsible for flats and houses on his patch, turned up to inspect the property. These individuals were normally Warrant Officers or Senior Non Commissioned Officers, placed on the Long Service List, having completed their regular 22 years' service. They had seen everything before and knew all the tricks. Their standards were very high and woe betide any family who were not up to the mark. Although he didn't know it at the time, Richard came to learn all about this, as he neared the end of his career.

The inspection took around 45 minutes and Birgit anxiously followed the estate warden around the accommodation. She was offended when she was politely asked to wait outside, as it was her husband's responsibility for the handover and was seething, as she stood outside the flat. How dare he! She had put as much, if not more, effort into the married quarter than Richard. Yet, this was always the way, the wives were always deemed subservient to their spouses, a fact that they were constantly reminded of, being referred to as the 'wife of' such a given soldier.

The inspection complete and the keys handed over, Richard joined Birgit outside, smiling at her, as he said, happily.

'That's it, we passed. He was especially impressed with the cooker.'

Birgit grinned back at him, proudly, because it was she who had cleaned the cooker. She had also done almost all of the painting. Richard had pleaded with her not to do so much in her condition but she was stubborn and had wanted to play her part.

The move was behind them. The family settled into their new, three bedroom home, in Warminster, on the edge of Salisbury Plain. They had been allocated a bigger house because of the imminent arrival of their new child. They knew it was going to be a boy, so they needed separate rooms for the children. This had been agreed to, so their new house was bigger than their last, in Germany. However, like all married quarters in the UK and unlike those in Germany, it didn't have a cellar.

They had made the place their own and were enjoying the peaceful, countryside surroundings, where they now lived.

Richard's new place of work was Harman Lines, situated on top of Sack Hill, bordering the edge of Salisbury Plain and accessed by road for the tanks to transit easily from their camp on to the Plain. He was based in a building to the left of the main Squadron offices and was one of only three members of staff to support the Squadron, with a WO2, Dai Evans, and a young Lance Corporal from Northumberland, Paul Stanford.

Dai was Richard's new boss and was a very laid back type from North Wales. The three got along straight away and quickly formed an excellent working relationship. Their job was to make sure the Squadron was fully operational, at all times. They stocked all the essential parts needed to keep the fleet of fourteen Challengers on the road. If they ran out of a part, they were given priority and would receive it within a maximum three days.

Richard set about computerising the stock system, to make it easier to check for parts in stock, rather than searching through volumes of folders, which held all the stock items on paper. This innovative move reflected well in his annual appraisal and he was, once again, put forward for promotion. The only stumbling block was his current back injury.

One morning, when Richard turned up for work, Dai pulled him to one side.

'The Squadron Leader has asked that you make your injury official, by making an appointment with the Senior Medical Officer (SMO). He's in the main Medical Centre, at Warminster Training Centre. I told him that you've been having private therapy, from an osteopath, but he wants you to go through the military channels,' Dai explained.

'Aye, no problem,' Richard muttered, knowing full well that Dai had been forced into this. Richard had, for the last couple of months, been receiving treatment from a local osteopath, at a considerable cost to himself, but felt it worthwhile, since it gave him relief. He got on the phone and made an appointment, for the next morning.

The following day, he booked into the WTC Medical Centre, where he waited to be called into the SMO's office. He had assumed that this would just be a brief examination and an assessment of his injury. As Richard's name was called, he was not prepared for what was about to happen.

Entering the SMO's office, he closed the door behind him, then was asked to take a seat, opposite a stern Lieutenant Colonel of the Royal Army Medical Corps (RAMC), who looked disdainfully at Richard, before speaking.

'I understand you have been receiving private medical treatment for your back injury,' he began, waiting for Richard to answer.

'That's correct, Sir,' he responded, wondering where this was going.

Then, like a volcano, the SMO erupted, his face turning crimson. 'Well! I'm not happy with that! I'm sending you for an x-ray,' he spat the words out venomously, as though he had been personally betrayed by Richard's actions.

Not knowing what to say, Richard simply nodded and took the tirade to be the end of the interview.

'I want the results to be dropped off at reception, when you return,' the SMO growled, as Richard left the room.

Seething with anger, Richard attended the appointment made for him, at the local hospital. As it was only a small establishment, so he was seen very quickly. Within an hour, he was back with the x-rays he had been given. He dropped them off at the Medical Centre, then returned to work, at Harman Lines.

Dai asked him how it had gone and Richard explained what the SMO had said. Dai shook his head, knowing Richard carried a genuine injury and should not have been treated this way.

Just before lunch, Dai's telephone rang and, after speaking for a moment, he handed it over to Richard, saying it was the Medical Centre at WTC.

Richard took the handset and answered, reciting his rank and name.

'Sure, no problem. I'll be there,' he said, returning the telephone to Dai, who looked at him, quizzically.

'Ding, ding, round two. The SMO wants to see me at 14:00,' he explained.

Reporting to reception at the Medical Centre, Richard was asked to take a seat. He had only just parked his backside, when his name was called. He took a deep breath and tried to calm himself down, before his second encounter with the obnoxious SMO. However, entering the room, he was aware that the demeanour of the SMO had changed, radically. He was cordially invited to sit.

'Corporal Hunter, I have had a look at your x-ray results and would like to go through them with you,' he waited for a moment, before taking the x-ray from his desk and putting it up on a screen, switching on a light. The illuminated black and white image of Richard's spine was clearly visible.

'Right, can you see your vertebrae here?' the Colonel indicated with his pen. 'Observe how appear nice and square, with spaces in between,' Richard nodded his affirmation. 'Well, look at these two here, looking like a piece of jigsaw puzzle. They simply shouldn't be like that!'

Richard looked blankly at the SMO, not comprehending what he was seeing. He gathered his thoughts, then answered, noting how the SMO's tone had changed, from one of arrogance that morning to one of concern.

'So, what is it you're actually saying?' Richard asked outright.

The Doctor went on to explain that Richard had, at some point in the past, received a compression fracture to his L4 and L5 vertebrae. He could only think that this had happened during the rugby match, a couple of years previously. He had been passed fit for remedial physical training, just after that, which meant that the fracture hadn't had time to heal. He realised that he had been lucky not to end up in a wheelchair. His blood boiled and he couldn't contain himself, any longer.

'So, what you're saying is I had an injury which was misdiagnosed?' Abruptly, he directed the question at the SMO, who was clearly uncomfortable.

He squirmed in his chair and went on to explain that it could have happened at any time, not wanting to drop the Regimental Medical Officer in the shit. Richard was having none of it but, happy that he had been vindicated, left the office, to return to work. He explained all that had happened to Dai, who was shocked and asked what was going to happen next. Richard said he had not waited to find out but had left before he said something he might regret.

Three weeks later, Richard had an MRI scan, which confirmed that he had indeed received a compression fracture. It was recommended he attend a course of rehabilitation, to be taken at the Defence Medical Rehabilitation Unit (DMRC), Headley Court.

Headley Court was located in the southern slopes of Epsom Downs and was the one time home of the first Baron Cunliffe - formerly Governor of the Bank of England and Chairman of the London and North Eastern Railway Company. Headley Court was purchased by the Institute of Chartered Auctioneers and Estate Agents who presented the estate to The Royal Air Force thro' the Air Ministry in 1946 to commemorate the Battle of Britain. During the war years Headley Court was the headquarters of The First Canadian Army firstly under General McNaughton and later under General Crerar. Soon after the war it became the rehabilitation centre for pilots and aircrew who had been injured during the war. Its role has changed somewhat and it is now functional to all three services in the rehabilitation of serving personnel who are undergoing recovery from injury or illness. It's mission, 'to provide clinical rehabilitation, training and personnel for the operational role and research in order to achieve optimal levels of health and fitness' (Headley Court, Website)

On arrival, Richard reported to reception, situated in a courtyard, just off the main road, running through the complex. He was booked in and given directions to his room, where he would be staying for the next four weeks. The rooms held four men. Richard found that his new roommates had already arrived and had unpacked. As was normal, introductions were made and the ice was melted in the bar, after the evening meal. They had been given a programme of activities for their time there and Richard, for once, decided this wasn't the time and place to kick the arse out of the drinking. He would assess if he needed to stick to this policy, over the next few days.

First thing next morning, the 'patients', as they were referred to at Hedley Court, assembled in the main gym, dressed in sports kit. It was a parade everyone had to attend every day, regardless of their injury. As they filed into the main hall, the instructors were waiting for them, all Physical Training instructors from the three services, Army, Navy and RAF. Richard was surprised to find amongst their number there were a couple of females. At the appointed time, one of the instructors called the roll call, to ensure no one was absent. Finding all present, he asked the patients to find themselves a space, with enough room to move.

Once all were in position, the instructors had them start running on the sport, to warm up their muscles and to raise their heartrates, before the lesson started, in earnest.

The lesson took the form of an aerobic session and each exercise was demonstrated by a different instructor. Copying their example, the troops began the first exercise, then eased into the next. This went on for thirty minutes. If an injury precluded a man from participating in a particular exercise, he was excused and moved on.

There was no room for slacking here, Richard thought. As he looked about the room, he saw soldiers with missing limbs getting stuck right into the routines. It boiled his piss, when he spotted a couple of young lads, no more than twenty or so, putting in less than 100% effort. They were obviously here for an easy time and had no intention of trying to get back to full physical fitness. Richard knew that this was required of him to ensure his eligibility for promotion and gave it his all.

The session over, the class left and made their way to their next lesson. The patients had been divided into groups, by their injuries. Richard was in the group of personnel with back problems and their first lesson was designed to assess how bad their injuries were. They were given a series of exercises and their results recorded by the instructor. These were put through abdominal and back strengthening exercises. Richard found some manageable but others almost impossible. The instructors asked that they tried their best. By the end of the four weeks, they hoped to see an improvement.

At the end of the first week, interspersed with small runs, gym work, back clinics, occupational therapy and sessions in the hydro pool each patient was assessed, by one of the Doctors.

Richard waited patiently, outside one of the offices, blissfully unaware of the news he was to be given. As the patient before him left the office, he stood, after hearing his name called. Entering the room, he was met an RAF Group Captain, the equivalent rank of a full Colonel in the Army. He introduced himself and invited Richard to take a seat.

'I have looked over your medical history, x-rays and MRI results. May I ask you how long you have left to serve, Corporal Hunter?'

Richard was taken aback by the question, wondering where it was leading. He thought carefully, working out how long he had left to serve, before replying.

'Six years, Sir,' he said, in a loud, clear voice.

The Group Captain looked down at the notes on his desk, before looking back up, at Richard. 'Corporal Hunter, do you wish to see your time out?'

This question was more ominous and sent a chill through Richard, 'Of course I do, Sir,' he heard himself say.

'Well, the injury you have sustained is not something we can fix. We can help you strengthen your back and teach you to manage the pain. If we are very lucky, we may even get you back to full fitness.'

Richard's heart sank as he heard this devastating news. He thanked the Officer for his time and left the room.

On the way to his next lesson, he determined, more than ever, to get back to full operational fitness, no matter how long it took, nor the effort required.

By the end of the four weeks, there had been a marked improvement to Richard's condition. He had successfully completed his first session at Hedley Court but would be destined to return another twice, before his injury would get to a manageable level.

On his return to camp, he drove his car up Sack Hill. As he drove, he saw the SSM, Robin Carter, marching two of the Squadron briskly up the hill. He giggled to himself, as he turned right, into the camp entrance. Parking his car, he walked into the stores office.

'Good to see you back!' Dai exclaimed, a broad grin spreading across his face.

'Good to be back, this will be a bit of a rest after the last four weeks. It was torture,' he cackled. 'What's the crack with the SSM marching those two cockwombles up Sack Hill?'

'It his new thing,' Dai said, raising his eyebrows, 'he calls it *Operation Grand Old Duke of York.* Any Squadron offenders are marched up every morning from the accommodation blocks, in best uniform. They get changed into work clothes, in the guardroom, at the top. Then, at lunch time, they get back into barrack order again and marched back down. He does this at the end of the day as well. He's fucking nuts but the boys are taking note. No one wants to drop a bollock these days, so he is doing something right.'

Dai and Richard laughed for the next five minutes over the SSM's crazy ways. Paul, who was also in the office, laughed with them.

The following day was St. Patrick's Day or Paddy's Day, as it was affectionately known in the Regiment. It was one of the main events of the Regimental Calendar and began with the Warrant Officers and SNCOs carrying around a green or silver container, filled with coffee or tea. One of their party was be loaded up with whiskey and brandy. They went round the single guys' accommodation block, to wake them up, pour them a cup of tea or coffee, topping it up with a generous slug of whiskey or brandy to liven their brews.

That duty performed, the SNCO went to the cookhouse, to serve the men breakfast. The Squadron then paraded on the tank park, where the Squadron Leader presented them with shamrocks. As soon as the formal part was done, they spent the day in sporting competitions, which involved consuming large amounts of alcohol. This year, it was decided that they should dispense with this and, instead, hit the pubs and bars in Warminster town.

As Richard and Paul were married men, they didn't get allocated "gun-fire", as the brew with alcohol was known. Instead, they decided to walk into camp and have a few quiet drinks, in the office. By the time it came for parade, they were already half cut.

In town, the first pub they chose to go in was the Bath Arms, a well-known watering hole for all soldiers, who passed through Warminster. The order of the day was Guinness, Richard's favourite tipple and to accompany this, only Irish whiskey would do. Despite it being only just after one in the afternoon, the singing had already started. Richard was, by this time, struggling to stand. He propped himself up, leaning on the bar, rather than risk sitting on a stool, which he would probably fall off.

Suddenly and inexplicably, he untied and removed his shoes, pulled down his jeans and boxers, which he placed them over two of the beer hand pumps. He stood smiling, wearing only a t-shirt, nowhere near long to cover his tackle and a pair of socks, one of which had a hole where a big toe poked through. People in the pub laughed and cringed, simultaneously. That was the last thing Richard remembered, as he was abruptly thrown out and dragged home by Paul.

Next morning, Richard sat in the office, his head in his hands. Inside his head, was a thumping like the big drum in one the Orange parades he had witnessed. He was nursing a hangover that would kill a civvy.

Dai and Paul were at the rear of the store, sorting out some of the equipment, on the shelves. As they banged and crashed about, Richard winced, the noise sending pains through his fragile head. Dai's phone rang and Richard called to him, to let him know. Dai entered the room and picked up the handset.

After a brief moment, he answered the caller, 'Yes, Sir, he's here. Do you want to speak to him?' Dai paused, then handed the phone to Richard. Not knowing who was on the other end, Richard stared blankly at Dai. The voice he heard was the unmistakeable tone of Thomas McCreedy, the new RSM, at Tidworth.

'Corporal Hunter, I have a question for you,' there was a moment's pause. 'I am in need of a new Provost Sergeant and I would like that person to be you.' There followed a deathly silence, while Richard considered his answer. 'Well, what do you say?' the Ulsterman urged.

'I would love the job,' Richard lied. He knew this was a way of getting the promotion he required, to move on. The RSM went on to explain that it would be a local rank, initially, which meant that Richard would carry the post and be paid for it, but that he wasn't eligible for further promotion, which could only be attained when Richard was back to full fitness. Richard agreed to the terms, thanked the RSM and placed the handset back on to its cradle.

That was it, then. In four weeks' time, he would move house yet again and would be living on the other side of Salisbury Plain.

Chapter 13 - Darkness Visible

It had a cold winter's evening and Richard had just returned from school. He had stamped his feet against the mat, in front of the door of the flat, shaking the snow from the soles of his shoes. The smell of stew had carried along the corridor, from the kitchen. He loved his mother's stews and had put his bag down, rushing towards the kitchen. When he had got there, his mother had had her back to him, stirring a pot on the cooker.

'Sit yourself down, it's ready, I'll dish it up, your dad's already had his,'

'Thanks, mum, I'm starving,' Richard had replied, taking a seat next to his brother, Mal, already eating.

Richard's brother was three years younger and had been due to start secondary school, the following year. The poor child hadn't known it then but he would have a reputation to live up to, as Richard had led a colourful life, since having joined the school, two years earlier. He had been a keen sportsman, who had represented the school in a number of sports. He had been captain of the rugby team and a favourite of Mr Knight, one of the PE teachers. Mr Knight had previously played for the Harlequins Rugby Club, in London, before going into teaching. He was a gentle giant and had been highly respected by the pupils. Mr Knight had later Christened Richard's brother "Marion" for his unwillingness to tackle, when playing rugby.

'I'm off, then,' had come his father's voice, from the kitchen doorway. He had been attired in a dark suit, had worn a Regimental tie and had carried a briefcase. Richard had stopped eating and had asked where his father was going.

'Mess meeting,' had been the reply.

Pausing for thought, Richard had questioned this. 'Mess meetings are Thursdays. It's Wednesday, today.'

'Just shut up, I'm off.' Kissing Richard's mother on the cheek, he had walked out.

Richard had asked the question because he had an inkling where his dad was going. A couple of weeks earlier he, his brother and sister had been searching for Christmas presents they had hoped were hidden in their parents' bedroom. Rummaging through a wardrobe, they had discovered a briefcase. Opening it, they had found a folder, with pages of writing which hadn't made any sense to them. They had looked at each other, inquisitively, as they read the strange words in front of their eyes. Under the paperwork, they had found a white fabric square with a light blue border, adorned with three light blue rosettes. Flanking these rosettes were two chains and, in the centre, sat a colourful, embroidered badge.

'Bloody hell, me dad's a pervert!' Richard had exclaimed and the boys had fallen about laughing. Richard's sister, too young to understand what was going on or what the word meant, had joined in, anyway.

So when the door had slammed, Richard had wondered if his father was going to a Mess meeting or to a meeting of a mysterious club.

On 24th June, 1758, the Most Worshipful Grand Lodge of Ireland granted a Warrant to establish a Masonic Lodge in the First Regiment of Horse, afterwards the 4th Royal Irish Dragoon Guards, and then styled the 4th/7th

Royal Dragoon Guards, and now styled the Royal Dragoon Guards,-it having ceased its role as a Cavalry Regiment and now operates as a unit of the Royal Armoured Corps

This Warrant was granted by the Right Hon. Charles, Viscount Moore, (Grand Master), John Bury, Esq. (Deputy Grand Master), Major Edward Windus and Charles Gardner, Esq. (Grand Wardens) to Brothers Andrew Watts, James Leathem and Robert Sanderson, to erect a Lodge of Freemasons in the 1st Regiment of Horse now commanded by Lieut. General Brown. It is dated 24th June, 1758, and is signed by MOORE, G.M. and E. WINDUS, S,G,W., and countersigned by' JOHN CALDER, G. Sec.

Viscount Moore was afterwards 6th Earl and 2nd Marquis of Drogheda and a Field Marshal in the Army.

The Warrant is the original and of the small size type as first issued by the Grand Lodge of Ireland. As was usual with Warrants at that time it had no distinctive name.

112 Members were registered by' Grand Lodge up to 19th June 1830 and on 6th May 1835 the Grand Lodge minutes record that the remaining members of the Lodge had sent in the Warrant to be laid up 'with a donation of one guinea to the Orphan School.

At the foot of the Warrant is the following Endorsement :~This Warrant re-issued January 1878 to Bros. Thos. Shaw-Hellier, John Hanly and Laurence Murphy (4th Royal Irish Dragoon Guards). Signed Saml. Oldham, Dep. Grand Sec., 11th Jan. 1878.
When the Warrant of 295 was resuscitated in 1878 the only member alive was W. Bro. Lieut.-General Sir

*Edward Hodge, who had commanded the Regiment with
great gallantry in the Crimea.*

*In reading these Notes it will be seen that being an
Ambulatory Lodge it was warranted in the Regiment and
generally speaking its activities have been largely
concerned with the areas in which the Regiment has served.
It does not (and never has done) work under any Province
or District as is the case with Stationary Lodges and is
controlled direct by the Grand Lodge of Ireland (St
Patricks Lodge 295 History)*

Richard looked up, from his book on the
Regimental Lodge, as Stan Horan entered the guardroom.

He didn't look very happy and pulled up a chair,
facing Richard. The two had first met just after the
Regiment had amalgamated and had struck up a friendship.
Stan's hair was quite thick and bushy, unusual for a soldier,
apart from a bald patch, on one side. As a young child, he
had pulled a pan of hot oil off the cooker, causing severe
burns, the scars of which he would carry for the rest of his
life. Stan had been glad when the two Regiments had
amalgamated. He had been a member of the Skins and, as
one of the few Englishmen in the Regiment, life had not
been easy.

Over a beer, he had once quoted an example to
Richard, which had stuck in his mind. When it had come
time for the Regiment to go on leave, those from 'over the
water' had been given special treatment. He had, on more
than one occasion, been denied leave, so his Irish
colleagues could have theirs.

Richard stared at Stan, waiting for him to explain
his demeanour.

'Didn't go well, mate,' he began, in an apologetic tone. The only reaction he got from Richard was a smile.

'I'm not joking, mate, you got black-balled.' Richard's expression changed to one of disappointment.

'We know who it was. He is due to go on a course in six months, so we will ballot you again, then.'

Richard paused before he attempted to answer.

'These things happen,' he said, trying not to show how upset he was. Stan had proposed him into the Lodge and was not happy about this stumbling block. As a 'Lewis' or son of a mason, he had expected that there would be no problem in joining and had not expected this news. Stan did his best to smooth things over, putting Richard's mind at rest.

Six months on and the day arrived for Richard and another from the Regiment to be initiated. The night before, he had ironed a white shirt, looked out a dark suit and his Regimental tie and had highly polished his shoes. Stan had told him the dress code and what he was required to bring with him, including a pair of pyjamas and slippers, which Richard thought was obviously a joke. However, he packed them into a carrier bag, anyway. Happy that he had everything, including a cheque for his subscription fees, he called out to Birgit.

'You ready to take me to the Lodge?' he asked.

A voice carried from a bedroom, at the top of the house. 'Won't be a minute.' Birgit made her way, down the stairs, to meet him. 'Are you nervous?' she asked, as they met, by the door.

'A little,' Richard admitted.

'It will be fine,' she said, kissing him on the cheek and pulling open the door, for them to leave.

The journey from their house to the Lodge building only took ten minutes and was taken in silence. Richard was wondering what would happen that evening. He felt better, knowing that someone else was going to be initiated with him and that they would go through the 'ordeal' together. Birgit applied her foot to the brake and the car came to a steady stop, outside the address Stan had given him. Richard had done a drive-by with Birgit the previous week, to check out where it was. His wife looked across at him and smiled, again kissing him on the cheek and wished him luck. She told him she would be waiting, outside at around 11:00 that night, to take him home. Richard thanked her, opened the door of the car and slowly made his way into the building.

The room he entered was already quite busy, with people bustling around. Stan caught Richard's eye and, smiling, came over. Richard was quickly led into a smaller room, where sat the other initiate, a newly promoted Sergeant from A Squadron, Paul Jones. He was slight of build, like Richard, and sported a massive, Mexican style moustache. He appeared even more nervous than Richard. They were joined by Steve Todman, a wild-eyed fella from Belfast. He was a gunnery instructor and had just returned from teaching at the gunnery school in Lulworth.

'What about ye?' he asked the Lodge's newest recruits, in his hard Belfast accent.

Richard tried to look confident, although his stomach was turning.

'We're great, Steve,' he answered, on behalf of them both.

Steve went on to explain that he was the Director of Ceremonies of the Lodge and that he would take them through their initiation. He looked at them both and, knowing, despite their military training, experience and the confidence which that develops in a man, they both now faced a journey into the unknown. That uncertainty had knocked the cockiness out of them and Steve felt sure he saw apprehension on their faces. He spoke words of re-assurance, advising them that they were about to take the same steps he and many others, had taken, years before.

They were prepared for the ceremony, then led to an adjoining room, in the corner of which was a battered, timber door. Steve opened it and invited them to step inside.

He left them in the confined, dark space, advising them that he would now give them time to reflect on matters material and spiritual.

It seemed an eternity passed, as they stood, not daring to speak or move, but, in reality, only a few minutes had gone. Their thoughts were disturbed by the sound of the handle being turned and the door was opened. Steve stood before them in his full Masonic regalia, a blue collar around his neck, with a silver ornament hanging from it and, around his waist and under his jacket, an apron, almost identical to the one Richard had unearthed, all those years before, in his father's hideaway.

He asked them to step out of the confines of the cupboard.

'Gentlemen, I am now going to take you into the Lodge room. Listen carefully to everything that is said,' Steve addressed them, formally.

Richard felt a hand on his shoulder, then someone take his right hand and they stepped forward.

Richard had no idea how much time passed nor did he fully take in what was said to him or where he was moved to, within the large hall. He learned, shortly afterwards, that Paul Jones was the same.

He did realise, however, that he had been through a ritual steeped in tradition and one which was handled with great dignity, almost a reverence. He knew, even after such a short time in the room, that things felt right. What he remembered of what had been said to him made sense and gave him a new perspective on his place in the world.

What most astonished Richard was that the person whose voice he had heard throughout the ceremony belonged to his childhood friend, Pete, the youth with whom he had travelled, to join the Army.

Pete smiled at him, from a large chair, covered in decorated carvings, on a raised platform. He shook Richard's hand and welcomed him into the Lodge.

Pete, now a Staff Sergeant, was the figurehead of the lodge, and was referred to as the Worshipful Master. He had joined as soon as he had been promoted to Sergeant, his father also being a member like Richard's. Richard felt proud that he was following on in his father's footsteps, and carrying on a Regimental tradition that had been in existence for over 200 years.

Richard, more than everything else, felt relief. When he finally looked round the room, he recognised almost every man in it. There was no-one below the rank of Sergeant, a requirement for membership of the Lodge. It had seemed strange to him that this was so, having spent many hours studying the principles of Freemasonry. Everyone was deemed to be equal and valued for his worth as a man. The reason for this caveat was explained to him, by his proposer, Stan. The members of the Warrant Officers' and Sergeants' Mess were seen to be experienced and educated enough by that stage in their careers, not to abuse the trust that they had entered into.

The ceremony had come to its conclusion and everyone filed out of the room. To a man, they lined up to congratulate Richard and Paul, shaking their hands and welcoming them into a fraternity that was dispersed all over the globe.

The Regiment was unique, in the fact that it was one of only two remaining military Lodges, which had a travelling or military ambulatory warrant. This meant that they would meet wherever the Lodge was stationed at that time.

When the congratulations had concluded, the two candidates were taken into another room. Tables had been laid out, complete with cutlery and glasses. They were invited to take a seat next to the Worshipful Master.

There was a single rap on the table and the announcement made that they would say grace before dining. This done, they sat down together, their glasses were filled by some of the Lodge members, acting as waiters.

They ate for a good hour, then Steve, the Director of Ceremonies, stood and requested silence, for the Worshipful Master. The room went quiet, as Pete stood up and asked them to rise and raise a toast to HM the Queen. As one, the members rose. Lifting their glasses in union, they toasted Her Majesty, then retook their seats. There followed a series of speeches and toasts, until it came to a toast to Paul and Richard, who were each, in turn, asked to say a few brief words in reply.

Richard took a deep breath and rose to speak.

'May I firstly start by thanking my proposer, Stan, for inviting me to join the Lodge. I thoroughly enjoyed the ceremony this evening and congratulate everyone who took part. I hope that I will be of service to the Lodge, in my time as a member. I know I have a lot to learn but am looking forward to the challenge and to spending many evenings with you all, in the future.' To a round of applause, he sat down.

Paul rose to give speak and the room again fell silent. Richard looked around the faces of the members, and thought that, not only were these gentlemen brothers in arms, they were now Brothers, of a different kind, a tie even more binding than he had experienced thus far. As the sound of applause for Paul's reply died down, Richard smiled to himself, content that he had made the right decision.

Chapter 14 - Warrant Officers' & Sergeants' Mess

Richard had made the move across Salisbury Plain. He and his family were now settled in the garrison town of Tidworth. The garrison, one of the biggest in the UK, included infantry, artillery, an armoured Regiment and a Brigade Headquarters. It was ideal for training, as Tidworth, like Warminster, was right on the edge of Salisbury Plain. Before Richard started his new job, he was first be introduced to the Warrant Officers' and Sergeants' Mess.

It was a Friday afternoon and all the newly promoted Sergeants, along with all mess members, were invited to the mess. This was a time honoured tradition, a way of celebrating the new Sergeants having attained their rank. It was also a way of welcoming them into this select club. Dressed in his barrack dress trousers and Number 2 shirt, Richard made his way towards the Mess. He was slightly apprehensive about the day ahead. Although he knew everyone who would be there, he, along with the other newly promoted Sergeants, would be in the spotlight. Richard had never been one for being the centre of attention and always tried to avoid it, if possible. This wasn't on today though, he thought. He took a deep breath, as he pushed open the double doors, at the entrance to the Mess.

The room was already almost full of senior ranks. Some stood at the bar, others lounged on the leather Chesterfield chairs and sofas. The room was festooned with paintings and statues, celebrating events and characters, past and present. Cigarette and cigar smoke hung in the air and Richard could just make out the figure of Stan Horan, who motioned him over.

'What you having, mate?' he asked.

'Just a beer, thanks,' Richard replied, timidly.

Calling the barman over, Stan ordered two pints, draining the glass he held, handing it back, to the barman. The duty of Mess barman was given mostly to Troopers who had proved inept at tank park life. Rather than discharge them as unfit for purpose, they were presented with this avenue, to allow them continued service. Some took to it with surprising ease and, in time, were promoted, for their efforts.

The glasses were placed on the bar, although Richard saw no money exchange hands.

'You not going to pay for those?' he asked, inquisitively.

'No, mate, I just put it on my Mess bill and pay at the end of the month!' Stan chuckled, as he explained.

It quickly became apparent that this was normal practice, as others ordered drinks and, like Stan, not pay in cash. Richard saw an inherent danger in this, especially if he was tempted to go on a bender. As the two friends chatted, they were disturbed by the sound of a bell, situated at the end of the bar. A great cheer went up from everyone in the room, as a hapless, newly promoted Sergeant, from A Squadron, stood rooted to the spot, his face scarlet. Richard had been warned never to ring the bell, as it incurred the penalty of buying everyone in the Mess a drink. As the laughter died down and the penalty drinks were poured, the room applauded. Richard turned back to Stan, who had already downed his pint, in anticipation of the freebie from the bell ringer.

'It's my round after this one,' Richard offered.

'Bollocks, you don't need to buy a drink tonight, mate. Do me favour while I bring over the pints; that picture over there has been bugging me all afternoon. Could you put it straight for me, before the RSM sees it?'

Richard turned, to follow his line of sight and noticed a small painting, of a cavalry officer dressed in scarlet. From the handlebar moustache, Richard guessed the subject must have been around the time of the Crimean war. He made his way toward it and angled it, slightly, so that it sat horizontal. He hadn't noticed the level of noise in the room had subsided and, as he turned, another loud cheer erupted.

'That will cost you a round of drinks for the room, Sergeant Hunter!' came the unmistakable, Northern Irish accent of Tom McCreedy, the RSM, over the noise of the cheering crowd.

Richard felt a right dick, but he was sure it wouldn't be the last time he would be tricked into doing something he shouldn't. 'Mess etiquette and traditions are a nightmare,' he thought to himself. Digging in his pocket, he turned to the barman and asked that he dish out a drink for all in the bar. The gesture was clapped by all the Mess members, as they filed their way to the counter, slapping him on the back and shaking his hand.

Once drinks was suitably replenished, the RSM raised his hands, then lowered them, to signal for the room to be quiet. The noise level dropped, until there was complete silence. All eyes were directed towards the RSM. Although only five and a half feet tall, like all RSMs before him, acted as though he were ten feet tall. He demanded the full respect of his Senior Non Commissioned Officers and, to a man, he got it.

'Gentlemen, you know why we are gathered here this afternoon, to celebrate the promotions of the following,' he began to read from a list and, as each name was called out, they were asked to put their hand up, so that everyone could identify who they were, if they didn't already know them. This was highly unusual, in a cavalry Regiment, as most soldiers began and ended their careers with the same bunch.

Introductions made, the newly promoted Sergeants were asked to turn around. They did as they were ordered to. Along the length of the bar was placed a shot glass, containing a golden liquid, for each of them. Richard knew from what his father had told him that it was Drambuie, a sweet liqueur, made from Scotch whisky, honey, herbs and spices. The barman took a match and lit the liquid in each glass, in turn. When he had finished, he nodded to the RSM.

'Okay, here are the rules. You have to down the Drambuie, every last drop, but the flame has to remain lit!'

He waited until the words had sunk in, before adding. 'If the flames goes out or you do not finish the drink, you will have to repeat the procedure. Are there any questions?'

A deathly silence descended, as the Mess members gathered round, in a semi-circle, to observe the spectacle.

One by one, the new made Sergeants attempted to drain their glasses, with varying levels of success. Most either burnt their lips on the glass or the sticky, hot liquid stuck to their faces. Richard smiled, as he waited for his turn. At last, the RSM turned to him, indicating it was his go. He had been prepared for this, knowing that it was coming. He produced a broken biro, from inside his pocket. The nib and plastic ink tube had been removed, which left a hard, plastic 'drinking straw'.

Moving towards the glass, he placed the biro tube in his mouth and inserted it into the glass, just touching the bottom. He could feel the heat rising from the flames searing his face. With one quick sip, he drained the contents of the glass, leaving the flame intact. He span round, to applause from the whole of the Mess, The RSM, not amused, was scowling at him.

'You will have to do that again!' he screamed out.

Richard simply smiled and said. 'You didn't say we had to touch the glass. Just that we had to drink the Drambuie and leave the flames burning, which I've done.'

He looked the RSM directly in the eye and watched, as his expresssion turned from a scowl into a grin.

'Good on ye, boy! I can work with someone who has some brains,' he laughed, as he shook Richard's hand.

'Unlike yourself,' Richard thought to himself, as the RSM was well known for not being the sharpest tool in the box.

The formalities over with, the job of serious drinking got underway. A long afternoon stretched into night. It was a Mess rule, no one could leave the building, until after the RSM had gone. Richard could see that some

155

of the SNCOs were nursing soft drinks, presumably under orders, from their other halves, to come back home sober. They constantly checked where the RSM was, to see if he was about to leave, so they could also cut away.

To their dismay, this particular RSM liked a drink, so they were in for a long wait.

As Richard chatted and drank with others at the bar, he spied a plaque, hanging in a prominent position. He was told it had been presented by Joe O'Connell, on leaving the Regiment. Joe had been the Sergeant who, with others, had crewed for Richard, in order that he could qualify for his Commander's pay on the ranges. That had been eight years ago. The inscription read ' *What you see and what you hear, When you leave, leave it here. Happy to meet, sorry to part, happy to meet again'*.

When Richard woke up the next morning, the pounding in his head and the dryness in his mouth confirmed to him that it had been a heavy session. He turned in the bed, to put his arm round Birgit, who, promptly removed it, from around her waist. He guessed at that point that in his drunken stupor he had done something to upset her.

'What's wrong, schatz?' he asked, using the German term for darling.

A short silence pervaded, until at last, she answered, curtly.

'You took a piss in the wardrobe, last night!' she hissed.

Richard's mind was working at full steam, trying to recall the events of the previous evening. Then, it struck him. He remembered getting up, in the middle of the night, to go to the toilet. Thinking he was opening the bathroom door, he had begun to urinate. A hand had gripped his arm. He had heard a scream.

'Richard what do you think you're doing?'

Taking a gulp of air and plucking up courage, he turned to Birgit, to apologise for his actions.

'I'm so sorry. It won't happen again,' he whispered, trying to rescue the situation.

As he said it and seeing the look on Brigit's face, he knew he was lying to her and to himself. He had heard so many stories of others in the Regiment, in similar states in the past, who had performed acts like this, or even worse.

A week later, Birgit and Richard were able to attend a formal dining function in the Mess. The occasion was the 'dining out' of one of the members, Ted Bowmore, who had completed his 22 years' service. These occasions were a recognition, by the Mess, of the service and dedication the person had made, not only to the Regiment, but to the Crown.

All the SNCOs wore Mess dress, with their tailored red jackets, waistcoats, tight fitting cavalry trousers and George boots, complete with spurs. Depending on the occasion, ladies wore either three quarter length cocktail dresses or full length ball gowns. Mess etiquette not only applied to the men, but also to the wives. If a wife was not correctly dressed or was involved in inappropriate behaviour, her husband was chastised. Many an SNCO had stood in front of the RSM, on a Monday morning, to receive a bollocking for the actions of his wife, at such functions. Richard had no fear of this happening with Birgit as, although she liked a drink and knew to party, she also knew how to behave. Birgit really liked these functions and was pleased when Richard gained his promotion. She had often seen some her friends, whose husbands were Sergeants or higher ranks, waiting outside their quarters, in full ball gowns, waiting to be picked up, to be taken to an occasion.

As she dressed, Richard gazed at her, in admiration. Although she had given birth to two children, she still had a shapely figure and looked good in her cocktail dress. When she finished putting on her jewellery, he asked her to straighten his black bow tie.

Fully dressed, they made their way downstairs, to where a friend's teenage daughter was sitting, watching over the two children. The girl was babysitting for them that evening and, due to the late hour they would be back, · would be staying the night.

'Okay, Ellie, you know where the fridge is. There are snacks in that cupboard. We also got some white chocolate and your favourite rice pudding,' Birgit said, pointing to a Schrank wall unit, in the living room.

'Thanks, Birgit,' Ellie replied, timidly.

Ellie was the daughter of one of Richard's friends, who had served with him, at the beginning of his career, in Berlin. It was normal practice for the teenage offspring of friends to babysit, while parents attending formal nights. Happy that Ellie had everything she needed, the couple left the house and made their way to the bus stop, where others were already waiting. The clip-clop of metal segs and the clanking of spurs on Richard's boots echoed in the street. The uniform he wore made him stand upright and proud. He thought of his father and mother and how they had looked, when they had attended nights like this.

The military bus arrived and, after a ten minute journey, making just one more stop to pick up others, they arrived outside the doors of the Mess. The passengers disembarked and, in all their finery, filed through the doors. The room was already half full of people, sipping on champagne. Richard looked across at Birgit, she was smiling like a Cheshire cat, obviously loving the experience. After a short time, a bugle sounded and the Mess Manager announced that dinner would be served, in ten minutes. The Mess members and their wives waited for the announcement to finish, then returned to their drinks.

Richard was getting slightly worried at this point. He had been told that, as the junior Mess member present, he would have to act as 'Mr Vice', meaning that, after the dinner, he would have to give a toast to the ladies, in itself a great honour. A bugle called everyone into the dining room.

The tables were laid out in the form of a 'U', with the RSM and the senior Warrant Officers at the top table. Richard took his place, indicated by a name card on the table. As Mr Vice, he was at the end of the right hand leg. As he stood, waiting for grace, he looked around the table. It was resplendent with silver, which glinted across the room, lit by the candles burning, in their decorative holders. Looking at Birgit, he knew that she was enjoying the formality of the occasion. Then, a voice brought him back to earth.

'Mr Vice, grace, please.'

He hadn't been told this was one of his duties, so the words hit him like hammer blows. Thinking fast, he uttered a quick prayer, acknowledged by an 'Amen' from those around him and everyone took their seats. The Mess members chatted amongst themselves and their partners, while Troopers from the Squadrons perambulated, serving wine.

This had been a 'duty' Richard had hated in his early years. On one occasion, when he had been 'chosen' to wait on, his father was still serving. It embarrassed him to have to serve his parents but it was all part of his education. At the end of the function, he was made aware of one great benefit. There was always drink left over and he got to nick as much wine and champagne as he could get away with.

The meal progressed, course after course and the wine kept on flowing. As soon as Richard took a mouthful or two, a waiter appeared, at his side, offering to top up his glass. It would be impolite to refuse, he felt, so he held up his glass each time.

As dessert was served, he felt a sharp pain in his bladder, and knew he desperately needed a piss. It was set in stone that no one left their chair, until after the meal was finished. To do so would mean a number of extra duties from the RSM. If anyone did manage to sneak away unseen, some joker would remove their chair, so they couldn't sit down again. They would send the absentee's name card to the RSM, so he was alerted to the fact that someone was missing. It was looked upon as all part of the fun of the evening. Richard had been told about these practices and determined to sit it out, trying to put the idea of pissing from his mind.

Before long, he could hold his water no longer and called over one of the waiters.

'Can you bring me an empty wine bottle, pronto?' he asked, in desperation. The waiter smiled and nodded, knowing full well why Richard had asked. He returned shortly and handed Richard a bottle.

Placing it under the table, out of site, he unzipped and positioned his manhood, on the narrow opening. It was an art in itself, pissing under a table, without looking at what you were doing. Richard occasionally felt a warm sensation, as the urine trickled over the hand holding the bottle, but he didn't care. Having relieved himself, he handed the bottle back to the waiter, who took it away, holding the bottle at arm's length. Richard wiped his hands, on the serviette, on the table. To his right, a colleague who recognised what was happening, pissed himself - although not literally.

The end of the meal was followed by the sound of a cavalry trumpet. One of the band stood, at the end of the room, near the top table and went on to play a piece known as the 'Post Horn and Gallop', a favourite throughout all cavalry Messes. Everyone gave the musician their undivided attention.

When he had finished, someone put up their hand, to indicate that they wanted to give it a go. As the would-be musician attempted his rendition, it came apparent that it wasn't as easy as it looked. The embarrassed soul sat down, to a little applause and a great amount of booing.

The moment came for Richard to give his toast to the ladies, the first of the toasts and speeches for the evening. Richard took a deep breath as the RSM called out:

'Mr Vice!' Richard was on.

He stood up, from his chair, and addressed the RSM, the Mess members and the ladies. For the next two minutes, he extolled the virtues of the wives, explaining how he and those like him would not be able to do their jobs, if it weren't for their partners' continued support. His words were greeted by tremendous applause, as he concluded and sat down. Looking across at Birgit, he could see that she was beaming at him, full of admiration and pride.

The speeches and toasts carried on, until it was the turn of Ted Bowmore, the man at the centre of the celebration. The RSM stood and presented a long overview of the soldier's career. The guest of honour was then invited to reply. By this time in the proceedings, Ted was pretty smashed and he staggered, unsteady on his feet. He was obviously enjoying his last evening in the Mess and was going out with a bang.

Ted regaled them with stories of events during his time in the Regiment. He was aware that this was his only opportunity to have full reign to speak his mind. Accordingly, he took full advantage, slating those against whom who he bore a grudge. Some in the room winced and looked away, as he continued. The RSM's face was betrayed his anger, but knew he could not stop him.

Sitting across the table from Richard was a member of the REME, who had recently been posted in. As Bowmore was giving his reply to his toast, the ignorant

REME fucker was chatting away, to his wife. Richard considered this was out of order, so leaned across and told him to shut the fuck up. As he sat back in his chair, Richard caught the eye of the RSM, glaring. Shrugging it off, he continued to enjoy the rest of the evening.

At the end of the meal and speeches, everyone was invited to an adjoining room, with a bar and dance floor. Those who had misbehaved during the meal were summoned to 'The Port Club', a tradition where they had to buy a bottle of port each and sit with the RSM, until the port was all gone. Richard would become a member of this select club, more than once in his career.

Next morning, Richard woke with a pounding hangover. 'Must have been a good night,' he thought to himself, although he couldn't remember a thing. He looked across at Birgit, still fast asleep. This was unusual for her, as she was normally an early riser. She must have really enjoyed herself too, Richard reckoned.

On the Monday after the function, Richard headed into the guardroom, to begin his day's work. As he walked in, one of the Provost staff looked up.

'Good night on Saturday?'

'Bazzin, marra' Richard replied, grinning from ear to ear.

'It must have been. The RSM's been on the phone. He wants to see you in his office, the minute you get here,' the Lance Corporal said, sympathetically.

Richard's heart sank and the smile disappeared. What the fuck had he been up to? Still questioning himself, he left the guardroom, walking in the direction of RHQ.

Standing outside the RSM's office, he waited, patiently, for the numerous people, either coming off or going on duty, to be briefed by the RSM. Finally, he heard his name called. He snapped to attention. Marching smartly into the office, he slammed his foot in, about three paces from the RSM's desk.

'Sergeant Hunter, I don't take kindly to people speaking in my Mess, when someone is giving a speech. Do you care to explain yourself to me?'

Richard gathered his thoughts, then realised what the RSM was accusing him of. 'It wasn't me, Sir. It was the REME punter, sitting opposite me. I leaned across, to tell him to shut up. That's probably when you saw me and assumed it was me,' Richard answered, in his defence.

The RSM scratched his chin, staring directly into Richard's eyes. He knew the incident was out of Richard's character, and decided to accept his version of events.

'Okay, Sergeant Hunter, I believe you. From what I know of you, it's not the sort of thing you would do. Your integrity is one of the reasons I asked you to be my Provost Sergeant. So you can go back to work and forget about this.'

'Thank you, Sir,' Richard breathed a sigh of relief, turned about, smartly, stamping his foot into the ground and marched briskly from the office.

Three weeks later, a games night was arranged, in the Mess. These were frequent affairs, sometimes between neighbouring units. This one was only for Regimental members and Richard was looking forward to it. Most of the games involved drinking copious amounts of alcohol and often got messy. The dress was casual and by the time Richard arrived, the Mess was already half full.

There was a board, situated inside the ante-room. On it, there was a list of the games chosen, for the evening. The competition was Squadron v Squadron. Richard browsed the board, to see which games he fancied participating in. He was surprised to find his name had already been submitted but wasn't surprised to see that his participation was in the drinking games.

Making his way to the bar, he noticed Pete was already there, smiling at him. Pete had reached the rank of Warrant Officer (WO2) and had recently been promoted to take charge of the forthcoming Standard Parade, the presentation of a new Regimental Standard by His Royal Highness, the Prince of Wales, Regimental Colonel in Chief. Pete had been awarded a great honour and one of great responsibility.

'What you having, mate?' he asked Richard.

'I'll have a glass of red wine, please,' Richard replied, taking a place at the bar.

He stood next to his childhood friend, waiting for the barman to serve the drink. When it arrived, the two raised their glasses and toasted each other. It had been fifteen years since two youths had left a garden in Germany, to begin their careers. Although Pete's career had progressed at a quicker pace than Richard's, he didn't bear any animosity but, rather, was pleased for his friend.

'What they got you down for?' Pete asked.

'I think the first one is wine draughts, that's why I'm warming up!' Richard replied, laughing.

'You'll smash it,' Pete predicted and the pair giggled, like schoolboys.

Richard had a reputation for being able to knock back large amounts of any form of alcohol, so a few wines would not present a challenge. The only problem was that the more intoxicated he became, the more obnoxious he got, sometimes leading to the "appearance" of Richard's legendary "twin".

Their conversation was interrupted by the sound of furniture being moved. Richard wondered what was going on, as different items were being set up, along the length of the room. He watched as 'obstacles' were put in place. A glass was then placed on the floor, at one end of the room.

The RSM, Tom McCreedy, went on to explain the rules. One man from each Squadron had to take a one pound coin, drop his trousers and place the coin between the cheeks of his arse. With the coin secured, he would then navigate the obstacles, making sure the coin didn't fall. Having managed to complete the course, he was required to squat and release the coin, into the glass, at the end of the course.

Richard had seen this played once before and had found it highly entertaining. He was glad, however, that he hadn't been chosen to represent his Squadron.

One at a time, the participants lined up, at the beginning of the course. With their coins secured between their butt cheeks, they began the tricky obstacle race. Some Mess members shouted words of encouragement, as others fell about the floor, in stitches. Richard was amazed at how skilled some were, in this strange game. All the competitors made it, apart from one. His forfeit was to have toilet paper stuffed up his arse, with a "tail" around two feet long, hanging down. The end of the paper was lit and the poor bugger had to navigate the course, again, before the paper burned its way to his anus. Lovingly known as the "Dance of the Flaming Arseholes", it set the tone for the evening.

Before long, Richard heard his name being called for the wine draughts. Emptying his glass, he made his way over to the area put aside for the game.

The rules were exactly the same as normal draughts, except that a table became the board and glasses of wine became the counters. One man moved glasses of white wine, representing white counters, the other red wine, representing black counters. As a participant jumped over his opponent's "counter", he drank the glass of wine he had just "taken". It was traditionally a messy game and one where the winner could get very drunk, very quickly.

Richard had been matched against a lad from B Squadron, also known to be a bit of a drinker. The match only lasted ten minutes and Richard was victorious, which meant that he progressed to the next round of the competition.

After two more rounds, he was feeling the effects of the mixture of red and white wine. He reached the final, which he won with ease. Unceremoniously, he fled from the table, rushing to the toilets. For the next five minutes he puked up all he had thrown down his neck, throughout the competition, but took consolation from the fact that, at least he didn't have to pay for it.

The remainder of the evening was spent in other drinking games, with a little singing thrown in. Richard sat at the bar, talking to Paul Jones, the man he had joined the Lodge with. Paul had started to study with the Open University, having spoken to Richard one night. Richard had begun his course with the Open University, three years earlier and hoped to finish in another two.

Their discussion became heated, as they talked about the contents of Paul's course. People around them noticed this and could foretell that something was going to kick off.

'Right, let's fucking discuss this outside!' Paul screamed at Richard.

'Don't be a dick, mate,' said Richard, not wanting to get into a fight over something so trivial.

Paul wasn't content to let it lie and began to poke Richard, in the chest. With a sigh, Richard rose from his stool and followed Paul outside the Mess.

As they stood facing each other, Paul took a swing, which Richard easily avoided. For the next couple of minutes, Richard dealt out a very harsh lesson to the pissed up Paul. Deciding enough was enough, they shook hands and Richard returned to the bar.

Accepting a drink from Pete, Richard explained the fracas was something and nothing. Then, out of nowhere,

Paul appeared back in the room, his shirt removed and blood running from his nose, matting in his chest hair. He began poking Richard vigorously, in front of everyone and bawling in his face, like a maniac. Richard attempted to calm him down but soon realised this was going to be impossible. With his left fist, he connected with Paul's right eye, launching him across the room. The room erupted as some from Pauls Squadron charged forward and the evening ended up in a massive bar-room brawl.

Next morning, Richard and Paul were summoned to the RSM. As they stood in front of him, Paul's face betrayed that he had come off second best, while there was not a scratch on Richard. The RSM screamed at the pair of them, demanding an explanation. To Richard's surprise and to Paul's credit, the beaten man confessed that it was all his fault. The RSM roasted them, then dismissed them.

Outside the office, the two shook hands and all was forgotten.

Chapter 15 - Provost Staff

On his first day in the job as Provost Sergeant, Richard didn't know what to expect. He had completed the course at Chichester, on to learn how to run a detention centre but his duties would entail more than this. The telephone rang in his office and, when he answered, he heard the dulcet tones of the RSM, asking him to pop up to his office. He replaced the handset, put on his Number 2 dress hat, straightened his tie in the mirror and checked his dress was correct. Finally, he picked up his blackthorn stick from the desk, placed it under his arm and marched briskly toward the direction of RHQ.

Reaching the door to the RSM's office, Richard came to a halt, outside. He could hear the RSM was in conversation, on the telephone. Spotting Richard, he beckoned him in, with his finger. Richard marched smartly into his office, slammed his foot in and stood to attention.

'Stand at ease, Sergeant Hunter,' the RSM invited Richard to relax, then continued his conversation.

'Billy, how do you spell together?' he asked the person on the other end. The only Billy Richard knew at the time was the RQMS.

'You know Billy likes to gather in sheep,' the RSM continued.

Richard almost burst into laughter, having realised what the RSM had meant. He came from an agricultural area of Northern Ireland and had used this metaphor to try and make his request clear. It wasn't the spelling of 'together' that he wanted but 'to gather'. As the RSM was legendary for his spelling gaffs in emails and memos distributed around the Regiment, this would become the in joke in the Mess for some time.

His conversation over, the RSM looked directly at Richard, standing patiently, trying hard not to reveal the smirk on his face.

'I have a wee job for you, Sergeant Hunter,' he began. 'I want you go up to the military cemetery, just outside of camp, by the entrance to Salisbury Plain.' He waited for Richard to nod, in recognition of his request so far. 'What I want you to do is inspect every gravestone and make a note of every man who was a member of any of our antecedent Regiments.' Again, after waiting for Richard to acknowledge his instructions, he continued. 'I want you to create a map, showing the layout and the rows of each of the fallen. This will make it easier on Remembrance Days, for us to lay a poppy, on their graves. Do you understand exactly what I want?'

The enormity of the task began to sink into Richard's brain. He had visited the cemetery before in the past and knew that there were hundreds, if not thousands of graves.

'Yes, Sir, no problem, Sir,' he gulped as he said responded. With that, he did a smart about-turn and marched from the office.

Arriving outside the cemetery gates, he could see the rows of gravestones, spread out before him. He had collected a couple of pencils and a large sheet of A3 paper from his office. This, he hoped, would allow him to make a rough sketch map of the area, noting any names from the Regiment's fallen members. He set out on his task, walking down each row in turn, checking the headstones. The task took him the whole of the morning, he didn't return to camp until two that afternoon. He then began transferring his sketch map on to his computer, so he could provide the RSM with the finished article. This took him till way past teatime but he was happy with the end result.

The following morning, he presented his map to the RSM, who was genuinely pleased with Richard's work and thanked him, accordingly.

He then told Richard that there was a prisoner to collect from a train at Andover Station, later that morning. The man had been AWOL for a number of months. When the RSM revealed it was David Ladd, Richard smiled, inwardly. It was David Ladd that Richard had escorted to the airport, before amalgamation. He had then been sentenced to a number of days in Colchester.

Richard knew, as he had heard on the Regimental jungle drums, that Ladd had been AWOL. On a leave, Richard had visited a friend in Leeds, who had informed him that David frequented the local Catholic Club. Richard had thought it would be amusing to show up, just to see the look on David's face. So, he and a friend had made their way to the club and had spotted David, supping a pint, without a care in the world. When he had seen Richard, David's jaw dropped, obviously thinking that Richard was going to let the RMPs know. Richard had simply smiled and had told him it was just a wind up, and they had spent the next couple of hours drinking and recalling old times.

Normally, Richard would have sent two of the Provost Corporals to meet the train but decided that he would go himself, with one Corporal and a driver. They mounted up in a Land Rover and started on the twenty minute journey to Andover. They arrived just in time to see the train pulling into the station. Two members of the RMP flanked David, one of them handcuffed to his prisoner. Seeing Richard, a broad grin spread across David's face.

'Looks like my luck ran out, mate but it was good while it lasted,' he said.

Richard tried to look professional and not smile, as he signed for the prisoner, from the miserable looking RMPs. He had a soft spot for the errant Leeds lad, having spent varying amounts of time, during his own formative years, in the Regimental prison. The paperwork done, the Provost Corporal with Richard handcuffed the prisoner to his right wrist and they hurried back to the Land Rover. They both jumped into the back, while the driver and Richard occupied the front seats.

'Sorry, mate, no beer for you this time,' Richard said, turning round and addressing the sorry looking individual, referring to the time, when he had escorted David, on his journey to the Military Correction Centre at Colchester. He had slipped David a few beers on the journey, knowing they would be his last, for many months.

David nodded his head and answered, 'It's okay, Richard, I know it's your job now and you have to follow the rules.'

On their return to camp, David was booked in and the necessary paperwork written up. He was put to bed for the night, after collecting all his military clothing, from his room. The last thing he did, before collapsing into bed, was to make sure his Number 2 dress uniform and shoes were up to standard, for Commanding Officer's orders, the next day.

David Ladd appeared in front of the CO the following morning and was awarded 56 days detention, once again in Colchester. As Richard marched him away, back to camp, he felt a certain sympathy and knew that this would probably be the final straw. He was to be proven right as, on his release, Ladd signed a 'premature voluntary release' and was discharged from the service, six weeks later.

Weeks turned into months and Richard was settled in his new job. He had three Corporals working for him, Tony Ganley, Cliff Richardson and William McCrae. Over the weeks, they moulded into an effective team, taking it in turns to 'educate' the soldiers under their charge. The aim of a military jail was not just to punish, but to train the soldiers, by use of military lessons and discipline.

One morning, Richard attended CO's orders and a bloke from C Squadron had been awarded seven days' jail, for disobeying a direct order from a superior. When the new 'Soldier under Sentence' (SUS) was marched out of the CO's office, he was handed over to Richard. From the look of disdain he gave, Richard knew immediately that this one was going to be trouble. What he needed was to be given a quick, hard shock. Drill was the perfect tool for this.

Recently, Richard had been sent to Pirbright to attend the all 'arms drill course'. He felt daunted at the prospect initially but soon got into the swing of things. It was like being back in training, although at an advanced level. This time, he was taught how to teach others the technical aspects of drill. He would never have imagined, all those years ago when he had stood in front of the Coldstream Guard Drill Sergeant in training, that he would be assuming his mantle. The course ended with a mock burial ceremony, which culminated in a 'wake', held in the Warrant Officers' and Sergeants' Mess.

Richard moved closer to the man in his charge.

'Right, you fucktard, get fell in, outside!' he screamed in the youngster's face, showering him with spittle.

The prisoner immediately began to make his way towards the stairs, at a brisk pace and descended them, two at a time, with Richard close on his heels, throwing obscenities at him, as he went. Exiting the building, the un-nerved soldier stood to attention, on the road, outside RHQ. Richard had become well known for his loud voice, when drilling unfortunates, either in jail or sent to him for punishment.

'Listen in to me, to my timing, by the front quick march!' His voice reverberated off the walls of the building surrounding RHQ and drew attention of many of the people either heading to work or travelling between the Squadron blocks.

'Left, right, left, right, left....!' His words melded into one and became almost indistinguishable.

After every ten paces, he commanded the prisoner to mark time, so Richard had time to draw level with him. Then, he placed his blackthorn stick in front of the offender, to make sure he raised his knees and thighs, parallel to the ground. Once Richard was satisfied the correct drill movement was being performed, he would step him off again. He repeated this again and again. By the time they had reached the drill square the poor sod was sweating, profusely.

For the next twenty minutes, Richard bounced the unfortunate bloke back and forward, across the drill square. He made sure every inch of it was covered. When he got him to mark time, Richard noticed that, due to fatigue setting in, the man couldn't raise his thighs level to the ground, which caused Richard to rain down a tirade of abuse on him.

Richard by surprise when the prisoner suddenly stopped in his tracks and sat down on the square. Richard was dumbstruck and, after gathering himself, he sped across the square, to confront the individual.

'Who gave you permission to stop, you fuckwit?' he bellowed, as he screeched to halt.

Staring down at the ground, the prisoner murmured, 'I'm refusing to soldier.'

The full impact of the sentence sank into Richard's mind, then he exploded.

'Don't be a fucking prick, you cockwomble! Get to your feet now!' Richard attempted to shock the guy into action but it was obvious, from his demeanour, he wasn't going to budge. 'Okay, if that's the way you want to play it, get up and we'll take a stroll to the nick.'

With that, the prisoner looked up and began to get to his feet. As he was refusing to be a soldier, Richard couldn't march him, but quickly formed a plan, in his head. Strolling slowly back to the guardroom, he took the bloke, now feeling a degree of cockiness, to the cells.

'Okay, take off all your uniform,' Richard requested.

The prisoner looked at him, confused, before answering.

'What do you mean, Sergeant?'

'I mean exactly what I said. Take off your uniform, it doesn't belong to you, it belongs to the Crown. As you are refusing to soldier, you are not entitled to wear it!' Richard's voice got louder, as he sneered at the fucktard.

Knowing he was beaten and had no choice, the prisoner began to undress. Luckily for him, he wasn't wearing army issue underwear. So, he stood there, wearing only his boxers. The floors in the jail were made of highly polished concrete, cold to the touch of bare feet.

'Army regulations state that we have to provide you with a blanket and water. So, here you are!' Richard threw him a blanket and left the cell.

He returned to the main guardroom. His staff were highly amused by what they had just witnessed. Richard picked up the telephone and rang the RSM, to inform him of the situation. After a brief conversation, he put down the telephone and informed his team that the RSM was on his way. They immediately began checking the guardroom, to make sure everything was in order, for his arrival.

Within minutes, the squat form of the RSM could be seen heading in the direction of the guardroom. From his crimson face, they could tell that the lad in the cell was going to get both barrels. He stamped into the guardroom and addressed Richard.

'Where the fuck is this retard, Sergeant Hunter?'

'He's in cell 2, Sir.'

With that, the RSM strode toward the cell area, motioning for Richard to follow him. For the next five minutes, the guardroom reverberated to the sound of obscenities hurled at the hapless individual. Richard's team winced at the verbal onslaught the prisoner was receiving. Then, there followed a deathly silence, until a couple of minutes later, Richard and the RSM returned to the main guardroom.

'Sergeant Hunter, that SUS is to receive only water, no meals or any other privileges entitled to a soldier. Do you understand?' The question was rhetorical, he knew that Richard understood the rules.

'Of course, Sir!'

The RSM turned his steely glare to the rest of the Provost staff. They fell silent and felt uncomfortable, under his scrutiny, the reaction RSMs received, when they addressed or looked at anyone. No more words were spoken. The RSM left the guardroom, returning to his office, in RHQ.

The prisoner lasted 36 hours, before hunger and cold got the better of him and he gave up his protest. He was given his uniform back. Added to his original sentence, were an additional 36 hours, for his time in the nick, when he had "not been a soldier". 'No one can beat the army system,' Richard explained to him, a fact he himself knew only too well, from bitter experience.

Chapter 16 - Standard Parade

It was a warm, June morning and Richard was putting the final touches to his dress, before the start of the working day. The sound of the Regimental band striking up, in the direction of the square, told him he would soon have to leave, to meet up with the RSM.

The Regiment was preparing to be presented with a new standard, in a week's time. For the last three weeks, at early o'clock, the whole Regiment had paraded on the square. Every man who was fit and at Regimental duty, including attached arms, were cordially invited to take part. The sick, lame and lazy didn't get off lightly, as they were given all the shit jobs to do, in preparation for the event, including providing security, erecting a collection of tents and the stands required for the spectators.

Richard checked himself in the mirror, placed his number 2 dress hat on his head and straightened his tie. Happy that he was correctly dressed, he picked up his blackthorn stick and tucked it under his armpit. Exiting the guardroom, he marched briskly in the direction of RHQ, where the RSM stood talking with the Adjutant. Halting smartly in front of the RSM, he saluted the Adjutant, who returned the gesture. The RSM smiled at Richard and bade him a good morning. Although a lot of people didn't see eye to eye with the RSM, he and Richard had developed a good working relationship. Finishing off his conversation with the Adjutant, the RSM asked Richard to follow him.

The pair marched, in unison, towards the drill square, where the Regiment had already formed up. It was Richard's job to attend on the RSM. If anyone didn't put in the required effort, the RSM would direct Richard, or one of his staff, to take them away to the nick. On the way there, they would be given a lesson in remedial foot drill, at a blistering pace.

Richard took his place, at the corner of the square, where the rest of his staff were already waiting. They were secretly waiting for someone to fuck up, so they could 'beast' them, which brightened up their repetitive, dull days. They weren't disappointed and, within fifteen minutes, the RSM singled out a couple of likely candidates he believed required some remedial foot drill. They were dispatched into the waiting arms of the Provost staff, who took it in turn to march them all round camp, before ending up in the nick, polishing anything that didn't move and even some things that did!

The parade rehearsal lasted two hours, by which time, Richard almost lost his voice because of the amount of 'customers' the RSM was sending his way. Thankful when the RSM handed back to the Squadron Sergeant Majors, Richard made his way back to the guardroom. Only one prisoner was in detention at the time, but Richard enjoyed it when he had more to do. He had become proficient in his new role and had devised a proper system of not only disciplining his charges, but giving them the tools to make them better soldiers, once released. There was not one part of their day, when they were not busy on an activity or lesson.

Richard had drawn up a training programme and it was displayed in the prisoners' cells, as well as in the guardroom, so the Provost staff were made aware of what was happening.

A typical day would begin with PT at 06:30 in the gym or Tony Ganley, one of his staff, taking the prisoners for a run. Tony was a Regimental physical training instructor, so was well suited to this role. After PT, the prisoners showered and then be marched to breakfast. Once they had eaten, they were given half an hour, to sort out their cell and equipment, which was then inspected. Richard, depending on his mood, regularly threw everything on the floor, not because it wasn't good enough, it was a method of keeping them busy.

After inspection, they spent an hour doing foot drill, on the square. They returned and were allowed a half hour break, during which, if they wished they could have one of their two rationed cigarettes for the day. After their break, they were given a military lesson, comprising anything from first aid, map reading, NBC to vehicle recognition.

Due to his time in Recce Troop, Richard had acquired a number of military instructor qualifications. Any he didn't have himself, were held by his staff. He didn't believe in just 'beasting' a prisoner, he was committed to making them more useful to their Squadrons and Troops, than they were when he got them. The training regime lasted the entire day, until final inspection, by the Orderly Officer at 18:00.

His methods were a far cry from when Richard had first joined the military, at the Apprentices' College of the Royal Engineers, at Chepstow. He had once been given a ten day sentence, a thing only Pete ever knew about. They had both, prior to Richard's incarceration, decided to transfer to their fathers' Regiment. Richard's time inside the college jail had been harsh, to say the least, and something which he didn't like to dwell on these days.

Breaking his thoughts from that time, Richard turned his attention to his present "guest", a young Trooper from C Squadron, Ted Wilton. Ted was the nephew of

Kieron Dyer, the soldier Richard had done his Junior NCO leadership cadre with. Dyer was also now a Sergeant, in B Squadron, and didn't particularly get on with his young nephew. He had told Richard to give the lad a hard time, during his detention. Richard was only too happy to oblige and, as he drank the remainder of his brew, he called out at the top of his voice:

'Wilton, get your NBC kit ready for this morning's lesson!'

'Yes, Sergeant!' came the prompt reply, from the cell area.

Richard smirked to himself, pleased that he instilled some sense of urgency in the young man. No matter what Kieron had told him, Ted wasn't a bad kid really, just a little misguided, as Richard had been, in his younger days. A little guiding hand was all that he needed.

'Right, Wilton, grab your kit and get fell in, outside!' Richard ordered, over his shoulder.

The sound of running feet coming along the corridor heralded the arrival of the young Trooper. He was dressed in full NBC kit, minus his respirator, gloves and boots. Richard gave him a quick once over, to make sure he had everything with him, then fell him in, outside. As soon as they left the guardroom door, Richard shouted:

'Gas! Gas! Gas!'

The prisoner immediately dropped to one knee and grabbed for his respirator pouch. Richard was counting slowly in the background. In an actual attack, a soldier had just nine seconds to retrieve his respirator and get it fitted before he succumbed to a biological or chemical agent. As Richard reached "Eight", the young Trooper stood up, indicating he had finished.

'What have you forgotten to do?' he asked the confused detainee.

There was silence, as eyes peered out, quizzically, from behind the respirator eye-pieces. The silence continued, until Richard cracked him, over the top of the head, with his stick. Realisation dawned on the prisoner and he quickly pulled up his hood and drew the cord tight, forming a seal.

'That's better,' Richard continued. 'Now, I will explain the rest of the lesson. Do you see that tank there?' He waited for Trooper Wilton to follow the path of his stick, pointing at the decommissioned tanks, which stood at the entrance to the camp gates. Wilton nodded his head.

'Well, what you are going to do is decontaminate it, from top to bottom,' Richard said, with a sneer.

From the look of dread in his eyes, Richard knew Trooper Wilton was not looking forward to this. The equipment had already been placed next to the vehicle and the detainee set about piecing it together. It consisted of a section of rods and a brush, with a hose, placed in a bucket of water with a chemical powder added. Along with this, was a stirrup comp, used to force the water into the hose and along the rods. Richard explained he would perform this duty for Wilton. Once everything was assembled, the prisoner climbed onto the top of the vehicle. It was already around 30° Celsius, as the summer sun burnt down. Richard noticed the youngster starting to labour, after fifteen minutes.

'If you're thirsty, you can drink as much water as you want, but you have to carry out the proper drinking drills!' he shouted up.

The lesson continued for another half hour, when Richard was disturbed, by a voice coming from the window of the guardroom.

'Sergeant, the RSM is on the phone. He wants to speak to you,' Tony Ganley called, from the open window.

Richard stopped pumping and told the prisoner to relax. He picked up his blackthorn stick and made his way into the guardroom. Putting down his stick and hat on the desk, Richard picked up the phone.

'Sergeant Hunter, the Adjutant has asked what you are doing with that soldier in this heat?'

The question took Richard aback and it was a moment before he managed to answer,

'Military training, Sir,' his reply was curt but respectful.

There was a moment of silence, before the RSM continued,

'I know how passionate you are about the detainees' training but the Adjutant has asked that you stop the lesson.'

Richard felt his blood starting to boil and his cheeks flushed red.

'Very well, Sir, right away,' Richard placed the phone in its cradle, gently, although he felt like smashing it into place.

'Tony, go and bring Wilton in, will you?'

Tony looked confused but did as he was told. For the rest of the day, Richard mulled over what had happened and decided it was time for him to change jobs. It was just a matter of getting himself upgraded by Hedley Court.

The Standard Parade had come around and they Squadrons were gathering. Richard dressed in his Number 1 dress uniform or 'blues' and was making his rounds. He was responsible for security for the event and, as HRH the Prince of Wales, their Colonel-in-Chief and the Duchess of Kent their Colonel Duchess would be in attendance, everything needed to be in order. He ensured that patrols were sent, to make sure the parade area was cleared and searched. Mobile and foot patrols were roaming round camp and the parade ground, located on the other side of the road. As he walked around, the mounted element of the parade, in their scarlet tunics and brass helmets, complete with plumes, were exercising their horses, prior to the parade. Richard felt a pang of jealously, as he had ridden when he was younger and would have loved to have been chosen to perform this ceremonial part of the day.

An hour later, the Regiment marched on to the parade ground led by the horsemen, on their black chargers. The Royal party arrived and were greeted with a Royal salute. The Regiment were then invited to inspect the Troops, which took more than 30 minutes to complete. After they had marched past, in slow and quick time, their new standard was presented to the CO. The day went off without a hitch, culminating in the Royal visitors taking a trip to the Warrant Officers' and Sergeants' Mess, where photographs were taken.

Richard would cherish his souvenir copy for the rest of his life.

Chapter 17 - Bosnia

Over the last nine months, Richard had attended two further sessions at Hedley Court, to continue his rehabilitation. He had improved enough, by the end of the first eight weeks, to be upgraded, to allow him to be deployed on operations. The added bonus was that he was, once again, eligible for promotion.

He arrived in work, one morning, to be told the RSM wanted to see him. He racked his brains to try and remember if he had done anything wrong. It was unusual for the RSM to ask for anyone out of the blue.

The RSM was at his desk, looking over papers. When Richard knocked on the door, he looked up and invited him in. As usual, Richard marched in, smartly, and came to a halt, a few paces from the desk. The RSM smiled and asked him to stand at ease.

'Sergeant Hunter, I have here your promotion to Substantive Sergeant,' he began.

Richard hadn't expected this but smiled at the news. Nor was he prepared for what came next.

'You have also been transferred to A Squadron, as a Troop Sergeant and will soon deploy, with them, to Bosnia,' he could see that the news had shocked Richard. 'I would just like to say it is my loss and their gain. It has been a pleasure working with you and I wish you every success in the future.'

Richard was still processing what he had just been told. He answered the RSM in a hesitant manner.

'Thank you, Sir. I have also enjoyed working with you.'

With that, the RSM fell him out and Richard did a crisp about turn and marched from the office, for the last time.

A Squadron were to deploy on *Operation Lodestar* in three months' time, giving Richard enough time to settle in, with his new Troop and Squadron, which would be part of SFOR and the only armoured asset in 'theatre'.

'The Stabilization Force (SFOR) was a NATO-led multinational peacekeeping force deployed to Bosnia and Herzegovina after the Bosnian war. Although SFOR was led by NATO, several non-NATO countries contributed troops.

The stated mission of SFOR was to "deter hostilities and stabilise the peace, contribute to a secure environment by providing a continued military presence in the Area Of Responsibility (AOR), target and coordinate SFOR support to key areas including primary civil implementation organisations, and progress towards a lasting consolidation of peace, without further need for NATO-led forces in Bosnia and Herzegovina".

SFOR was established in Security Council Resolution 1088 on December 12, 1996. It succeeded the much larger Implementation Force IFOR which was deployed to Bosnia and Herzegovina on 20 December 1995 with a one-year mandate. The commanders of the SFOR, who each served one-year terms, were General William W. Crouch, General Eric Shinseki, General Montgomery Meigs, Lt. General Ronald Adams, Lt. General Michael Dodson, Lt. General John B. Sylvester, Lt. General William

E. Ward, Major General Virgil Packett and Brigadier General Steven P. Schook

Troop levels were reduced to approximately 12,000 by the close of 2002, and to approximately 7,000 by the close of 2004. During NATO's 2004 Istanbul Summit the end of the SFOR mission was announced. (Wikipedia)

Their operational training was over. They arrived in Bosnia in sub-zero temperatures. Richard was dreading the tour, in these conditions. His left foot ached after a couple of hours, reminding him of the frostbite injury contracted, a few years earlier, on the plains of Alberta. They were taken by truck from the airport, up into the mountains, to a place called Barice. The journey was long and the roads were treacherous, not only because of their condition, but also from the danger of mines.

They arrived at their new home at midday and began the handover of vehicles from the outgoing unit. They formed part of the 9th/12th Lancers Battlegroup, the main armoured asset. The handover takeover was swift and they were finished by last light. The snow had continued to fall throughout the day, setting the pattern for the next few months. The outgoing Troops took great joy in taking the piss out of the incoming Squadron, as was to be expected. It was just before Christmas and they would be home to celebrate with their families.

The tanks were housed in an old, bombed out factory. It had been a job to shoehorn the tanks into it. So tight was the space, they had literally scraped the paint off the bazooka plates. Maintenance on the vehicles was further made difficult as there was very little or no light, and the temperatures so low.

The accommodation was basic, with everyone sleeping in Corramecs (converted containers). They were warm and dry, and to the men, that was all that mattered. The ablutions were also Corramecs, with sinks and showers accessed by a run through the snow.

The Squadron Leader was a Major Crawford, who was renowned for having things done his way. He was very strict with his commanders, which sometimes led to heated discussions, behind closed doors. These were one way conversations and the Major's word was law. If there was a saving grace, it was that the Second in Command was Andrew Halifax, now a Captain, who had been RSM shortly after amalgamation. He was level-headed and tried to get the OC to compromise on some of the decisions he made. The SSM was an old friend of Richard's, with whom he had served in Berlin and the SQMS was an old Troop Sergeant from Command Troop, Steve Orchard.

The Squadron also had a Troop location on the IEBL (Inter Entity Boundary Line) called Cold Hussar, about 30 minutes' drive from Barice. The Troops loved it there, as it offered a bit of normality, away from "Crawford's World". They bought bread from the bar owner. Everyone made out it was lush but it was fucking bogging. The bread runs took a couple of hours and incorporated tasting sessions of the local, high-in-alcohol drink, Pivo.

It was important to gather information from the locals and the best way of doing that was to drink with them. Each Troop had a designated Slivo drinker, about whom the OC knew nothing. Slivovitz, a local plum brandy, was made in three batches: one for everyday drinking, which tasted like rocket fuel; one for special occasions, which was marginally easier to drink and one for VIP occasions, which was highly potent.

On one patrol, Richard was the designated Slivo man. They rocked up, in a village, which happened to be distilling a VIP batch. Richard got chatting and was offered a drink of the everyday crap, which was grin and bear it stuff. Emboldened by the drink, he asked to sample the VIP batch. It wasn't the done thing to get out the good stuff, unless something special was going on, but Richard had made a good impression so, on the village elders say so, the rules were bent.

He was handed a glass about the size of a port glass, filled straight from the still. He did the squaddie thing and downed it in one. On first impression, it was fantastic, unlike the first, rough stuff he had swallowed. A lovely taste of plum came through and it went down really smoothly.

Within seconds, all Hell was let loose. The scene which followed was like the bit in *The Great Escape* when Steve McQueen made potcheen. Richard couldn't fucking talk. The "brandy" completely messed up his vocal chords! Then, he felt a burning sensation start in his chest and work its way up to his throat. He thought he was melting, sweat ran from his forehead. The locals just pissed themselves laughing and offered him a second glass, which he refused, scared of what it might do to him.

Two of the SQMS staff later found themselves in the shit for getting rat-arsed on Slivo. They worked in the Ops room and, hearing of the Slivo trips, decided to go on a patrol with a Troop, to sample the booze themselves. The effects were catastrophic, they got legless and had to be brought back. They were punished by being put on a chain gang, literally breaking rocks for two weeks, to fill the massive holes made by the tanks.

Christmas was tough, the Squadron was trapped in Barice, as the snow was so deep. But, as is always the way, the cooks pulled out all the stops and a really good Christmas dinner was served to the men, by the officers and SNCOs, in the mess.

After a while, the Squadron moved from Barice to Mrkonjić Grad, down a single track road, not meant for heavy traffic. Warning signs for landmines ran the length of the road. They knew some stretches had yet to be confirmed but they were treated as "live". They dared not deviate from the road, because of the threat of mines, so a plan was devised, with recovery assets split along the convoy of tanks, to hook up any broken down vehicle and tow it, to designated REME assistance points.

To lower the risk of a breakdown to a minimum, each Troop ran their vehicles over to Glamoc, about 15kms away, every week, so the engines were bedded in and got used to being used, rather than sitting still for days or weeks on end.

After weeks of preparation, the OC decided to take a chopper and photograph his Squadron, from the air. The Squadron was led down by the Ops Officer, who commanded the OC's tank. The move was controlled from a Land Rover, by the 2i/c and REME Sergeant, sweeping the route in front of the Squadron, to ensure it was clear. They were watched, all the way, by the local Militia and the Serbian Army, so reputations were on the line. Despite a great deal of snow and severe ice, the route was cleared by the engineers, followed by the 2i/c.

The Squadron made it down, safe and sound, without one breakdown or incident, passing the front gate of their new home, where they were greeted by the CO of the 9/12 Lancers, who toasted to their success.

The small town of Glamoc was a constant reminder of how vicious and deadly the conflict was. It had been cleared of inhabitants and mined, to render it useless to anyone. Every building was covered in graffiti and had been looted or burnt out. To enter the village was to risk serious injury or death yet, on a number of occasions, soldiers saw local militia, walking around the ruins, thinking they were invincible.

The Squadron and the 9th/12th Lancers were involved in a couple of incidents, over the next few months.

There was a rumour going around that a fully bombed up tank had been hidden in the Tactical Area of Responsibility (TAOR.) Word reached the 9/12L, who went searching for it. They found it, in a very high risk area, which was suspected to be mined. Ignoring the dangers, they approached it. As they did, one recce car hit a mine, killing one and severely injuring another two.

The Squadron itself was only called out once, when the Serbs decided to steal a T55, kept under NATO control and take it out of the barracks, as a show of strength; A Troop from the Squadron was deployed, to deal with this, which resulted in the Serb taken tank hurriedly being left to be returned, to its proper place.

The Squadron Leader decided to hold a firing camp, to ensure all drills were up to speed, with the local Serbs, on Glamoch ranges. They were living in a tented camp, at the rear of the ranges. The camp backed on to minefield, which meant there was no margin for error, when firing at stationary or moving.

Loads of spectators came to see what SFOR had up its sleeve. They both had Soviet built T55s and turned up gobbing off about how good they were. When they stood on the back decks of a Challenger letting rip, their minds were instantly changed. They tried to keep up the pretence but it was clear what they were thinking, especially after seeing a Challenger let one go, down range.

Canadians, operating nearby, had been invited to join in the fun. Their OC mentioned that he would like to watch a single tank shoot from the turret of the Squadron Leader's tank. He was so impressed by the speed of the Squadron Leader's loader that, after the crew were given 'Crew, crew, 'shun,' and de-briefed, the AIG asked the crew and the Canadian OC if there were any questions.

'Just one,' piped up the Canadian OC, referring to the overweight loader in Major Crawford's tank, 'how does that big fucker move so quick, in that little space? I don't even know if you hit anything, I was too busy watching that big fucker!' Everyone laughed, except Major Crawford.

At the end of the ranges, the Squadron had a smoker with the Canadians to end the firing camp. The SQMS put two of his staff in charge of prepping the fire, two Northern Irish guys, from opposing cultures. It was natural that they would have a pissing contest on how big this thing could get. One thing they did agree on was how to light it .... a petrol bomb! So, just as it got dark, one of them hurled said petrol bomb, primed with petrol, diesel, paint thinners, paint and fuck knows what else, at the firepit. The whole of A Squadron stood back, as they knew what was likely to happen. The fire erupted four feet in the air and scorched every Canadian near it.

One lad, the Squadron Leader's loader, started singing and most joined in. A Lance Corporal from 3rd Troop perfomed a display of Morris dancing, which left the Canadians thinking 'What the fuck?' A great time was had by all and it concluded a successful, if very cold, operational tour in the Balkans.

Chapter 18 - Iraq

The Bosnia tour was long behind him. Richard and the rest of the Regiment prepared to move back to Germany. They had just returned from Northern Ireland, where they had been responsible, amongst other things, for supervising the March at Drumcree. They had sustained some casualties but thankfully no fatalities. It was all change again, from being foot soldiers back to their beloved Challenger tanks. Ulster had been their only posting in the UK and Richard was glad to be going back to Germany. There was also the added bonus that he would be around £350 better off, due to the 'Local Overseas Allowance' (LOA).

The handover went smoothly. Before long, Richard and his family were 'marching into' their new quarter, to be their home for the next few years. Birgit and the two children had come accustomed to this nomadic lifestyle. Yet, some military families, especially the younger ones, found it more difficult. For some, this would be their first time out of the UK, away from their family networks. This brought its own challenges and the Welfare department would certainly be kept busy. Richard didn't know it yet but this would play a major role in the last part of his career.

No sooner had they settled in, than Richard was promoted to Staff Sergeant and sent away on an RQMS course, designed to teach prospective Warrant Officers how to account for Regimental equipment. The course itself was tedious and Richard was preoccupied with what the Regiment were doing, while he was sitting on his arse in the UK.

The Regimental Battlegroup deployed to Iraq in 2004 (*Operation Telic 5*) and assumed control of the area south of Basra, close to the border with Kuwait. The main tasks were to mentor the newly formed Iraqi Police Force and provide security for the first presidential elections in the country since the US led invasion in 2003.

The conflict saw over 100 fixed-wing aircraft and over 100 rotary-wing aircraft of virtually every type in the British inventory deployed. It also saw a 33 ship fleet, which was the largest taskforce deployed by the UK since the Falklands War. Some 120 Challenger 2 main battle tanks, 150 Warrior infantry fighting vehicles, 32 AS-90 self-propelled 155 mm howitzers and 36 105 mm towed howitzers were deployed with the land forces, with reconnaissance vehicles and everything else that makes a modern mechanised and armoured force function.

During the post invasion phase, and following a number of British casualties blamed on inadequate equipment, a great deal of new equipment was purchased to help deal with the threats posed by insurgents. These included 166 armoured Pinzgauer Vectors PPV, 108 Mastiff PPV, 145 enhanced FV430 MkIII "Bulldogs", Desert Hawk UAV and 4 additional Britten-Norman Defender observation aircraft. (Wikipedia)

Richard watched the news and studied the newspapers, at every opportunity. He listened intently for any news of his Regiment, hoping not to hear bad news. The loss of a friend or comrade, although part of the job, is something no soldier ever wants to endure. It was all part of what they had signed up for, made worse by some craving the excitement of proving themselves in a combat zone.

The course dragged on but finally it reached its conclusion and, with a distinction, Richard passed. He returned to Germany and took up his new role of SQMS for

B Squadron. He had briefly been part of B Squadron, on his first operational tour in Northern Ireland, so many years ago. Faces had changed and only a few of his original contemporaries were still around.

The next eighteen months were spent in a non-operational role, meaning they were not deployable into a conflict zone. They carried out normal, everyday training which some found boring. Even in the years since Richard had joined, the Army evolved and the modern tank soldier was now multi-roled. He was able to fight as an infantry foot soldier, as an armoured reconnaissance asset or, indeed, in his Challenger 2.

On a set day, the Regiment were told they were to deploy to Iraq, once more, on *Operation Telic 11*, as part of the 1st Battalion Scots Guards Battlegroup. Once again, a buzz of excitement filled in the air, as the training and preparations began. Training could last anything to up to six months but, by the end of it, the troops were ready for any eventuality. Richard was secretly pleased that they were to deploy again, having missed out on the last one. He kept this little nugget of information to himself and didn't mentioned it to Birgit.

The Regimental Battlegroup took over from 4 Rifles, in November of that year. 4 Rifles had faced a tough summer and had a number of fatalities and a larger number of wounded. The area of operations spanned both Basra and Maysaan provinces. B Squadron landed in Kuwait, in a comfortable 25° C. For the first week, they acclimatised in camp Buehring in Kuwait, undertaking the reception staging. After that week, they departed and arrived in Basra, to finally get on with what they had trained so hard for.

Richard looked around the camp, which seemed comfortable enough. The guys quickly got settled in. As SQMS, it was Richard's job to see that the administration of the Squadron was taken care of and, for the first few weeks, he busied himself, putting everything into place. Once this was sorted, he and his staff could relax a little. The Squadron settled into a routine, with one entrepreneur making himself a small fortune, cutting peoples' hair. A bodybuilding club was also been set up, with several trying to look like Adonis, for the end of the tour.

From the first week, they had taken Indirect Fire (IDF) from rockets. This was happening at least three to four times a week and was a concern. The Squadron deployed, in various guises, to try and halt this.

One particular day, Richard and one of his staff were crossing the compound, when they came under fire from a 107mm rocket. It struck on the far side of the compound and one of the Squadron was hit, by the flying shrapnel. Richard and his storeman ran to the bloke, who was writhing about, on the ground. Their Team Medic training kicked in and they dealt with the casualty, who, thankfully, recovered quickly from his injuries. It had been the first time, since Richard's last time in Iraq, that he had witnessed and had to deal with something of this nature.

Later, as he laid on his camp bed, the incident began to play on his mind. What if....? No one dwelt on the thought that it would ever be him who would be injured or killed but the fear was always lurked in the back of their minds.

Christmas arrived and the Squadron celebrated this emotionally trying period, as best they could. After it, the names of the first group to go on R&R was announced.

In January, a decision was made that some elements of the Brigade would return home. However, the frequency of the IDF, if thankfully not the accuracy, had picked up. Some of the patrols were under constant threat of IEDs. On one such occasion, two members of the Squadron were on the receiving end. Due to their training and well-rehearsed drills, neither was seriously injured and they were casevaced back home.

In late March, the Squadron was heavily involved in supporting the Iraqi army in *Operation Charge of the Knights* destined to be the Squadron's biggest test of the tour, so far. They were on constant standby for strike operations, which, sometimes, never took place. It was a testing time of patience and willpower, as they were on a constant 30 minutes notice to move. This lasted the final three months of their operational tour.

The operation itself regularly involved the Squadron leading US and Iraqi Special Forces into Basra. Their primary role was that of 'bullet catchers', a form of protection against the IED threat. This showed the utility of heavy armoured vehicles in this type of operation, enabling them to deliver men on the ground to their objectives.

One such morning, a Sergeant from 3rd Troop was involved in an operations to lead the American and Iraqi Special Forces, to arrest a key Iraqi Hezbollah commander. They were warned, over the radio, there was a possibility of sniper fire, so they closed down the hatches. Just before dawn, the vehicles moved out, with Sergeant Richard Christian leading the column.

As they trundled up the road, in the direction of the house that the suspected Hezbollah commander was located, all around was eerily silent. This was in stark contrast to the amount of traffic being sent over the radio. Negotiating a series of obstacles placed in the road, the column of British armoured vehicles pushed on. They reached an intersection in the city and Richard Christian ordered his driver to take a left turn. The driver revved the engine and pulled his tiller, slewing the vehicle round the intersection. As it straighten up, a loud explosion broke the silence, instantly followed by another. The Challenger rocked under the explosions and the crew inside were deafened but uninjured. Assessing the situation and the need to keep up momentum, Sergeant Christian ordered his driver to advance. As it continued up the street, it hit another IED, which exploded under its right track. Undeterred, the commander continued to advance, until they reached the target house to be entered.

An FV432 Bulldog Mk3 armoured personnel carrier turned left, into the street, and men of the Reconnaissance Platoon dismounted. One had a battering ram, lovingly named a 'thumper', slung on his back. The Bulldog is mounted with the Remote Weapon System (RWS), operated by the Recce Platoon commander. They pulled up, just behind the Challenger. Above them, a C-130 gunship was firing on designated targets and all hell was breaking loose.

The American and Iraqi Special Forces assaulted the house, killing a number of gunmen and arrested the Hezbollah commander. For his actions that day, Sergeant Christian received the Military Cross, for enormous bravery and leadership. When they returned to camp, they were received with great applause, epitomising the bravery of the British armoured soldier.

Earlier in the tour, Battlegroup Headquarters, HQ Squadron and C Squadron departed early from Iraq, in direct consequence of the gains made in Basra. The decision was met with mixed emotions. On one hand, they were going home to their loved ones, on the other, professional pride meant that they would have wished to have remained, to the end of the tour.

Richard made frequent trips to the Ops room, where he was engaged at time in the role of Watchkeeper, monitoring all activity in the Battlegroups area of responsibility. He always liked to know what the rest of the Battlegroup was up to and keep up any news of his friends.

A Squadron was carrying out border operations, on the far side of the Shatt al Arab waterway. They were pretty much on their own, not with the rest of the multi-national forces. As such, they were physically and geographically cut off from any immediate, intimate support from friendly forces. It could take anything up to an hour, for the immediate response helicopter to reach them, depending where they were at any given time.

Their tasking was either mounted in their Warriors or in the dismounted role. On foot, they had to carry all their equipment and food, in case the helicopter couldn't resupply them. Their Bergens normally weighed in excess of 60kg. In the hot, desert climate this made for tough going, as the temperatures sometimes reach over 40° C. The ground was like concrete and the job of 'digging in' was extremely difficult, which amused the Iranians on the other side of the border, observing them, from a mosque. They would blast out gunfire, the sound of aircraft strafing and explosions from the PA system, normally used to call the faithful to prayer. The Troops quickly realised that this was meant to annoy them. An NCO suggested that they line up, drop their trousers and 'moon' at them but, although he did find the idea amusing, this was rejected by the Squadron Leader.

Daily, they deployed multiple foot patrols, along the border and the crossing point at Salamchen. These patrols were supported by quad bikes, used to move the heavy stores. There was a local smuggling trade and business was brisk. These local patrols damaged and discouraged it. Mst locals were friendly enough and would warn of any danger to the Squadron.

The men were only supposed to be operating in that area for an initial six days but this turned into a month. The final operation they took on was the Iraqi re-intervention in Basra. They were required to prevent any assistance to the insurgents from entering the city from Iran or, from any wanted men, fleeing the city. This was a difficult task, as the area to cover was massive. They also mentored the Iraqi border force, who were based at the crossing point.

They were hit by a sandstorm, one day, so fierce that it took a sheet off one of the REME vehicles, anchored down with 20kg weights. Coils of barbed wire, left over the Iran/Iraq war, were blown through the air, smashing into vehicles and causing considerable damage.

In support of *Operation Charge of the Knights,* one of the vehicle commanders spotted a pair of suspected IEDs. He had observed them, using the thermal sights of his warrior vehicle. They were buried in the uprights of two lampposts. He engaged the lampposts with his 30mm Raden cannon, which allowed the safe extraction of a number of Iraqis. While there were a number of injuries during this operation, they were mostly suffered by the Iraqis, firing their weapons in the air.

Richard smiled to himself, as he read through the log of the previous Watchkeeper. The Regiment had done itself proud, during their time on tour. In only another week, they would be boarding the plane, back to their families. It couldn't come soon enough, he thought, as he tussled his hair, in an attempt to get the sand out of it.

Chapter 19 - Home

Richard sat in his armchair, a beer in hand, watching TV. They had been back a number of weeks and had quickly fallen into their old routine. It was a difficult time for families, when the men returned from operations. It took a while for the men to adjust to the company of their families, having been in an almost exclusively male environment, during their time away.

Birgit had noticed a change in Richard, ever since he had returned, from his time in Bosnia. He had become more withdrawn. He had sleepless nights and, alarmingly, had begun to drink more and more. They would often argue and he would fly off the handle, for no reason at all. Since he had returned from Iraq, the situation was becoming worse and she attempted to find out what it was.

The enquiries only led to another argument, as Richard fervently denied there was anything wrong. She pleaded with him to open up to her or to go and see someone about it. Like all soldiers, he was too proud to admit he had a problem. Richard also had in mind that he might be looked down upon by his superiors or, indeed, his peers. So, he kept it all bottled up, letting the alcohol try to erase the bad memories, from his mind.

As she looked at him, sipping his beer, a smile crossed his lips.

'What you thinking about?'

Richard turned to her, the smile still evident.

"I was just thinking about the guys who did that video at Al-Fawr,' he answered.

While they had been in Iraq, one of the Squadrons had made a parody of the Peter Kay cover of the Tony Christie song *Amarillo*. It had been the brainchild of the SQMS, a guy from Liverpool, full of humour. They had shot video and it had gone viral, on the internet. So popular had it become that it crashed the Army servers. The news got round and some of those, including Richard, who had taken part in it were asked to appear on *Good Morning Britain*.

In stark contrast to some of the horrors they went through, things like this just showed the lengths that soldiers would go, to keep up morale and typified the humour of the British soldier. No matter what the circumstances, they just got on with the job, poking fun at it, when the opportunity arose.

As quickly as Richard's mood had lightened, it changed again, as he returned to his bottle of beer. Standing up, he moved to the kitchen and withdrew another bottle from the fridge. Taking off the top with his teeth, he returned to his seat, not even acknowledging Birgit's presence. His brain felt fuzzy, as the alcohol consumed him and, after a few moments, he drifted off to sleep, the bottle still in his hand.

Birgit quietly moved towards him and retrieved the bottle. She placed it in a container in the kitchen, with the other empties. Richard had polished off a dozen beers that night. She returned to the living room, turned off the TV and lights and made her way upstairs. She knew if she woke him, it would only lead to another argument or, perhaps worse than that, he would continue to drink. Things were starting to get unbearable.

The following week the Squadron were preparing to go away, on a couple of weeks adventure training. This was always a good way for the Troops to relax and let off a little steam. Richard was really looking forward to it, anything to be out of camp and away from family life. All he wanted was to be in the company of his 'brothers', nothing else mattered. He knew he had a problem but pushed it to the back of his mind, hoping everything would turn out okay.

Vogelsang was a former school, where the elite of Hitler's future leaders were taught. It had been used as an adventure training establishment by the British Army, for a number of years.

'In 1934 work began on three construction projects to build "Order Castles" or "School Castles" where the future leadership of the Nazi Party would be trained. These projects were under the direction of Dr. Robert Ley, head of the Deutsche Arbeitsfront (Labor Front). These Ordensburgen were built at Sonthofen in the Allgäu (Bavaria), Crössinsee in Pomerania (now in Poland), and Vogelsang in the Eifel (North Rhein - Westfalia).

The Vogelsang Ordensburg was designed by architect Clemens Klotz, built on a hillside overlooking a large lake valley. The school was completed in 1936 and the first class of "Junker" (cadets) began training immediately. The overall project as planned was never completed, with a large "House of Knowledge" hall, a 2000-bed hotel, and other buildings being omitted. During World War II the site was used for military purposes and to house refugees from bombed German cities. The U.S. Army overran the area in February 1945 and briefly occupied Vogelsang, before turning it over to the British military. In 1950 Vogelsang and the adjacent military training area

207

were turned over to the Belgian Army, who controlled the
area until 1 January 2006.'
(http://www.thirdreichruins.com/vogelsang.htm)

Richard arrived at Vogelsang camp with his staff and, as SQMS, was responsible for taking over the accommodation the Squadron would be using. He also had all the adventure training equipment to check and prepare for issue to the various instructors. The advance party had set off the day before the Squadron was due to arrive. By the end of the day, Richard had taken over the rooms and had issued out all the equipment.

The rest of the Squadron arrived by bus, just before lunchtime and Richard showed them around the accommodation. The Troop Sergeants signed for the rooms and the Troops were allowed to chill out, for the rest of the day.

Next morning, they were wakened at 06:30, for breakfast. Last night had been a heavy session in the bar. There was no Sergeants' Mess, so the SNCOs drank with the men, in the only bar. An American Unit was staying at the same time. Richard noticed there had been a bit of friendly banter bandied about, the previous evening, all taken in good spirit.

The Squadron finished breakfast and were assembling, at the appointed place, to be taken to the day's activities. With nothing to do, now that the stores were all squared away, Richard decided he would try scuba diving.

He waited outside the accommodation, with the rest of the group participating, some keen on the idea, some who had been 'volunteered'. It was one of the few things that Richard had never attempted, although a strong swimmer, he had a fear of open water. He also had an inherent fear of sharks, which had always prevented him from taking part.

Richard was feeling apprehensive, as the troops loaded the truck with air tanks, wetsuits and the rest of the equipment needed for the day. The instructor, born in Liverpool, was nicknamed Scouse, an epithet totally lacking in originality. He had been in the same Squadron as Richard, prior to the amalgamation but had been in a different Troop, so Richard had hardly ever seen him.

Scouse was an instructor in many outdoor pursuits, from winter activities, like skiing, to water sports, such as windsurfing, canoeing and, of course, sub aqua. His Troop was lucky if they saw him three months out of the year.

The journey from camp to the lake, where they would carry out the diving, took less than ten minutes. The lake, itself, was turquoise in colour and was surrounded by hills, on three sides. The water was tranquil, with not a ripple on its surface. It was the perfect place for novices to learn the techniques of sub aqua. Scouse handed out the wetsuits, flippers and masks and asked that they get ready. Richard took his equipment, sat down on the ground and began to struggle into his wetsuit. It wasn't easy for a novice and, before long, he was sweating and swearing like a madman.

'For fuck sake, Scouse, is there not an easy way to get into this thing?' he screamed across at the instructor.

Scouse turned his attention to Richard, thrashing about. He burst into laughter at Richard's predicament. Making his way across, he leaned down.

'Here, mate, let me help you there,' he said, in a calming voice.

With Scouse's help, Richard managed to get the wetsuit on. When everyone was ready, Scouse went through how to operate the air tanks and the buoyancy vest, which allowed them to descend and ascend the depths. He established had done sub aqua before. Accordingly, he concentrated his efforts on those who hadn't. After explaining what he wanted them to do, he asked that they all put on their air tanks.

Richard placed his arms through the straps, as he lay on the ground and secured them at the front, making sure the belt was tight and that the tanks didn't move about. He then attempted to get up but found, due to the weight, he couldn't. He looked like a tortoise that had been flipped on its back, as his legs thrashed, in an effort to try and right himself. Finally, Scouse, seeing his predicament, held out a hand and pulled him to his feet.

'Thanks, mate,' Richard said, gratefully.

'I think you'd better stick with me,' Scouse advised him.

The students made their way to the water's edge, under Scouse's direction. Those who had dived before were asked to go through their drills and begin to dive. Scouse then turned to Richard and asked him to follow, wading out into the lake, until the water was up to their chests.

'Right, what I want you to do is to put the mouthpiece in and get used to breathing through it, then, slowly submerge your face, under the water,' Scouse mimicked the actions, as he spoke.

Richard did as requested but, as soon as he started to suck on the mouthpiece, he began to panic. He couldn't breathe! He spat it out.

Scouse circled him and put his hand on the air tanks, slowly turning the valve.

'You forgot to turn on the air, you fecking knob jockey!' he said, pissing himself at Richard's stupidity.

Now that he could breathe and, feeling embarrassed, Richard regulated his breathing and slowly re-submerged his head. After a short while, he became accustomed to the strange feeling. He returned his head above surface, waiting for Scouse's next instruction.

'Okay, now, I want you to follow me, so we're not touching the bottom,' Scouse led him out further into the lake, until they were both treading water.

'Right, I want you to lie flat on the surface of the water, looking down. Then, swim down to the bottom. You okay with that?' He asked. Looking at Richard's widened eyes, Scouse could tell he was nervous.

'Yeah, okay. Let's give it a go,' Richard replied, shakily.

Putting the mouthpiece back in, he positioned himself on the water, looking down. He then attempted to submerge himself, to kick off, for the bottom. Yet, no matter what he did, he was going nowhere. He looked at his air gauge and saw it was steadily moving, due to the rapid gulps of air he was taking. He felt a hand on his shoulder. Scouse pointed to the valve on Richard's flotation vest. Not understanding what he was indicating, Richard shrugged. Then, Scouse depressed the valve, letting air out of the vest, allowing Richard to submerge, slowly. His breathing returned to normal, as he descended into the depths Scouse remained no more than an arm's length away. It was a strange, surreal experience but Richard was loving it. For the next fifteen minutes, the pair explored the bottom of the lake, until Scouse gave a thumbs up, letting Richard know they were to return to the surface. He pressed the air canister attached to Richard's vest, filling it, once more, with air.

The sun shone in Richard's eyes, blinding him as he spat out the mouthpiece, having broken the surface of the water.

'Well, how did you find that?' Scouse asked, having appeared in front of him.

Richard waited until his breathing was back to normal before answering.

'Fucking great but I don't think I'll become the second Jacques Cousteau, any time soon!' Richard was grinning from ear to ear.

For the remaining days in the camp, the Squadron rotated through the various sports on offer. Richard took part in as many activities as his free time allowed. He had always loved walking and noted, with some anticipation, the added bonus that there were plenty of pubs on each intended route. He also tried his hand at windsurfing, something else he had always wanted to do but had never got round to. However, he spent more time in the water than on the board, so, after a day, gave it up as a bad job.

The two weeks passed rapidly. It was the evening before they were due to depart, back to their camp in the north. The Squadron had arranged a get-together in the canteen bar. By the time Richard arrived, the party was already in full swing. He went to the bar and grabbed himself a beer, turning to chat with the SSM, standing watching the troops enjoy themselves.

'All right, Steve?' Richard enquired, as he started on his beer.

'Yes, mate. I'm just keeping an eye on these dickheads, you know what they're like when they kick the arse out of it,' he smiled.

Richard knew exactly what Steve meant, as the lads could be quite boisterous, to say the least. He glanced over in the direction of four tables the Squadron had pulled together. They'd begun to stack their empty beer cans into a pyramid and it had already reached an impressive height. It was a testament not only to their artistic ability but also to the amount of drink they had poured down their necks, in such a short space of time.

'We going to join them, then?' Richard asked Steve, who nodded and they sauntered over, to take a seat with the rest. The only ones not in attendance from the Squadron were the Officers, probably under instruction from the Squadron Leader to steer clear. He could be a bit of a prickly fucker at the best of times, so Richard assumed they had probably not wanted to rock the boat.

For the next couple of hours, the beer flowed freely and the singing began, a usual occurrence at these sort of get-togethers, each Troop taking it in turn to lead the way. There was always one in every Squadron who started it off and, in Richard's Squadron, it was Mike McGregor, a big lad with Scottish and South African parents. He was a keen rugby player so his repertoire consisted of the ballads heard in the bars of rugby clubs, everywhere. Mike was atop one of the tables, giving a rendition of *'We are Warriors'*, much to the delight of the crowd. Without stopping for breath, he kicked off into *'Father Abraham'* and the noise level rose, as others joined in.

Richard glanced around the room and spotted that a group of around twenty Americans were looking more than a little pissed off, at the British taking over the bar. They had come in for a quiet drink, which had been spoiled by the Squadron's behaviour. As Richard pointed this out to Steve, he noticed Pete Holdfast, one of 3rd Troop, trying to get to the bar. His way was blocked, by a group of six burly American infantrymen. Pete had been a Great Britain junior karate champion and was shaped like an inverted pyramid. He was mild mannered but Richard had heard rumours that if Pete was pushed too far, things were likely get interesting. He watched, as Pete tried to make further progress to the bar. He began to talk to the six guys. They were looking at Pete as though he were a piece of shit and Richard feared the worst.

Pete turned, to walk away, when one of the Americans grabbed his shoulder. In the blink of an eye, Pete swivelled, on the ball of his left foot, his leg extended parallel to the ground. Then the leg drew back and extended itself again, in rapid fashion, felling three instantly. He head-butted the fourth and, with the back of his hand, struck a blow to the throat of the sixth. It was all over in seconds. Six bodies were littered across the floor and Pete strolled towards the bar, not seeing a group of Americans nearby were making their way towards him.

Mike McGregor, who loved a good tear up, spotted this and hurtled towards them, with other members of the Squadron close behind. He smashed his fist into the face of the first Yank, dropping him immediately. The others, behind Mike, were getting stuck in.

Although Richard tried to avoid getting involved, it was too late, as the Squadron, to a man, entered into a pitched battle with the Americans.

The melee was broken up by the arrival of the camp MPs, who managed, after a struggle, to pull the combatants apart. After calming the situation down, they ordered everyone to return to their accommodation.

The combatants reluctantly made their way back, under the watchful eye of the MPs. Entering the block, the Squadron began to climb the stairs but were alerted to the sound of running feet, below them. Turning, Richard saw a group of Americans, around twenty in all, who had been roused from their beds, by the group who had started the fight in the bar.

Thinking that numbers counted for everything, they stood, goading the British troops. Richard turned to the SSM, who shrugged his shoulders and descended the stairs, towards the aggressive looking Yanks, who halted in their tracks, at his stocky, six feet frame and the deep, red scar, which crossed his face.

The rest of the Squadron followed the Steve's lead and joined him, in confronting this new threat. As the SSM's foot reached the bottom of the stairs, a fire extinguisher was thrown, directly towards his head. Lifting up his arm, to protect his face, he knocked it aside, as if swatting a fly. The looks on the faces of the Americans was a picture, as the rest of the Squadron tore past Steve and got stuck into the unprepared aggressors. Another massive fight broke out. The Squadron was outnumbered by two to one but that made little difference, as they knocked seven bells out of the American Troops.

By the end of the scrap, bodies were strewn all over the corridor and blood splattered the walls and floor. One of the Americans, who instigated the original trouble, held up his hand, in surrender. The SSM called to the boys to cease fighting which they immediately did. He walked to the American and extended his hand. They shook hands and agreed the fight was over and that they should forget about the whole incident. The Yank complimented Steve on the Squadron's fighting spirit, which drew raucous laughter, cheers and whoops of delight from the bloodied Troops.

Morning came and the Squadron handed back the accommodation to the camp Quartermaster. They had to pay for the damage done to the canteen bar, although this would be taken from Squadron funds. They had received the mother of all bollockings from the Squadron Leader, earlier that morning but weren't prepared for what would happen when they got back to camp.

As the bus pulled up, outside the Squadron block in camp, they were greeted by a stern looking RSM, waiting in the car park, with the Adjutant. Richard thought to himself this wasn't going to end well. As the SSM got off the bus, the RSM called him over. After a brief and somewhat heated conversation, Steve nodded and turned, to go back to the Squadron, who were wondering what was going on.

'Right, guys, get your bags off the bus and put them in the Squadron entrance. We need to be in the RHQ lecture room in five minutes!'

The Squadron groaned and hastily removed their luggage, from the compartment under the bus. The SSM was not in a good mood, as he hurried them, shouting abuse at those who had not taken his order seriously.

The Squadron, including the Squadron Leader and all the Troop Leaders, assembled in the lecture room. Everyone was thinking the same thing, had the Regiment been informed of their little altercation, the previous day? They were soon to find out, as the RSM called them up to attention and, as one, they stood up, from their seats.

The unmistakable form of the Commanding Officer, followed by the Adjutant and RSM, entered the room. Taking his place, behind the lectern at the front of the room, the CO turned, to face them. His face was the colour of the crimson on the Regimental flag. He paused and, before speaking, surveyed every man in the room.

'It was brought to my attention very late last night, in fact in the early hours of this morning, this Squadron was involved in a fight with American Troops in Vogelsang. To say that I was embarrassed is an understatement!' he began, the spittle from his rant covering the lectern. 'When you leave these camp gates, you are representing the good name of the Regiment and that, I'm afraid, on this occasion, you have failed to do. As far as the Camp Commandant is concerned, we are nothing but a bunch of animals and he has no other choice but to ban us from using his facility, for the foreseeable future!' he went on, his anger growing. 'So, not only have you discredited yourselves, but also the Regiment's name!' He paused, looking for further words to

217

continue his berating, but they seemed to evade him. 'You are all scum, get out of my lecture room! I want to see all officers in my office, directly after this. Now, get out!' He ended his tirade by gesturing with his hands, shooing the Troops from his sight.

The Squadron stood and hurriedly left the lecture room. Once outside, on the way back to the Squadron block, laughter broke out but they knew that wasn't the end of the matter and that there would be repercussions.

Richard thought to himself that, all in all, it had been a pleasant distraction and had taken his mind off the demons growing inside him.

Chapter 20 - Reflections

Three months had passed since the incident in Vogelsang. Richard received the pleasant news that he was to be promoted to Warrant Officer Class 2 (WO2) and that he would take over, as Squadron Sergeant Major, D Squadron, the following month. The Regiment had also been informed that they were to deploy to Afghanistan, the following year on *Operation Herrick*. There was a definite buzz around the camp, as they began to prepare to undergo the Mission Specific Training (MST).

Richard sat at home one night and, as usual, started on the booze, as soon as he finished his tea. There was a familiar silence in the room, as Birgit sat in an armchair, opposite him, watching the television. He took the top off another bottle of beer, placing the empty one next to his chair. Birgit knew not to comment on the amount he was drinking, as it would only lead to another row. As the golden liquid slipped easily down his throat, Richard's mind drifted back to that time, all those years ago, before joining and to the things that had happened during his career, so far.

It was summer and his father had led his fifteen year old son, up the stairs in A Squadron's block. Richard was not due to join up for another year. His father had thought it might be a beneficial for Richard to see what the social side of the Army was like. They had reached the top of the stairs and his father had turned right, down a corridor. Richard had followed on, dutifully, behind him. As they had neared one of the doors, on the left hand side, the noise had got louder and louder. His dad had pressed down on the handle and, with a flick of his head, had invited Richard to follow him in.

Entering the room, which, like all the other Squadrons, had a purpose-built bar, his father had been surrounded by members of his Squadron. He was a popular figure and much respected, not only in his own Squadron, but throughout the Regiment. One of the guys had immediately bought him a brandy and coke, his favoured tipple. They had then asked Richard what he wanted. Richard had looked at his father, who had smiled.

'I'll not tell your mother, if you don't,' he had shouted, above the hubbub in the busy bar.

Plucking up courage and trying to imitate his father, he had asked for a double brandy and coke. He had been half expecting his father to rebuff him, for the cheeky request, but Tommy had simply handed him the drink, poured by the barman.

After a few more drinks, Richard had begun to loosen up and chat with some of the lads from his father's Squadron. They had seemed genuinely interested in the fact that he was thinking of joining up. They, jokingly, had told him not to join 'this Regiment'.

Yet, when Richard thought back about it they had been serious, which caused him to chuckle, in his chair.

Birgit looked round at him. She liked to see him smile, it didn't happen too often these days. She left him to his memories and returned to her programme on the TV.

Richard's mind returned, to that first day in the Squadron bar. He remembered an empty fire bucket had been produced, from out of nowhere. It had been handed over the bar and the barman had begun to fill it with Double Diamond draught beer, from the pump. When the beer level had reached halfway, he had poured in bottles of brandy, vodka and any other spirit he could reach.

A space had cleared in front of the bar and around a dozen of the revellers had sat on the floor, in a circle. Richard had been invited to join them. He had looked at his father, who had nodded his head, a wry smile on his face. It had all seemed like good fun, as the bucket had passed round the circle, everyone taking a gulp, then passing it on.

Once it had completed one revolution, one halfwit had decided to wash his hair in it. As soon as he had finished, the bucket continued round the circle. Then, another bloke had taken off his socks, had dipped them in the mixture and had wrung them out, in the bucket.

Richard had thought he was going to throw up, at that sight. The others had just groaned but had continued to pass the bucket round. The only rule in this lunatic drinking game was that, if a man quit or puked, then he had to buy the next bucket.

By the end of the evening, Richard had been in such a state that he couldn't remember a thing, apart from his younger brother turning up. Their mother had sent him to bring back Richard and his father. However, his father, instead, had bought him a drink which, of course, he had taken. By the end of the night, Richard hadn't been able to walk. The last thing he had remembered was the Squadron bar door crashing open, his mother standing there, her face like thunder. She had dragged her errant husband, by his hair, out of the bar, kicking his arse down the corridor. The two brothers had staggered on, behind.

Richard's mind drifted forward to training and an incident when he had convinced a rather naive bloke from the West Country that there were two types of razor, a facial one and its counterpart, the anal razor. The hapless young man had taken it all in. Richard had found him, the next day, with his arse hovering over a wash basin. Looking over his shoulder, he had been dutifully shaving his arse cheeks and crack. Richard had run out the room and had collected everybody, to watch the spectacle. It hadn't long, before the youngster, had realised that he had been the butt of a joke. Richard giggled, as he remembered the incident, and took another mouthful of his beer.

He recalled the story of Mick Ovenden, from Leeds, who, while on leave, had been in a nightclub in the city centre, in the early 1980s. As he had ordered a drink at the bar, he had spotted the lead singer of the synth-pop band *Mixed Nuts*, Matt Arnolds. Arnolds was a flamboyant, openly gay man, something that didn't sit right with Mick, coming, as he did, from a strict, no-nonsense upbringing. In his eyes, men weren't supposed to be attracted to, far less have sex with, other men. Watching Arnolds act as he did had made Mick mad. He had got very drunk and he had followed the singer into the toilets of the club and had then given him the kicking of his life.

From his early years, Richard had been passionate about Rugby, both the Union variety and League, the thirteen-a-side version, predominant in the North of England. He had once lived in Castleford, when his father recruiting for the Army in Wakefield and Leeds. From this time, his passion for the game was born and, later, he had even been offered trials at the Castleford Academy. His father had been due to be posted back to the Regiment, at the time, so he had had to decline the offer. He still followed the sport on TV, when he could and a group of friends from the Regiment had organised a pilgrimage to watch the Challenge Cup Final at Wembley.

The minibus had been waiting on the Regimental square. The ten friends, making the trip, had loaded jerry cans of diesel, meaning they wouldn't have to pay for fuel, on their journey. Richard had been forbidden from driving; on a previous outing, his driving had been so galactically shite, the group, unanimously, had sworn that he would never do it again. He had been given the much more important job to load the crates of beer into the vehicle.

They had set off from camp, in Germany, and had set a course for the Dutch border. By the time they had reached Calais, the friends were, well and truly, in high spirits.

They all had sported t-shirts, which Richard had designed.

Leaving the ferry at Dover, they had taken the main motorway towards London. On this occasion, the final was to be held at Twickenham, rather than the usual Wembley venue.

One of the guys had crapped himself, shortly after leaving camp. The cream chinos he had been wearing had been discarded on the ferry but a combination air freshener, after shave, beer and his excrement had still pervaded the air in the minibus.

As they had left the orbital M25, which surrounded London, Richard had felt the urge to piss. He had decided, in his infinite wisdom, that he would open the door of the minibus and let fly, as they moved. Getting down on his knees he had opened the fly of his off-white denims. Sliding open the door, he had steadied himself with one hand, the other holding his dick. As the urine had left his body, he had felt a great sense of relief but he hadn't known about the roundabout ahead. As the driver had navigated the vehicle around the junction, he had almost fallen out of the open door. He had been saved by someone grabbing hold of him, at the last minute. As they had dragged him back inside, he had seen that piss covered his white jeans. He had prayed that it would dry, by the time they reached the stadium.

The minibus had pulled up, in a barracks where they had booked in, to stay for the weekend. As soon as they had dropped their bags off in the rooms, they had headed straight to the tube and into Twickenham.

They had made great timing and first pub they had come to, had only just opened and was relatively quiet. They had got in a round of drinks and had stood in a position where they could observe all that was going on. The beauty of Rugby League is that the supporters are a universal family. No matter which team anyone supported, generally there was little animosity between fans. The pub had filled with shirts of many different clubs, not just the two in the final. Over the next hour, friendly banter between opposing fans had started. Richard's lot, by this time, were well on their way, after almost twelve hours of drinking.

One of the group had gone to the bar, to order another round. When he had returned, he hadn't looked best pleased. Richard had asked what was wrong, thinking there might be trouble about to kick off.

'I'll tell you what the problem is, you feckin' cockwomble! Look what you've had printed on these t-shirts!' he had exclaimed, pointing at his own.

It wasn't until everyone checked that instead of saying "Twatted at Twickers" Richard had spelled it "Twated at Twikers", which had made him the object of everyone's abuse.

The atmosphere in the stadium had been unrivalled by any other sporting event Richard had ever been to. Unlike a lot of football grounds, beer had been on sale. There was rarely trouble between fans and the need to segregate them was not an issue. The game had been a one-sided affair, with Leeds Rhinos taking the Cup, for the third time in four years. As the friends had departed the ground, they made the decision to dive into London. One of the party had been an officer in the Regiment, who had said that he knew a great pub, off the King's Road. As this was an affluent area, Richard hadn't been sure they would want ten drunken squaddies frequenting any of their establishments. The officer had said it wouldn't be a problem, as he knew the owner.

On their arrival, two doormen had tried to bar them from entering, until the Officer had told them that the party was with him. Recognising the Officer, the doormen had stood aside, allowing them to enter. The pub had been full of well-dressed and well-heeled members of the upper class of London. Richard had felt slightly out of place but had soon relaxed, as the group consumed glass after glass of Champagne, with Guinness chasers! There had been a lot of 'top totty' in the bar, staring over at the 'pieces of rough' the Officer had brought with him.

One of them, always up for a laugh, had decided that they should do a 'Full Monty' strip on the stage. Richard had been one of the six volunteers, who had stepped forward, at the suggestion.

As they had taken the stage, to perform their 'act', there had been a hushed silence. The Officer had arranged for the people running the pub to play the theme tune from the film. As the guys had acted out the final scene in the film and had begun to slowly disrobe, the females in the bar had, suddenly, expressed an interest. The strippers had got down to their boxers and some women had been staring through open fingers, in a feeble attempt not to be seen looking. As they had ripped off their boxers, a great cheer had gone up from the crowd.

For the next hour or so, the guys hadn't had to buy another drink, as the owner and some of the guests were sending drinks over to them.

Richard chuckled to himself, once more, as he sipped on his bottle of beer, his mind drifting back to another funny moment.

He was back in Northern Ireland, on a 'Quick Reaction Force' (QRF) in the town of Portadown. They had had a call that a suspicious package had been discovered on the high street. The four man patrol had been crashed out to assess the situation and had begun to cordon off the area and assist the Police (RUC). After having established the cordon, the RUC could not make the decision whether or not to call in the bomb disposal. As Richard had watched, one of the Police Officers had approached the plastic shopping bag, left at the corner of a junction on the high street, his heart had begun to race. This was either a very brave or a very stupid thing to do.

The police officer had picked up pace and, with a mighty swing of his right foot, had kicked the bag. The contents of the suspect 'bomb' had been emptied out, on to the street. Potatoes, carrots, onions and all the ingredients needed to make a nice Irish stew had littered the pavement. With comic timing, an old lady had appeared from around the corner and had begun to lay into the policeman.

It turned out that she had left her shopping bag there, as it had been too heavy to carry up the hill, where she lived. The team had been stood down and, on their return to camp, they had almost crashed, as the driver couldn't see for the tears that had been streaming down his face.

Yet, for every humorous moment, Richard's career had a horrific counterpoint and his mood quickly changed, as he slipped into the darker reaches of his memories.

Sounds of gunfire and explosions reverberated through his head. Images of the dead and dying, in conflicts all over the world, came to his mind. Charred remains of Iraqi soldiers, on the road north from Basra, their clawed, blackened hands reaching out to him, for help; mutilated bodies of women and children in mass graves in Bosnia; images of the injured and the dying swam around, inside in a pool of despair; the soldier sitting, staring into space, looking past him and through him, as if he wasn't there, searching for answers that would never be revealed.

Man's inhumanity to man was the one factor that Richard would never come to terms with. He was a soldier: this was his job, his life, his being so why did it torment him? Faces of friends and colleagues no longer here, slowly cleared from his thoughts, like morning mist on a sunny spring morning. The sound of the programme on the TV broke his train of thought and he was back in the room.

Chapter 21 - Afghanistan

The intense, arid heat of the Afghanistan summer burned Richard's skin, as he walked down the stairs of the aircraft.

Their Mission Specific Training (MST) had begun some nine months earlier. They had been equipped with Viking armoured vehicles and had completed a Combined Arms Live Firing Exercise (CALFLEX) in Castlemartin, Wales. There, they had lived in a makeshift Forward Operating Base (FOB), built on the side of a blustery Welsh hillside. The Troops had spent four days there, rotating through, a Troop at a time.

Squaddies played the role of insurgents and made up a real life opposing force and friendly forces of Afghan National Police (ANP), Afghan National Army (ANA), Local Nationals (LNs). This had allowed the Troops to be tested thoroughly. They had fired a series of different scenarios, both day and night, and had been faced with the complexities of mounting a Counter-Insurgency operation (COIN). They had had only seven Viking vehicles to work with and it had been a massive task for the REME to ensure they were at 100% availability. A lot of the commanders in the Squadron were new and the lessons they had learned on these exercises would reap rewards in the future.

The final training had culminated in an event known as an MRX or Multi Task Force operation. It had involved the majority of the Brigade and had been held on Salisbury Plain. It had been primarily focused on the ground holding Battlegroups, about to deploy. It had been a valuable lesson for all involved and had taken Richard and his Squadron to the level they were at now.

Their first task was the incredibly important one of protecting, sometimes even taking part in, Combat Logistic Patrols (CLP). They transported from the airport to their different locations. Half the Squadron travelled to work with the Royal Ghurkha Rifles (1 RGR), while the remainder, including Richard and the Command element, moved to the desert, to protect a CLP.

The Squadron arrived safely at their designated areas and quickly fell into a well-practised routine. They weren't due to officially take over their responsibilities until the 12th of June. However, they were given a task to provide Troops, to form part of the defence around Lashkar Gah Agricultural College, during a visit by the Prime Minister. They saw to it that this went off without incident.

Once the Squadron had officially taken over their area of authority, they went straight into providing the support for the CLP. During the operation, the Squadron suffered several IED strikes and a number of the boys were injured, keeping the Squadron medic extremely busy.

Only a week later, the Squadron received devastating news.

The other half of the Squadron, working on different tasks, were also being kept extremely busy. They were being 'smashed' on a daily basis, with regular contact and firefights with the insurgents. One of the troops heavily involved was 4th Troop. On the afternoon on 18th June they were tasked to provide support to Combined Force Nahr-e Saraj (South), in the vicinity of Patrol Base 1 (PB1). The Troop had been tasked to provide protection for a patrol conducting a clearance operation, in order to increase security for the local population. This was in the vicinity of Check Point KINGSHILL. On that afternoon, while carrying out this operation, one of the Troop, an unassuming but likeable character, Trooper Aiden Jones, was killed in an IED strike on his vehicle.

When the news reached the Squadron it was like a hammer blow. Although they had received casualties in their first few weeks, this was their first fatality. Morale was low and a sombre mood descended on the Troops.

Richard, although shaken up, made it his mission to get around the boys and make sure that everyone was all right. He spoke to them on a personal level, one by one, reassuring them that young Aiden, who had only been 21, had not died for nothing. When Richard returned to his bed space, he sat, staring into space. His hands began to tremble and the emotions welled up inside him.

The Squadron Sergeant Major was seen as the father figure of the Squadron. This was the mantle and facade that Richard had to portray. He had heard himself being referred to as the 'epitome of a fighting Sergeant Major' by the Squadron Leader, who had stated that Richard was morally and physically fearless, in protecting his boys and was held in the highest regard by the Officers and men. This accolade was little comfort for the way he felt right now.

For the next few days, 4th Troop were given little time to reflect on the death of Trooper Jones. They were, immediately, involved in the protection of route TRIDENT, a route that linked Gereshk and Lashkar Gah, the two economic centres of the Task Forces area of operations. The route itself represented progress and the insurgents targeted it, on a daily basis. The troop used the mobility of their vehicles to interdict the insurgents. Taking the fight to the enemy ensured that they were kept away from the road, thereby protecting it. This also gave them an opportunity to get among the local people and interact with them, which all helped support the Battlegroup plans.

Their Troop Leader was an inspirational man and led from the front. This attitude culminated in him and another from the Troop being injured and casevac'd out, by helicopter. The Troop Sergeant, a bloke from Doncaster called Dave Welsh, didn't hesitate to take over responsibility of the Troop. Shortly after the Troop Leader had been extracted, they found themselves in an IED minefield. Dave Welsh, aware that the Troop nerves were fraying under the stress of the past few days, made an extremely brave decision. He had been advised to stay where he was for the night. He took the mine detector from one of the soldiers, whose job it was to clear routes. Dave selflessly and in darkness walked the Troop out of the situation.

The Squadron Leader made the decision to rest 4th Troop after this and SHQ, along with 1st Troop, convoyed off to PB1. They moved to either end of route TRIDENT, to oversee and give protection to the build. Other elements entered into what was called the OMID or 'Hope' operations, which included working with the Afghan National Army, seen as critical to be able to partner with the local forces. This was Richard's and SHQ's first real contact with the insurgents. For days and weeks they attacked a series of enemy compounds, which gave the Company of the Mercians, at PB1, a little breathing space, to build another checkpoint, to enable them to expand their influence and the security 'bubble', in their area of operations.

The first few days were hectic, with the Squadron coming under constant RPG and small arms fire. One of the

Vikings was hit, by a well-executed insurgent ambush, and was destroyed. To call in air strikes and artillery, including mortars, was a necessity. At times, the rounds landed dangerously close to the friendly troops. The insurgent positions were quickly neutralised, surrounded and destroyed by the ground forces. The smell of cordite drifted in the air and, at times, was so thick it choked the advancing troops. On one of those days, in the space of a few hours, the Squadron suffered four casualties, two of which were never to return to the fray, due to the severity of their injuries.

For 72 hours of hard fighting, the ground holding troops thanked God for the armoured support the Squadron's Vikings were giving them. This became the norm for the tour and SHQ would move to where the main effort was needed, to plan any future operations, until the Troops were ready to deploy again.

Elsewhere in the Squadron, 1st Troop were in the rural area of Laskar Gah. They were commanded by a raw 2nd Lieutenant and, under him, more young commanders. They were underpinned by the experience of their Troop Sergeant and senior Corporals, who provided the stability needed for the dangerous operations. During operations, two of the Troop were killed in action and they suffered many casualties.

During one intense action, Corporal John Staindrop noticed that one of the ground troops had been hit. With scant regard for his own safety, he moved his vehicle, to shield the wounded soldier. He jumped from the vehicle and climbed on to another. He was firing a machine gun, to protect a gunner tending to the casualty, when he was shot dead. A young Scots Guardsman had also seen the predicament and had ably assisted Corporal Staindrop but was also killed. The wounded soldier survived, due to their bravery. Corporal Staindrop was later awarded a posthumous Military Cross, for his actions that day.

It wasn't all bombs and bullets for 1st Troop, who employed the clever tactic of setting up a 'compensation' scheme for the locals, in recompense for any damage caused by their tracked vehicles. This won over a lot of the locals and brought in a great deal of intelligence.

They were involved in an operation known as *Advance to Shura*. Here, they managed to win over the trust of the local villagers of Poplezai and Khan Keyl, who had been sheltering the insurgents who had killed Corporal Staindrop and the young Guardsman. Not only did they find and clear a huge weapons cache and IED factory but they also arrested all the insurgents involved. This later reaped benefits, as the constant small arms fire and IED attacks almost ceased, due to the insurgents having no ordnance.

There was a break in hostilities for a few days and the Squadron regrouped, to rest and take stock. They had been hit hard and had suffered almost 27% casualties, in the past three weeks. This brought the guys even closer together, determined that they would see their task to the end, in memory of those who had paid the ultimate sacrifice.

Since part of Richard's job was not only to look after the discipline of the troops but also to be a father figure, he ensured his door was always open, if anyone wanted to talk about how they felt. He had always been an approachable character and good listener. Yet, while he tended to the men's needs, he wondered who would tend to his? The strain of the operations were starting to tell on him. The nightmares were coming more frequently now, but, still, he kept it locked up inside.

It was the Brigade Reconnaissance Force's job to establish what was going on in the area of Gereshk and other places in the area of authority. They did this, by not only engaging with the insurgents but with the local population too. However, firefights and attacks were commonplace and it was on such a day Richard received terrible news about a friend.

Robert Nunthorpe was a giant of a man in stature and character. When Richard had first met him, on amalgamation, the two hadn't really see eye to eye. Rob was a colourful soldier, with a past history to match. He loved to have a drink or two and had been known for getting into the odd altercation, in the local German hostelries. He hailed from the West of Cumbria and spoke his mind, as a lot of the people from that area do.

As he matured, Rob gradually settled down, was promoted and reached the rank of Sergeant. He was responsible for overseeing the running of the Regimental Medical Centre. He married and, before long had a daughter. His child became biggest calming influence on his life and he adored her deeply. Over this time, Richard came to respect and befriend the big man, who had mellowed so much. When Rob asked if he could join the Regimental Lodge, Richard was only too pleased to propose him.

A few days before he was to be initiated into the Lodge, Rob called Richard to ask if he needed to bring anything with him. When Richard told him that, apart from turning up smart, he should bring something to wear to relax in, later in the evening.

The official part of Rob's big day had come and gone smoothly. Later, they had gone to their separate rooms in the pub, to change into casual gear for a few drinks and a midnight curry, which would be the highlight of the overnight stay. Rob had been last back down and none of the lads could believe the sight in front of them. At the foot of the stairs had stood a six feet two inch Rob, dressed in pyjamas and wearing bright yellow Homer Simpson slippers.

'What are you staring at?' he had grinned. 'You told me to bring something comfortable to wear! Now, get me a pint in.'

2nd Troop of the BRF was tasked to clear a compound designated (CP9), to be used for firing mortars at the coalition forces. A section from the Troop were tasked to clear a route into the compound. Once there, they conducted an all-round defence. One of the sections was positioned in the tree line covering, to the east. The Troop Leader's section, which included Rob and the Troop medic, were in reserve. One man cleared the route up to the compound and up to the western wall, going firm at the north-western edge covering north. The Troop Leader's section or multiple was covering south, so it looked like they had all bases covered.

It was not yet first light and, due to orders that they were not to enter compounds at night, they waited. They remained in position for almost 90 minutes, until the sun broke over the horizon, in the east. Another Section, on the southwest corner of the compound, was asked to enter but their Section Commander informed the Troop Leader that, if they did, they would have no cover. It was therefore decided that all the Sections would remain in their positions and the Troop Leader's multiple would push through the Troops already holding their ground.

At around 04:30, the Troop Leader led his Section through the multiple, at the south-west corner. Rob was fourth, in the line of march. The Troop Leader had a brief discussion with the Section Commander, at the south-western corner. He advised him that, as the compound seemed to be unoccupied, they should perhaps go over the wall. After a couple of minutes, it was decided against this and the Troop leader led, on a cautious slow advance, to the doorway of the compound, ten metres from the south-western section.

Rob was lagging behind slightly, due to the massive load he was carrying, which not only included his trauma bag but mortar rounds and extra ammunition or 'link', for the machine guns. He passed by the Section Commander of the south-western corner, who pointed him in the direction of the doorway. Rob nodded and pushed on past him, struggling under the weight on his back.

Three of the Section passed through the doorway. Rob followed and, as he approached the men waiting in the compound, a loud explosion was heard. Rocks and debris rained down on the Troops, inside and outside the compound. Smoke and dust obscured their views, adding to the confusion. Without hesitation, some rushed to the fallen Rob and began to drip feed him. One of the Section covering to the east, informed the Troop Leader of suspicious activity.

The Troop Leader and the Section Commander on the south-western corner quickly assessed the best place for the Emergency Helicopter Landing Site (EHLS). 200 metres to the west, in a field, which had a large mound on it, was the nearest spot. They were told, on the net, transmissions from the local insurgent commander had been intercepted. He had informed his men not to fire on the troops, he wanted more of them to step on IEDs, or 'Water Melons', as they were affectionately known.

The route to the EHLS was cleared, ready for the extraction of Rob. One man marked the safe route with cyalume glow sticks. Within moments, some of the section carried Rob, from the compound, towards the HLS. The helicopter carrying the Mobile Emergency Response Team (MERT) landed at the HLS. It had been only nineteen minutes, from the point of the detonation, to their wheels touching down on the desert sands.

As the lads carrying Rob handed him over to the MERT, they noticed that he was still breathing and gave a sigh of relief. The one who had cleared the route was sitting on the ground, his head in his hands. The Section Commander, who had been at the south-western edge of the compound, went across to console him.

'It's not your fault, mate. It was probably a low metal content IED.'

He put forward his hand and helped him up from the ground. The patrol moved off.

The Troop was informed that Rob never regained consciousness, on the flight to Bastion. Rob was a big man in more ways than one. It was a massive blow for the Troop. He was loved by the guys and rated the best medic in the BRF. He would be sorely missed by not only them, but anyone who knew him.

When he heard the news, Richard sank to his haunches, vomit welling up inside his stomach, forcing him to gag. The news hit him hard. He sat, staring into space, through tear-filled eyes and wept, uncontrollably.

A week later, Richard was called to see the Squadron Leader, who informed him that he was to be commissioned, as a Captain, on their return to camp. He would cover the role of Unit Welfare Officer. Although this was the pinnacle for any soldier, to take the Queen's commission, Richard listened to the news, with mixed emotions.

Just after the meeting with the Squadron Leader, by chance, Richard bumped into the Troop Leader of the BRF. They got talking about the incident with Rob and, after giving Richard all the facts, confirming what he had already been told, the Troop leader continued.

'I remember the day before he died,' he said, 'we were running across open ground, while under fire. Rob was running alongside me, firing his shotgun, with a big, shit-eating grin on his face. He turned to me and said:

'This is the best day I've had in the Army!'

Richard and the BRF Troop leader couldn't help themselves. They burst into laughter, the story just summed Rob up to a T.

The months carried on as before, with constant patrols and other taskings. The Squadron, thankfully, sustained no more fatalities, only a few minor injuries. It wasn't long before they were boarding the plane, on the way home. As Richard settled into his seat, he surveyed the Troops in the compartment and stared at four empty seats, symbolising the men who would never again drill, train, fire a weapon or crack open a beer. Their memory would go on forever, in the history of the Regiment. Soldiers never die, they just 'reorg' on the plains of Heaven.

Chapter 22 - Welfare & Goodbye

Only two months after they had returned from Afghanistan, Richard had been commissioned and was now the Unit Welfare Officer. He attended a week's course, to help enable him to understand some of the Welfare issues he might have to deal with, on a day-to-day basis. He listened to lectures on primary welfare support, good practices and how to build a case study. An essential part of the job was being able to listen, so a lot of time was spent developing listening and helping skills. The subject of death and how to support those going through a bereavement was a particular skill Richard dreaded putting into practice.

The most challenging areas Richard had to learn to deal with included domestic violence, child abuse, self-harm and depression. He knew, only too well, that the last subject was prevalent throughout the British Army. He also recognised traits which reflected his own moods and situation. He questioned his suitability for the post but knew he owed it to the soldiers and their families, to give them the support they needed.

On his return to camp, Richard arrived in his new office and met his members of staff, who comprised a Sergeant Marchant, his driver, Jimbo and his secretary, Andrea. Morris had attended the same course Richard had just been on and had been in the job for six months. He would be a great asset to Richard, as a source of information and they would need to work very closely together in the next two years. They would take it in turns to be available 24/7, each doing a week on call, at a time. Richard would need to be available for anything which his Sergeant couldn't handle. For the next two years, his life wouldn't be his own, which was going to put even more stress on his already delicate family life.

No sooner had he sat at his desk, than a knock on the door made him raise his head, from the paperwork, waiting to be filled in. In front of him stood a familiar figure, almost 6ft tall, with long, dark, curly hair. The glasses she wore gave her a studious, secretarial look. Her demeanour was far from that of a helpful secretary, though. Richard knew, only too well, how confrontational she could be, as he was acquainted with her husband, an SNCO. She was German and came from not far from where they were stationed, at that time. She stood, her arms crossed over her chest, her appearance almost intimidating. Without knowing what was on her mind, Richard knew he could have had an easier start to his job.

'Yes, Bianca, what can I do for you?' he asked, smiling.

'I'll tell you what you can do for me. I need you to get my husband back from exercise.'

Richard had been briefed by his predecessor that this was one of the most common complaints or requests he would have to deal with. He paused a moment, hoping that this might give time for Bianca to calm down a little, before he answered.

'Can I ask why you need him back, Bianca?' he asked, not really wanting to hear whatever excuse she would come up with.

When she did speak, Richard was lost for words.

'Well, I have just started lessons to enable me to get my civil bus driver's licence. As the lessons are at different times of the day, I don't have anyone to look after our children,' she said, as if this was the most important thing in the universe.

Richard had to pause for a moment, to let the preposterous excuse sink in. He leaned back in his chair, sucking on the end of his pen. He was fighting hard not to let a smirk cross his face or even laugh out loud, at the request. He took a deep breath and began to deliver his answer.

'Well, you know that the exercise the Regiment is on at the moment is classed as an operational one?' he posed the question, throwing the ball back into Bianca's court.

It wasn't embarrassment which made her face turn the colour it did, it was rage, building inside her. Richard knew her character from old, from when she had stormed into the RSM's office and asked why her husband had to attend drinks in the Mess, one afternoon. This was only one of many altercations she had had, with the establishment. Most of the wives, although they didn't agree with some army ways, generally got on with things. Bianca was an exception, one who made it her mission in life to try and upset the apple cart, whenever she could.

'I don't give a fuck about a fucking exercise! I want him back now or I'm going to see the CO!' she screamed at Richard.

Richard smiled openly, knowing full well that she wouldn't carry out her threat. Even if she did, the CO was away, with the Regiment on the exercise. One of the

242

Squadron Leaders was standing in, as rear party officer in command. If she had have gone to him, he would only have echoed what Richard was telling her, that the excuse she was giving was not a valid one.

'Firstly, Bianca, you knew this exercise was coming up, for the past few months, so I cannot understand why you arranged to do this course, knowing full well that your husband would be away. Secondly, you could arrange for someone to look after your child, while you are doing the lessons. I know you have family close by, so can't see that being an issue.' Richard stared at her, as he spoke.

Bianca knew what he was saying was true and, in a rage, turned around and stormed out of his office.

'Welcome to the Welfare Office, Sir!' came a voice from next door.

Richard stood up and entered the office next to his. His new working buddy was sitting in his chair, laughing his head off. Steve Marchant had been a member of C Squadron, on the last tour of Afghan. He had been injured in an RPG attack and had been flown back to the UK. His injuries prevented him from going back to front line service, so he had been given the welfare job, to see out his last two years of service. He was an amiable character, perfect for this line of work. He was well known by both the men and the wives and would be invaluable, in helping Richard in his new job.

'What have you got on this week?' Richard asked.

'Well, we have a new family arriving, later this morning. I'm meeting them for the march in of their new quarter. Get this one, he is only 22 years old and his wife the same age and they have five feckin' bin lids!' Steve answered, using the army slang. They've got a five bedroom house on my estate, just up from the RSM's house. I'm off over there, in about half an hour.'

'Is there anything I need to be aware of, for this week?' Richard enquired, again.

'No, not really. I've got the phone this week, so you can relax. We do have a hospital visit every Friday, though. You should come along, so you see how things go. We normally get a list of those in hospital, from the Med Centre.'

Richard recollected when he had been in hospital, the Welfare Officer visited him, to see if he required anything. It hadn't clicked that it was going to be a regular part of his new job.

'Yeah, that sounds good. I'll put it in my diary,' with that, he returned to his office.

Steve left half an hour later and got into the car used for welfare purposes. He drove the short distance to the estate where the new family would be taking over their quarter. Already waiting outside, the family looked slightly bewildered. Steve introduced himself and immediately tried to put their minds at rest. He understood, from the countless families he had dealt with, what an alien situation they were in. This young couple had never left their county, never mind their country, so were understandably like the proverbial fish out of water. The five kids were running riot, while their mother tried to calm them down.

As they were talking, a car pulled up. Out stepped Pat Lavery, the estate warden for that patch. Pat was ex-

Irish Guards and was now on the long-service list. These were usually senior ranks, who had finished their full 22 years and were given an extension to their service. He walked over to Steve and shook his hand, then introduced himself to the young couple. In the six months Steve had been working with him, they had struck up a good working relationship. He was strict but fair when it came to marching couples in and out of the married accommodation.

They began in the kitchen and Pat went through the 'get you in pack', which newly married couples were issued with. This was a kind of start-up set that included all the crockery, cutlery, pots and pans a family would need. These were carefully inventoried and would need to be handed back, either during the couple's occupation or when they marched out of the quarter. The soldier signed for the items, knowing anything missing or damaged would have to be paid for, when they left.

Pat then took them round each room and went through an inventory, marking down the cleanliness and any damages. While it was expected a family moving out had to leave the quarter in the same condition as it had been in, when they took it over. Sometimes, they were actually handed back in better order. Steve had found this was not always the case. Richard would learn very quickly it would take up a great deal of their time.

The walk round finished, the checking of inventory and damages recorded, the soldier signed the required paperwork and was handed the keys for the house. Steve and Pat explained that, if there was anything they needed, to simply call or drop into their respective offices. The family thanked them and saw them to the door.

As they walked to their cars, Pat turned to Steve.

'I think you may have a few problems with that family,' he remarked, 'who the hell has five kids, at their age?'

Steve knew Pat was right and would report the same to Richard, when he returned to the office. A lot of marriages in the army didn't survive long, for various reasons, such as infidelity while the soldiers were away, homesickness or the wives being young and unable to cope, without immediate family support. It could take new wives a long time to settle in and make new friends.

Richard and Steve held weekly meetings, to discuss any concerns they had, about particular families. It was a proactive way of hopefully getting to the root of any problem, before it worsened. Richard made a decision that he would arrange to visit those families he deemed not to be settling in or struggling.

For the rest of the week, Steve and Richard went through the case files they had opened on some of the families. Most was run of the mill stuff but Richard needed to be brought up to date on everything, in case the CO asked him about something he felt Richard should know.

Friday came around in no time and Richard checked with the Medical Centre for a list of military personnel in the local German hospital. When the list had been faxed over, he and Steve got in the car and, with Steve driving, sped north, up the Autobahn.

The journey to the major hospital, where British patients were treated took 45 minutes. They parked the car, made sure it was locked and walked inside. Richard knew, from his list, there was just one soldier and one wife to be visited. He didn't recognise the soldier's name but he certainly knew the woman's. She was the wife of a friend of his and lived not far from Richard and Birgit, on the estate. They had spent a number of afternoons in their back gardens, having barbeques. She was from the West Country and had the strong accent associated with there.

They asked at the reception, for the room numbers of both patients. Richard decided they would visit the soldier first. They found his room without a problem and Richard introduced himself, in case the young lad didn't know who he was. He had broken his leg, having fallen off the back of a tank, as they were refuelling, at night. He had been in for a couple of days and was hoping to be released. Richard made small talk for a while and, confirming the young man didn't need anything from him, left, with Steve, to look for the next patient.

As they entered the room, the woman, Stacy, opened her eyes wide, seeing Richard.

'Feckin' hell, what you doing here?'

'I'm the new Unit Welfare Officer. Didn't you know, Stacy?' Richard asked, knowing that, at times, she was a bit slow on the uptake.

'Oh, that's right, you took over, just after Afghan,' she cackled, like a witch.

Richard was wondering what she was in hospital for but, before he could ask, she blurted out.

'I've had my gearbox out,' Stacy hollered, referring to her recent hysterectomy.

Before Richard could ask how she was, after the operation, she lifted her nightdress.

'Do you want to see the scar?'

Richard and Steve tried to avert their eyes and, looking at each other, tried not to laugh. Asking her to pull down her nightie, Richard turned back to her.

'Is there anything you need that I can arrange for you?' he asked, trying to return the situation back to normal and banish the sight he had just seen from his memory.

'Nah, I'll be out in a couple of days. Mark is visiting tonight and bringing me a few things,' she said, referring to her husband.

'Okay, that's great. We'll love you and leave you, then,' Richard replied. He and Steve exited the room and, once they were out of earshot, burst into uncontrollable laughter.

Thing were quiet. Richard hadn't received any calls from Steve, who had been on call that weekend. On the Monday, he took the phone off him and was informed there had not been any problems. Richard hoped his shift would be the same, but that wasn't to be.

The following Friday night, Richard took a call from the Guard Commander, who told him someone had reported a possible "domestic", at one of the quarters. Richard jumped in his car and hurried off to the address given. As he drove, his mind raced, thinking about the different scenarios he might come across and how he would deal with them. Parking the vehicle outside the married quarter, he locked the door and approached the house. He could hear the screaming voices, before he reached the door. He waited, listening. As the voices got more agitated, he rang the bell. The voices stopped but no one came to the door. He rang the bell again, but still no one came. Making a fist, he banged it against the door. After a few moments, it was opened and a sheepish looking young man peered out.

'Trooper Studley, we have had complaints about raised voices. I was wondering if everything was okay?' Richard asked, politely.

There was a slight pause, before the young soldier answered.

'Aye, Sir, everything's fine,' he whispered.

'Then, you won't mind if I come in?' Richard spoke in such a way that it was not a question but an order.

Opening the door, the embarrassed looking Trooper let Richard enter. Walking into the living room, Richard faced a young woman, with a kitchen knife in her hand. As Richard turned to look at the soldier, he noticed blood on the lad's shirt.

'Are you all right?' he asked, now concerned.

'Aye, Sir. She just caught me on the side,' he indicated a small wound.

Richard went on to ask what had caused the argument. It came to light that they had been drinking heavily. They were newly married and it was the first time his wife had been away from home. She was finding it hard to cope with their newly born son. The young lad had just returned from a six week course in the UK, during which she had been left at home on her own, with the infant.

Richard ensured the wound was superficial, tidied it, then sat the couple down and had a frank discussion with them. He managed to defuse the situation and insisted that they see him, the next day. They both agreed and thanked Richard for his understanding.

As Richard left the quarter, towards his car, he thought to himself, that this was going to be a hard couple of years.

The incident with the young couple was one of many the Welfare Office had to deal with, during Richard's time as Welfare Officer.

A more serious and disturbing case happened, not long after he had taken over. He was still living in the same quarter as before, there were no Officer's houses available, at the time.

A young couple moved in next to them, he was a member of the REME, from Richard's Regiment. They had a young child and everything seemed to be great between them. One night, Richard was home, drinking a bottle of beer, as Steve was on call. Richard was drinking more than ever and, as was now commonplace, his mood turned darker, with every sip. Things were not going well between him and Birgit and the arguments between them were more frequent and more heated.

As he sipped his beer, his mind went back to that last tour in Afghanistan. The sights, sounds and smells were still vivid. The faces of the four they had lost, during the tour, flashed in front of him, like eerie spectres, forming out of the mist. Rob's face, smiling at him, gave him some succour, remembering the good times they had shared together. Then, he fell back into despair, as he thought of Rob's young daughter, now without her loving, doting father. As Rob had been a single parent, his best friend had taken over guardianship of the young girl, as requested by Rob, in a letter he had written, before the Regiment had deployed.

The sound of raised voices and the shattering of glass tore Richard away from his thoughts. He looked across at Birgit, who shrugged her shoulders. He put down his bottle and rose from his chair. Putting an ear to the wall, he could hear a male and a female voice, in heated discussion. As the voices got louder, breaking glass could be heard, again. A young child was crying loudly and added to the mix. Richard knew that the couple next door had a six month old infant, so he decided to take action.

Standing outside their door, he hammered on it, swaying slightly, as the alcohol kicked in. He steadied himself by leaning against the wall and the door opened. The young REME Lance Corporal stood there, surprised to see Richard.

'We heard raised voices and the sound of glass breaking. Is everyone all right?' Richard asked, calmly.

There was a stunned silence and the guy looked back, over his shoulder, before answering.

'Yeah, me and the wife were just having a bit of a disagreement.'

The sound of the baby screaming gave Richard cause for concern.

'I suggest I come in,' he stated.

'Err, of course, Sir,' came the guarded response.

Pushing past him, Richard walked toward the living room. As he did, he glanced into the kitchen. Wine and vodka bottles covered the table. As he made his way into the living room, his foot kicked a shard of glass from an empty vodka bottle on the floor. The wall, to his right, was wet with its contents. The sound of the baby crying upstairs was deafening. The wife of the timid Lance Corporal sat on a chair, on the opposite side of the room. Her eyes were puffy and red, her mascara had run, confirming to Richard that she had been crying.

'Are you all right, love?' Richard asked.

The young wife looked up at him, trying to focus. He could tell that she was angry, so was cautious with his next question.

'Do you mind if I sit down?' he asked, in a quiet voice, aware of the mood in the room.

The distressed young girl shook her head and he took a seat opposite her. For the next half hour, they chatted. Richard came to the conclusion that she was possibly suffering from post-natal depression. He had asked the husband to go and see to the baby, which gave him the opportunity to talk candidly to the wife. Although she may have been suffering from depression, there was something else Richard couldn't quite put his finger on. When he was satisfied that the situation was calm enough, he left the couple and returned to his own house.

Over the next few weeks, things escalated with the couple with, yet again, more shouting matches, which resulted, on one occasion, with the lad being assaulted by his wife. On yet another night, the disturbance got so bad that Richard attended the incident, as he was on call. After leaving the couple, having calmed things down, he returned next door. Not ten minutes later, Richard's ground floor toilet window shattered, causing him to rush to his door. He opened it, to see the young woman about to enter her own house. She turned and hurled a tirade of abuse in Richard's direction. Enough was enough, Richard thought, they had attended a session with a local social worker the week before and had been warned that their child was close to be taken into care.

This was the last straw. Richard called for an ambulance, fearing for the child's safety. When it arrived, the woman was taken away, kicking and screaming. She was later psychiatrically assessed and sectioned, as it was deemed she was a danger, not only to herself but to her family too.

It was revealed later that, as a child, she had been abused by her father. This, coupled with the depression, had manifested itself in a deep rooted psychosis. The poor woman spent the next few weeks in hospital, until she was deemed ready to return to her family.

This was one of the most disturbing cases Richard had to deal with, in his time as Unit Welfare Officer. It was not the last one by a long way and he wondered if the Regiment really knew the things that went on, behind closed doors.

Two years had come and gone. As Richard sat at his desk, he stared out of the window, at the men working on the tank park. It was scary to think that all those years ago, he had lived in a caravan, with his parents, on that very spot not 200 metres from where he now sat.

He had come full circle. That evening, he would be dined out and leave this life forever. He opened a drawer in his desk and withdrew a small bottle of whiskey, pouring a shot into his coffee. His hands shook as he did so and the sweat trickled down his brow.

The Mess was full of Officers and ladies of the Regiment. The ladies' jewellery sparkling in the light from the candles, lined up, along the long table. Richard sat, pride of place, next to the CO and made pleasant conversation with his wife. The champagne was flowing and Richard's head started to swim, as it mixed with the whiskey he had put away, during the day. Birgit sat next to him, her hand squeezing his thigh, confirming that she still loved him, despite all the problems they had faced, during their time together. They had handed over their quarter the day before and had moved into a hotel, for that evening, before leaving for the ferry, the following night. She knew that she would probably have to drive, as Richard wouldn't be in a fit enough state.

The sound of the Adjutant striking his glass, with a knife, caused the room to fall silent. He prayed silence for the CO, who rose from his chair. For the next ten minutes, the CO spoke about Richard's colourful career, which drew more than one laugh, from the assembled Officers. As he drew his speech to a close, Richard prepared to give his reply. He had thought long and hard about what his parting words would be. As he rose to speak his mind went blank. He winged the speech and, as he resumed his seat, hadn't a clue what he had said. The cheering and the applause let him know he must have done all right, though.

His spurs rang on the concrete steps. With his arm linked through Birgit's, he stumbled on to the minibus waiting outside and, with the help of the duty driver and Birgit, fastened his seat belt.

The vehicle left the camp. A tear formed in Richard's eye, as he looked back, over his shoulder. As the red and white barrier closed, it closed on that part of his life.

Epilogue

Richard woke from his nightmare. Although the cold, November wind cut through his wet clothing, he was sweating profusely. The images of burnt bodies and severed limbs would not dissipate from his mind. The faces of so many friends and comrades flashed before his eyes, then all merged into one. He saw, clearly, the faces of those who had made the ultimate sacrifice. His heart was racing, and fear gripped him, as it always did. The smell of vomit, which stained his sweatshirt, wafted up, from under the blanket, in which he was wrapped. He shuffled back further into the doorway, where he had located himself the previous evening. He reached out, for the remnants of the cheap bottle of vodka, which lay just within arm's reach. His hands shaking, he unscrewed the cap and, lifting the bottle to his lips, he gulped down the fiery liquid. As the clear liquid trickled down his throat, he shuddered. The cheap booze helped to mask the images in his head, if only for a short time.

It had been 18 months since the breakup of his marriage, after leaving the military. The warning signs had been there, five years before he left. Yet, like most soldiers, he had tried to put them to the back of his mind, too proud to admit there was a problem. He had experienced flashbacks, nightmares, repetitive, distressing images and sensations, and pain and nausea, sometimes leading to vomiting. He had suffered severe mood swings, the lows vented on Birgit and the children. He had had continual negative thoughts of events from the past and had never really come to terms, with some of the horrors he had witnessed.

Why had these things happened to him? Had there been anything he could have done to prevent them? The questions had led to feelings of guilt, then shame, which manifested themselves in uncontrollable rages. Birgit had pleaded with him to see a doctor, but he had blankly refused, thinking it would have had a detrimental effect on his career.

She had first noticed a difference in him when they were in the Warrant Officers' and Sergeants' Mess and someone had begun to speak of an incident, where one of the Regiment had been killed in a firefight. Richard had become withdrawn and had immediately changed the subject. He had become more involved with his work, often not coming home until late at night. This was one way of dealing with the problem by 'emotionally numbing'.

He had started to avoid certain members of the Regiment, at social gatherings, as a coping mechanism. This was a major warning sign to Birgit, as Richard had always been a social animal.

Over the years, they had become more and more distant and, after leaving the service, things had come to a head. In his job, at the hospital, he had been given two written warnings, for turning up at work, reeking of alcohol. Then, finally, after having been given a driving ban and losing his licence, for driving under the influence, he had been sacked. Being unable to deal with his constant, aggressive outbursts and habitual drinking, Birgit had, reluctantly, filed for divorce.

There began a rapid, downward spiral. Not seeing any way out of his predicament, the drinking had got worse. When most of his savings were gone, he had found himself homeless. He had spent a short time with his parents and his sister but they, like Birgit, had found it difficult to deal with his emotional outbursts. Not taking their advice of seeking medical help, he had ended up alone in a doorway, fighting his demons.

Gone was the warm embrace of his Regimental family. He had been let loose in Civvy Street, to fend for himself. He was not the only one to be in this situation. The military had tended to their every need, while they were serving but had not taught them how to survive in the 'outside world'. Once they had left, they were expected to fend for themselves. Any time on a Long Range Reconnaissance Patrol course and the demanding environments he had lived in hadn't prepared him for this ordeal.

The British Government had set out a 'Military Covenant', stating its commitment to looking after members of the Armed Forces, after leaving the Services. The Armed Forces Covenant sets out the relationship between the nation, the government and the Armed Forces. It recognises that the whole nation has a moral obligation to members of the Armed Forces and their families, and it establishes how they should expect to be treated:

The Covenant's principles are that:

'The armed forces community should not face disadvantage compared to other citizens in the provision of public and commercial services

Special consideration is appropriate in some cases, especially for those who have given most such as the injured and the bereaved

The covenant exists to redress the disadvantages that the armed forces community may face in comparison

to other citizens, and to recognise sacrifices made.'
(https://www.gov.uk/government/publications)

Richard had read these words many times and, every time, laughed sarcastically, believing they were not worth the paper they were printed on.

He took another swig of the clear liquid and, as he did so, his attention was drawn to the sound of coins being dropped into the box, laid at his feet. Next to the box was a hastily made sign, stating that he was a 'Homeless Veteran'. As he looked up, to thank the individual who had kindly donated to his plight, he stared, speechless.

The gigantic frame, dark hair and brown eyes were so familiar. Those big, brown eyes stared into his own, with the same look of recognition. A moment passed, before any words were exchanged. Then, an unmistakable grin, this time tinged with sadness, crossed the face of Mark Newbottle.

It had been 25 years, since those days back in training, when the pair of them had pounded the drill square, their first steps on the path to a military career.

'Is that you, Richard?' came the familiar, deep Geordie accent.

This affirmed Richard's suspicions that it was indeed Mark. 'It is, marra,' Richard replied, using the Geordie word for friend. As he spoke, the look between them needed no explanation. Tears began to roll down Richard's cheeks and he began to sob, uncontrollably.

The gentle giant stooped down, took Richard's hands and hauled him to his feet. They embraced in a way that only brothers can. He gripped Richard tightly and whispered in his ear that everything was going to be all right. The embrace seemed to go on forever, until, at last, Mark asked him to pick up his belongings and led him off down the street.

For the next week, Richard stayed with Mark, who had moved from his home town of Ashington to the bright lights of Newcastle. He had done well for himself, after leaving the military, and was manager of a local Tesco.

He had made many connections during his time in Civvy Street and persuaded Richard to accompany him, to a local military charity, which helped ex-soldiers find their feet again, after falling on hard times. Within a couple of weeks, Richard had been given accommodation and had found himself a job. He began a course of counselling, which was helping him to deal with his issues.

If it hadn't been for the chance meeting, on the streets of Newcastle, the outcome might have been so different. It showed the compassion and brotherhood which existed between soldiers, even after leaving the Forces. The Americans had a saying about "never leaving a man behind". This was eclipsed by the love and respect the British soldiers had for their comrades.

Richard was contacted by the Regimental Association, asking if he wanted to be added to their mailing list. He agreed, and began to receive newsletters, about the Regiment and events involving past members. These events normally took the form of social gatherings, organised by ex-members. Richard had never attended since his departure and, was apprehensive, as he ironed his trousers and shirt and packed his bag. He felt his pulse start to race, emotions started to well up, once again. He took a deep breath and continued with his packing, calming himself, as he did so. Although he was not totally over his illness, he was on the right road. This could be the last piece of the jigsaw, to finally put to rest the ghosts of the past.

His driving ban over, Richard climbed into the run-around he had bought for himself. The drive, from his flat on the outskirts of Durham, to the venue, a pub in a small village, on the edge of Halifax, took around an hour and a half. Richard pulled off the motorway, and into the car park of the hotel, where he would be staying for the night. Opening the boot, he took out his bag and the trousers, blazer, shirt and Regimental tie, hanging in the back of the car. Closing the boot, he hesitantly made for the entrance.

As he stood at the reception desk, waiting to be seen, he surveyed the room. There were a number of guests, at tables, chatting and drinking. Richard recognised a few faces, but was taken from his train of thought, by the receptionist asking for his name.

'Richard Hunter,' he replied. The young girl typed his name into her computer.

'That's room 203,' she said, handing him a key and giving him directions to his room.

Thanks to social media, he found that the event had drawn a lot of interest. On the list at reception, there were many names that he recognised, not only from his own era, but also those who had served with his father.

Richard thanked her, picked up his bag and walked towards the lifts. His room was comfortable and clean. He quickly showered and got dressed into his trousers, shirt, blazer and Regimental tie. Closing the door behind him, he chose the stairs and descended, feeling apprehensive, as he did so. It had been almost two years, since he had any contact from either serving or ex-members of the Regiment. He took a deep breath, as he entered the main foyer and bar area. The bar was void of the faces he had recognised earlier and, looking at his watch, he realised that the function had already started. He spotted a phone hanging on the wall, by reception and hurried, to call a taxi.

The taxi arrived within minutes and, giving the driver the address of the pub where the event was being held, he settled down, in the back seat. He was alone with his thoughts, during the ten minute journey. As the cab pulled up at the pub, Richard saw a number of people outside smoking and chatting. He paid the driver and stepped out of the vehicle. As he strode towards the pub, he found himself looking at the smiling face of Pete.

'Long time no see, stranger,' he said, welcoming Richard with a firm shake of the hand. Richard replied that it had, indeed, been a long time, since they had last met.

Within the space of ten minutes, Pete brought Richard up to speed, with what was happening in the Regiment, who the CO, the RSM, the Squadron Sergeant Majors and other key personalities were. The names were all too familiar to Richard and he wondered how some of them had attained the positions they had. It had only been two years since he had left but the makeup of the Regiment had changed massively. After finishing their conversation, the pair went inside.

The room was full of old, familiar faces and, as they made their way to the bar, they were stopped a couple of times, by people saying that it was great to see Richard again. It took almost another fifteen minutes before they actually made it to the bar. As Richard took a sip of his Guinness, he looked around the room. All the fears and anguish he had felt, prior to walking in, had evaporated.

That question that he had asked, all those years ago in the garden in Germany was finally answered. 'Would he ever feel this same bond with others as he did now with these three friends?'

Of course, he felt the same bond but it was even stronger than his childhood friendships. He was home in the bosom of his Regimental family.

Who could separate them?

Quis Separabit.

Other books by the author:

Denim to Khaki

"Fare Thee well"